GOD WAS HERE BUT HE LEFT EARLY

NOVELS

Evening in Byzantium
Rich Man, Poor Man
Voices of a Summer Day
The Young Lions
The Troubled Air
Lucy Crown
Two Weeks in Another Town
Beggarman, Thief
The Top of the Hill

SHORT STORY COLLECTIONS

God Was Here But He Left Early
Love on a Dark Street
Sailor Off the Bremen
Welcome to the City
Act of Faith
Mixed Company
Tip on a Dead Jockey
Five Decades

PLAYS

Bury the Dead
The Gentle People
Sons and Soldiers
The Assassin

NON-FICTION

In the Company of Dolphins
Paris! Paris!

God was here but He left early

❖ ❖ ❖ ❖ ❖ ❖ ❖

FIVE SHORT NOVELS BY

Irwin Shaw

PRIAM ⚬⚬ ⚬⚬ BOOKS

Arbor House   New York

TO DAVID SHAW

Contents

Preface 9

PART I

God Was Here But He Left Early 19

Where All Things Wise and Fair Descend 51

PART II

Whispers in Bedlam 77

The Mannichon Solution 148

Small Saturday 192

Preface

❖   I MET Somerset Maugham once. He said to me, "Young man, I envy you."

Suspecting irony, but prepared for flattery, I asked, "Why do you envy me, Mr. Maugham?"

"Because you are an American and write short stories. There is a short story on every street corner in America. I have to go through a whole country to find one."

This was before World War II, as can be guessed from Mr. Maugham's addressing me as "Young Man." It occurred to me then that perhaps the old gentleman's trans-oceanic *politesse* was more the result of his own temperament than our native abundance. I had been on a lot of street corners in America by then and it never seemed that easy to me. Still, if one remembers how many stories were being published every week in those days, and on what a variety of subjects, Mr. Maugham's estimate is understandable.

One is astonished now to remember the number of magazines that were open to assault—and the supply was there to meet the demand. My first story, for example, was published in *The New Republic*—and who can recall the last time that magazine published something that was candidly labeled as fiction? A second story of mine was published in the Sunday supplement of the New York *Herald Tribune* and how long now has the *Tribune* itself been gone?

In those days, too, there was often heard the cliché, especially among Europeans, that the American genius, whatever that might be, was most accurately expressed in the short form. Although I was aware that Scheherazade had not gone to the University of Chicago and that neither de Maupassant nor Chekhov had grown up in San Francisco, I had not yet written any novels and I was inclined to be pleased that my work was in the mainstream of American letters. Now that I have six or seven novels behind me I am not so sure that it should have been a source of pleasure to us that others found us at our best in sharp bursts and over moderate distances.

The publishers of books also contributed to the vitality of the craft. In the Thirties and Forties a publisher did not suggest that you were attempting to take the bread out of his family's mouth when you showed up in his office with a volume of stories. Nor did he expect that when he brought forth the volume the reviews would be, with certain honorable exceptions, relegated to the back pages usually reserved for the notices of the how-to books and ghosted autobiographies of obscure generals and disgraced politicians.

Today, a new man arriving in a publisher's office with a sheaf of stories under his arm is liable to be regarded in much the same manner as a young inventor approaching the president of the Chris-Craft corporation with an advanced design for a trireme. All this has not deterred me, as the publication of this book demonstrates. I am used to sinking ships. I started my professional career in the Broadway theater and no one has to be reminded about what has happened to that institution. I supported myself, after the failure of each of about ten plays, by working in Hollywood, and the cries of famine that emanate from that center of culture these days are heart-rending. And even before I wrote the first paragraph of *The Young Lions* I had read a hundred critics who assured me that the novel was dead.

The truth is, of course, that drama is not finished, although Broadway may be; that while fewer movies are being made than heretofore, the good ones that are produced each year are in a respectable ratio to the overall distribution. People still read novels, and while the outlets for stories have been reduced there are just as many and perhaps more stories being written than ever before in America.

There is no denying, however, that there has been an appreciable decline in the *appreciation* of short stories in the past forty years. But that decline is not the consequence of a corresponding falling-off in quality. The good stories of today are as good if not better than those of the period when it seemed that hundreds of stories were published every week, and even the *bad* stories that appear today seem to me to be an improvement on the bad stories of the booming epoch.

Fashions change, of course, currents alter, styles become over-familiar, the works we read today are certainly different from the ones we read then. The stories that used to appear in *The New Yorker*, for example, were accused of being formless as today they are accused of being written to a formula, and in each case the accusation was and is unjust. But the level of the writing, the *performance*, in our sadly diminishing list of magazines, seems to me to have remained fairly constant, or as constant as one could expect in anything so chancy and unpredictable as modern literature. People may not like to read short stories as much as they once did but writers devote as much enthusiasm and care to them as they ever did when Katherine Anne Porter was making her debut and Wilbur Daniel Steele was represented in each edition of the *Best American Short Stories* of the year.

The reasons for this can hardly be mercenary. The writing of short stories is not, except for certain freakish exceptions, a lucrative profession. I received twenty-five dollars for that story in *The New Republic*. My rate went up when I finally broke into *The New Yorker*—I received a check for seventy-five dollars. Editors, then as now, were firm in their belief that short story writers did not live by bread alone.

I must admit that prices have risen somewhat since that happy time. But even in my most prolific period, before the novel began to absorb the greatest part of my time, there never was a year in which I could meet my bills solely from the proceeds of the short stories I had written in those twelve months. This was not entirely due to the minginess of editors, although I have chided them gently from time to time on their thrift. For most writers, myself included, the completion of a short story that one is ready to send out into the world involves a formidable number of working hours. Occasionally there are prodigies like the late Sally Benson, who would come into *The New Yorker* office around eleven o'clock, sit down at her desk without taking her hat off and tap out a charming story before leaving for lunch. And John O'Hara once told me he could have dinner, with several drinks, and go home and start and finish a story, and a very good one, indeed, before going to bed. Once or twice in my life I have been briefly blessed by this enviable facility, but the usual process is one of long, slow accretion and even longer and slower construction.

More often than not, I have struggled with an idea for six months, give or take a few weeks, and there is one story of mine that was published not so long ago that I had on and off my desk for twenty years. None of this, of course, presupposes excellence. We all know writers who have dedicated lifetimes to trash.

With all that, the medium exercises an inordinate attraction for writers. A.J. Liebling, a modest and retiring man, whose work makes a good deal of the so-called new journalism sound like the effusions of stunted children, boasted only once in my presence—on the occasion of having a short story of his included in an anthology. And John Gunther, who had invented a gigantic method of assimilating information about entire continents, once told me that it was the dream of his life to get a story into *The New Yorker*.

Obviously, the rewards of the trade, while for the most part intangible, are many. I shall mention the most mundane and least elevated one first. If a critic dislikes your novel he is likely to dismiss you and all your works completely, in the strongest and least amiable terms of which he is capable. (Needless to say, this has happened to me.) But even the most intemperate critic, confronted with a book of short stories, is liable to be attracted to at least one of them and speak kindly of it, so that some shred of value is still attached to several years of your work. (This has happened to me too.) My first book of short stories, while not unanimously greeted with hosannas, was the occasion for the one review I have received over the years that I remember most fondly. It was written by Otis Ferguson and it seemed to me to reveal marvelous intentions in my work that I myself had not fully understood until then. Ferguson, naturally, was the first and I imagine the only critic who was killed in World War II.

Other rewards are more profound. There is the reward of the storyteller seated cross-legged in the middle of the bazaar, filling the need of humanity in the humdrum course of an ordinary day for magic and tales of distant wonders, for disguised moralizing which will set everyday transactions into larger perspectives, for the compression of great matters into digestible portions, for the shaping of mysteries into sharply-edged and comprehensible symbols.

Then there is the private and exquisite reward of escaping from the laws of consistency. Today you are sad and you tell a sad story. Tomorrow you are happy and your tale is a joyful one. You remember a woman whom you loved wholeheartedly and you celebrate her memory. You suffer from the wound of a woman who treated you badly and you denigrate womankind. A saint has touched you and you are a priest. God has neglected you and you preach atheism.

In a novel or a play you must be a whole man. In a collection of stories you can be all the men or fragments of men, worthy and unworthy, who in different seasons abound within you. It is a luxury not to be scorned.

❖   ❖   ❖

So with this book. The reader will easily see that it is divided into two distinct and unequal sections. The two shorter stories are realistic, with tragic or at least pathetic overtones. The three longer ones, of a length which editors are tempted to call novellas, are satiric and fantastic in tone and deal, in a roughly systematic fashion, with three of the major preoccupations of our age—Science, Sport and Sex. My British publishers, representatives of a comparatively homogeneous society and disturbed by the thought of including disparate elements between the same covers, have elected to bring out the three last as a separate book. My American publishers, victims of or contributors to the most various society on the face of the earth, have bravely thrown them together. Conscious of the difference between the nations, I have allowed myself to be persuaded by their separate arguments.

Ah, that Ferguson were still alive!

—I. S.

PART I

God Was Here
but He Left Early

❖ BE LUGUBRIOUS, Love," she remembered, as she rang the bell. Bert had said that on the phone, when he had called her back from London. "They dote on sorrow. Suggest suicide. Just the merest hint, Love. Name me, if you want. Everybody knows how weird I am, even in Geneva, and they'll sympathize. I'm sure it'll be all right. Three of my friends have been and have lived happily ever after."

Bert's vocabulary was airy but he was familiar with trouble in fifteen countries; he was a friend of outlaws; the police in several cities had taken an interest in him, he knew everybody's name and address and what they could be used for. Thinking about Bert, his pleasure in complication, she smiled in the dark corridor before the closed door. She heard steps. The door opened. She went in.

"You are how old, Mrs. Maclain?"

"Thirty-six," Rosemary said.

"You are American, of course."

"Yes."

"Your home?"

"New York." She had decided not to let him know she spoke French. It would make her seem more helpless. Adrift, non-communicating in foreign lands.

"You are married?"

"Divorced, five years ago."

"Children?"

"A daughter. Eleven years old."

"Your . . . uh . . . condition dates back how far?"

"Six weeks."

"You're sure?" He spoke English precisely. He had studied in Pennsylvania. He was a small, youngish, precise man with neatly brushed brown hair in a neat brown office. There was a pale ceramic blankness about his face, like a modestly designed dinner plate. He was alone. He had opened the door for her himself. Diplomas and degrees in several languages hung on the brownish, neutral walls. There was no noise from the street. It was a sunny day. She didn't feel lugubrious.

"Perfectly," she said.

"Your health?"

"Physically. . . ." She hesitated. There was no sense in lying. "Physically—I suppose I'd say normal."

"The man?"

"I'd prefer not to talk about it."

"I'm afraid I must insist."

Inventions. *We were to be married but he was killed in a car crash. In an avalanche. I discovered in time that there was a strong streak of insanity in his family. He's a Catholic and Italian and married and as you know there's no divorce in Italy and besides, I have to live in New York. He was a Hindu. He promised to marry me and disap-*

peared. It was a sixteen-year-old boy in a wagon-lit and he had to go back to school. Absurd. All absurd.

The psychiatrist sat there in his brown office, patient, in ambush, prepared for lies.

"He's married." The truth. "Happily married." Perhaps more or less the truth. "He has two small children. He's much younger than I." Demonstrably true.

"Does he know?"

"No." Absurdity, too, has its limits. A senseless weekend in the mountains with a man you never had met before in your life and finally didn't much like and whom you never really wanted to see again. She had always been a fastidious woman and had never before done anything like that and certainly would never do it again. But you couldn't go surging in on a man ten years younger than you, bear down on him in the bosom of his 16th Arrondissement family, and whine away like a schoolgirl about being seduced because of two meaningless nights during a snowstorm. Caught. She frowned as she thought of the word. The vulgarity was inescapable. She wasn't even sure she had his address. He had written it down the last morning, she remembered, and said that if she ever came to Paris . . . But she had been sleepy and glad to get him out of the room and she wasn't sure whether she had put the slip of paper in her bag. His business address, he had said. The sanctity of the *foyer*. Frenchmen.

"No, he doesn't know," she said.

"Don't you think you ought to tell him?"

"What good would it do? Two people worrying instead of one." Although she couldn't see him worrying. Shrug. American women coming to Europe not even knowing how to. . . . "You see," she said, "it was terribly casual. In a ski resort. You know how ski resorts are . . ."

"I do not ski." He said it proudly. He was a serious practitioner. He did not devote his time to frivolity. He did not pay good money to break his legs. She began to dislike him in waves. The brown suit was hideous.

"I was drunk." Not true. "He helped me to my room." Not true. "I didn't know it was happening, really." The brown suit twitched. "He behaved in a very ungentle-manly fashion. . . ." Was it really her own voice? "If I *did* tell him, he would only laugh. He's a Frenchman." Perhaps she had something there. The mutual loathing of the Swiss and French. Calvin versus Madame de Pompadour. Geneva humiliated by Napoleon's troops. One Frenchman less in the world. Or demi-Frenchman. "By his attitude, I could tell he would have no sense of re-sponsibility." Now she sounded as though she were trans-lating from a policeman's testimony. She hoped the brown suit didn't notice. It was important to seem spontaneous, too distraught to be artful. Besides, what she had said was probably accurate. Jean-Jacques would have no reason to feel responsible. As far as he knew she might well go to bed with three different men a week. She had taken him to her room after knowing him only twenty-four hours. *Pourquoi moi, Madame? Pourquoi pas quelqu'un d'autre?* She could imagine the polite, disinterested tone, the closed-down, non-giving thin expression on the thin, handsome lady-killer face, still tan with the mountain sun. Jean-Jacques! If an American woman had to take a French lover, the name didn't have to be *that* French. The hy-phen. It was so banal. She cringed now, thinking of the weekend. And her own name. Rosemary. People called Rosemary do not have abortions. They get married in white veils and take advice from their mothers-in-law and wait in station wagons in the evenings in green suburbs for commuting husbands.

"What are your means of support, Madame?" the psychiatrist asked. He sat extraordinarily still, his hands ceramically pale on the green of the desk blotter before him. When she first had come into his office she had been aware that he had swiftly made a judgment on the way she was dressed. She had dressed too well for pity. Geneva was an elegant city. Suits from Dior, Balenciaga, Chanel, glittering in front of the banks and advertisements for chronometers. "Does your ex-husband pay you alimony!"

"He pays for our daughter. I support myself."

"Ah. You are a working woman." If his voice were ever allowed to express anything, he would have expressed surprise.

"Yes."

"What is the nature of your work?"

"I am a buyer."

"Yes?" Of course she was a buyer. Everybody bought things.

She knew she had to explain. "I buy things for a department store. Foreign things. Italian silks, French antiques, old glass, English silver."

"I see. You travel extensively." Another mark against her. If you traveled extensively, you should not be made pregnant while skiing. There was something that didn't hang together in the story. The pale hands, without moving, indicated distrust.

"I am in Europe three or four months a year."

"*Donc, Madame*," he said, "*vous parlez français.*"

"*Mal,*" she said. "*Très mal.*" She made the *très* sound as comically American as she could.

"You are quite free?" He was attacking her, she felt.

"More or less." Too free. If she hadn't been so free, she wouldn't be here now. She had broken off a three-year affair, just before she had come to Europe. In fact, that was why she had stayed in Europe so long, had asked for her holiday in winter rather than in August, to let it all settle down. When the man had said he could get his divorce now and they could marry, she had realized he bored her. Rosemary was certainly the wrong name for her. Her parents should have known.

"What I mean is the milieu in which you live is a liberal one," said the doctor, "the atmosphere is tolerant."

"In certain respects," she said, retreating. She wanted to get up and run out of the room. "Do you mind if I smoke?"

"Forgive me for not offering you a cigarette sooner. I myself, do not smoke, so I sometimes forget." He didn't ski and he didn't smoke. There were probably many other things he didn't do. He leaned over and took the lighter from her hands, steadily held the flame to her cigarette. Her hands were shaking. Authentically.

There was a little flare of the psychiatrist's nostril, disapproving of the smoke in his office. "When you travel, Madame, who occupies himself with your daughter? Your ex-husband?"

"A maid. I have full custody." Americanism. Probably

stir up some subconscious European aversion. "He lives in Denver. I try to make my trips as short as possible."

"A maid," the man said. "Financially, you could bear the expense of another child."

She began to feel panic, small electric twinges behind her knees, a tide in her stomach. The man was her enemy. She shouldn't have depended upon Bert. What did Bert really know about these things? "I'm afraid if it was discovered that I was to have a child I would lose my job. At my age. Ridicule is as dangerous as. . . ." She couldn't think of a forceful comparison. "Anyway, America isn't as free as all that, Doctor. And my husband would sue for custody of my daughter and would most probably win it. I would be considered an unfit mother. My husband is very bitter toward me. We do not speak. We. . . ." She stopped. The man was looking down at his immobile hands. She had a vision of herself explaining it all to her daughter. *Frances, darling, tomorrow the stork is going to bring you a present.* . . . "I can't bear the thought," she said. "It would ruin my life." Oh God. She had never thought she would ever bring out a sentence like that. *He isn't going to do it, he isn't going to sign the paper, he isn't.* "As it is, even now, I have days of deep depression, I have unreasonable fears that people come into my room when I sleep, I lock the doors and windows, I hesitate to cross streets, I find myself weeping in public places, I. . . ." Be lugubrious, Bert had said. It wasn't difficult, it turned out. "I don't know what I would do, I really don't know, it's so ludicrous. . . ." She wanted to cry, but not in front of that glazed face.

"I suggest these are phases, Madame. Temporary phases. It is my feeling that you will recover from them. It is also my feeling that neither your life nor your mental health will be put into serious danger by having this child. And as you no doubt are aware, I am only permitted, by Swiss law, to advise interruption of pregnancy when. . . ."

She stood up, stubbing out the cigarette in the ashtray. "Thank you," she said. "You have my address. You know where to send the bill."

He stood up and escorted her to the door and opened it for her. "*Adieu, Madame.*" He bowed slightly.

❖   ❖   ❖

Outside, she walked quickly down the steep cobbles, toward the lake. There were many antique shops on the narrow street, clean, quaintly timbered, eighteenth century. Too picturesque by half for a day like this. She stopped in front of a shop and admired a leather-topped desk, a fine mahogany sideboard. Swiss law. But it had *happened* in Switzerland. They had no right to, it wasn't *just*. When she thought this, even the way she was feeling, she had to laugh. A customer coming out of the shop glanced at her curiously.

She went down to the lake and looked at the fountain frothing in its snowy column, a flag for swans, high out of the water, and the excursion boats moving sedately, like 1900, out toward Ouchy, Vevey, Montreux, in the sunshine.

She felt hungry. Her appetite these days was excellent.

She looked at her watch. It was time for lunch. She went to the best restaurant she knew in the town and ordered *truite au bleu*. If you're in a country try the specialties of the country. She had a bottle of white wine that was grown farther down the lake.

Travel in Europe, the advertisements in the magazines announced. Relax in Switzerland.

The afternoon loomed before her, endless.

She could get on one of the steamers and throw herself overboard, in her smart suit, into the blue, polluted lake. Then, when they fished her out, she could go, still dripping, to the man in the brown room and confer once more with him on the subject of her mental health.

❖   ❖   ❖

"Barbaric," Jean-Jacques was saying. "It is a barbaric country. In France, of course, we are even more barbaric." They were sitting at a table on the *terrasse* of the Pavillon Royal in the Bois de Boulogne, overlooking the lake. The trees were mint-green, the sun surprisingly hot, there were tulips, the first oarsmen of the season were gliding out on the brown water in the rented boats, a young American was taking a photograph of his girl to prove when he got home that he had been in the Bois de Boulogne. The girl was dressed in bright orange, one of this season's three colors, and was laughing, showing American teeth.

Rosemary had been in Paris three days before she had called Jean-Jacques. She had found the scribbled piece of paper in her valise. Business address. Legible foreign handwriting. *Très bien* in *orthographe* in the Ecole Communale. The good little clever boy at the small desk. Finding the folded scrap of paper had brought back the smell of the tidy, scrollwork hotel room on the mountain. Old wood, the odor of pine through the open window, the peppery tang of sex between the sheets. She had nearly thrown the address away again. Now she was glad she hadn't. Jean-Jacques was being human. Not French. He had sounded cautious but pleased on the phone, had offered lunch. In Paris his name hadn't seemed too—too, well, foreordained. In Paris the hyphen was not objectionable.

She had spent the three days without speaking to anyone she knew in Paris. She had used the telephone once, to call Bert, in London. He had been sympathetic, but useless. He was on his way to Athens. Athens was swinging these days. If any ideas occurred to him among the Greeks, he would cable. Never fear, Love, something will turn up. Enjoy Paris, Love.

She was in a hotel on the Left Bank, not her usual hotel on the Rue Mont Tabor where she was known. She didn't want to see anybody she knew. She was going to think everything out sensibly, by herself. Step one, step two, step three, step one, step two, step. . . . Then she had the sensation that her brain was turning around on itself, inverting, like an Op Art painting. Whorls and squares, making illusory patterns that started and ended at the same point. Then suddenly she had to talk to someone. About anything. She hadn't really meant to tell Jean-Jacques. What was the use? But then, in the restaurant near her hotel (*sole bonne femme*, a bottle of Poully Fumé), he had been so solicitous, he had guessed so quickly that something was wrong, he was so good-looking in his dark suit and narrow tie, so *civilized*, it had all come out. She had laughed quite a lot as she told the story, she had made a humorous character out of the man in the brown suit, she had been brave and worldly and flippant and Jean-Jacques hadn't asked *Pourquoi moi?*, but had said, "This must be discussed seriously," and had driven her out to the Bois in his lady-killing British racing green sports car for brandy and coffee in the sunshine. (They must have a four-hour lunch period in his office, she thought.) Sitting there, watching the young men row past the tulips, she didn't regret the snowy weekend quite so much. Maybe not at all. It had amused her, she remembered, to take him away from the tight-flanked young beauties who were lying in wait for him. She remembered the ignoble sense of triumph with which she had managed it, older than all the rest, a hesitant novice skier approaching middle age, not swooping down the slopes like those delicious, devouring children. Jean-Jacques held her hand lovingly on the iron table in the sunshine and she felt wickedly pleased all over again. Not pleased enough to go to bed with him again, she had made that clear. He had accepted that graciously. Frenchmen were much maligned, she thought.

When he had taken out his wallet to pay the bill in the restaurant she had gotten a glimpse of a photograph of a young woman behind a celluloid shield. She had insisted upon his showing it to her. It was his wife, a smiling, serene, lovely girl, with wide-spaced grey eyes. She didn't like the mountains, she hated skiing, he said. He went on weekends alone. Their own business. Each marriage to its own rules. She, Rosemary, would not intrude, could not intrude. Jean-Jacques was sitting there, holding her hand not as a lover, but as a friend whom she needed, who had committed himself, unselfishly, to help her.

"Of course," Jean-Jacques was saying, "whatever it costs, I will. . . ."

"I don't need *that* sort of help," she said quickly.

"How much time do you have?" he asked. "I mean, when do you have to be back home?"

"I should be there now."

"And America?"

She took her hand out of his. She remembered some of the stories friends of hers had told her. The darkened rooms in doubtful neighborhoods, the money paid in cash in advance, the sleazy nurses, the criminal doctors, the staggering home two hours later, hurried out of doors which bore no nameplates. "Anything better than my sweet native land," she said.

"I've heard," Jean-Jacques said. "A little." He shook his head. "What countries we inhabit." He scowled, looking across the blare of tulips at the idiocy of nations.

Her mind began to feel like Op Art again.

"I am to go to Switzerland for the weekend. Spring skiing." He gave an apologetic little shrug. "It has been arranged weeks ago. I will stop in Zurich. I have friends there. I will try to find a more sympathetic doctor."

"Psychiatrist."

"Of course. I will be back on Tuesday. Can you wait?"

More Op Art. "Yes." Another week.

"Unfortunately, I must go to Strasbourg tomorrow,"

he said. "On business. I am to go on to Switzerland directly from there. I will not be able to entertain you in Paris."

"That's all right. I'll entertain myself." Entertain, there's a word. "It's very good of you." Inane, but she wanted to make up in some way for earlier, unspoken judgments on him.

He looked at his watch.

There is always the moment, she thought, when a man, the best of men, looks at his watch.

❖ ❖ ❖

The phone was ringing in her room when she opened the door. "Eldred Harrison here," a soft British voice said in the receiver. "I'm a friend of Bert's. Like everybody else." A little laugh. "He said you were alone in Paris and I must take care of you. Are you free for dinner?"

"Well. . . ." She prepared her refusal.

"I'm dining with some friends. A small party. We could come by your hotel and pick you up."

She looked around her hotel room. Stained, Watteauesque wallpaper, bulbs too dim to read by. The room joined her brain in Op Art patterns. A week to wait. She couldn't just sit in the room and wait seven days.

"That's very good of you, Mr. Harrison."

"I look forward to it." He didn't say it heartily, but softly and tentatively. "Shall we say eight?"

"I'll be ready," she said.

At five minutes to eight she was sitting in the hotel

lobby. Her hair was pulled back severely and she had put on her most shapeless dress. She didn't want to attract anybody this week, not even an Englishman.

Exactly at eight, a couple came into the lobby. The girl was young, with pale hair and Slavic bones. She was pretty, a little chubby, like a child, and seemed anxious to smile. She obviously didn't have much money to spend on her clothes. Jean-Jacques would have liked her, but he would take her to out-of-the-way restaurants. The man was tall, with greying, well-brushed hair and his hint of a self-deprecating stoop, the discreet cut of his patterned grey suit, went with the voice on the telephone. After the first glance, Rosemary sat there, her ankles crossed primly, waiting. The man spoke to the concierge in French and the concierge indicated Rosemary, sitting near the window. The couple came over. They both smiled.

"I hope we haven't kept you waiting, Mrs. Maclain," Harrison said.

She stood up and gave him her hand, smiling back. There wasn't going to be any trouble tonight.

❖   ❖   ❖

She hadn't counted on the drinking. Harrison kept to a schedule. One whiskey every fifteen minutes. For everybody, including the girl. Her name was Anna. She was Polish. She had come from Warsaw four months ago. Her papers were doubtful. She worked as a receptionist because she spoke five languages. She wanted to marry an American, for the passport, so she wouldn't be sent back to Warsaw. Strictly a marriage of convenience, she wanted that understood from the beginning, and a quick divorce and the passport.

Harrison did something in the British Embassy. He smiled benignly at Anna, relieved, Rosemary thought, that Anna would not settle for a British passport. He was on the watch for a likely American. He ordered another round of whiskeys. They seemed to make no difference to him. He sat straight, his hands did not tremble as he lit cigarettes, his voice remained low and cultured and club-like. The Empire had not crumbled because of the likes of him.

They were in a small dark bar near Rosemary's hotel. Convenient little spot, Harrison had said. There were a thousand convenient little spots in Paris for Harrison, Rosemary was sure. He knew most of the people in the bar. Some other Englishmen, about Harrison's age, in their forties, some young Frenchmen. The whiskey arrived on schedule. The bar became somewhat hazy, although Rosemary felt that her eyes were growing dazzlingly bright. Dinner was for the future. They were to dine with a young American. Rosemary couldn't quite make out just where they were to meet him.

They spoke about Bert. Athens. The Army had just taken over in Athens. Bert would like that. He swam in trouble. "I fear for him," Harrison said. "He is always being beaten up. He likes rough trade. One day, I'm sure they'll find him floating in the harbor of Piraeus, some harbor. A peculiar taste."

Rosemary nodded. "I've felt the same thing. I've talked to him about it." Oh, Love, Bert had said, a boy does what a boy has to do, Love.

Anna smiled over her fifth whiskey. She reminded Rosemary of her own daughter, smiling over the rim of a glass of milk at some secret eleven-year-old joke before bedtime.

"I knew somebody else like that," Rosemary said. "An interior decorator. A small, pleasant man. Over fifty. Quiet. Not blatant, like Bert. American. He was beaten to death by three sailors in a bar in Livorno. Nobody ever could figure out what he was doing in Livorno." What was his name? She knew it. She *knew* she knew it. She had met him dozens of times, had talked to him often at parties. He had invented a chair, she remembered. She was annoyed at not remembering his name. A bad sign. If a man you've talked *hours* to, a man who had done something important like inventing a chair is murdered, the least you can do is remember his name. A very bad sign.

Another round of drinks. Anna smiled. The bar grew appreciably darker. Rosemary wished Bert weren't in Athens. Tanks on the streets, curfew, people being rounded up at the point of a gun, nervous soldiers not likely to understand an English fairy's jokes. Be lugubrious, Love.

They walked across a bridge. The river flowed among monuments. Paris is a Bible in stone. Victor Hugo. A taxi driver nearby ran them down and shouted, "*Sales cons,*" at them. The voice of Lutetia.

"*Ta gueule,*" Harrison called, out of character.

Anna smiled.

"The streets are dangerous." Harrison held her elbow protectively. "Chap I know, Frenchman, got into a tangle with another car on a side street near the Opera, the other driver came raging out, hit him once and killed him on the spot. In front of his wife. Turned out to be a karate expert, something along that line."

Anna smiled. "It's worse in Warsaw," she said.

She had been in prison in Warsaw. Only for forty-eight hours, but in prison. They were in the restaurant by this time, but waiting at the bar, with the whiskeys still coming. The American hadn't shown up yet. The restaurant was a small one off the Champs-Elysées, with men sitting alone reading newspapers. On the front page of one of the newspapers there was a large photograph of two fattish middle-aged gentlemen gingerly poking rapiers at each other. There had been a duel that morning in a garden in Neuilly between two representatives of the Chambre des Députés. A little blood had been spilled. A nick in the arm. Honor had been satisfied. France.

"I am only sixteen at the time," Anna was saying. "I am invited to party. A diplomat from Italy. I am in demand in foreign circles because of my languages." She was a mistress of the present tense, Anna. "I still drink only juices of fruit. All the Poles present are arrested."

"*Encore trois whiskeys, Jean,*" said Harrison to the barman.

"The diplomat is smuggling works of art out of Poland," Anna said. "He is lover of art. The police talk to me for ten hours in small room in prison. They want me to tell them how I help smuggle out works of art and what I am paid. They say they know I am spy, besides. All I can do is cry. I know nothing. When I am invited to party I go to party. A girl goes to party when she is invited. I want to see my mother, but they say they will lock me up and keep me in prison until I talk, they do not tell nobody I am there. Forever." She smiled. "They put me in cell with two other women. Prostitutes. Very bad talking. They laugh when they see me crying, but I cannot stop. They are in prison three months already, they do not know when they must get out. They are crazy for man. Three months too long to go without man, they say. Out of cloth, twisted around, they make an," she hesitated, searching for the word, "an object," she said modestly, "shaped like sex of man."

"Penis," Harrison said, helpfully British.

"They use it on each other," Anna said. "They want to use it on me. I scream and the guard comes and they laugh. They say in three months I be screaming for them to lend it to me." She sipped her drink, smiling. "The next night, I am set free. I am not to tell anybody where I have been. So now I am in Paris and I would like to marry American and live in America."

On cue, the American entered the restaurant. There was a young blond-and-pink *Journey's End* kind of Englishman with him. The American was called Carroll and had a long, gaunt, sunburnt face. He was wearing a leather jacket and a black turtleneck sweater under it. He was a news photographer working for a big agency and had just come back from Vietnam and he explained he was late because he had been waiting in the office for blowups of some of his shots. They hadn't arrived yet. The Englishman had something to do with the BBC and seemed shy. The American kissed Anna, a brotherly kiss. He was not the type to enter into a marriage of convenience.

More whiskey appeared. Rosemary felt radiant. The

young Englishman seemed to blush again and again, whenever she caught him looking at her. How much better this was than sitting brooding alone in the hotel room, with lights too dim to read by.

"Prison is the ultimate experience," Harrison was saying, on his schedule of whiskey. Anna's reminiscence had set him off. He had been in a Japanese prisoner-of-war camp for three years. "It is more of a test of character, it is more essential than combat, even."

They were at table. They were eating hors d'oeuvres. The restaurant was famous for its hors d'oeuvres. There were two large carts loaded with plates of tuna, sardines, little radishes, céleri rémoulade, eggs with mayonnaise, raw mushrooms in oil, ratatouille, a dozen different kinds of sausage and pâté. The armies of the poor could be fed indefinitely on these tidbits of Paris. The young Englishman was sitting next to Rosemary. When his knee touched Rosemary's accidentally under the table, he pulled his leg back frantically, as though her knee were a bayonet. The whiskey had been transmuted to wine. New Beaujolais. The purple bottles came and went.

"The guards had a little game," Harrison was saying. "They would smoke a cigarette, very slowly, in front of us. A hundred men, starving, in rags, who literally would have given their lives for a cigarette. There wouldn't be a sound. Nobody would move. We just stood there, our eyes riveted on a little man with his rifle, looking at us over the smoke, letting the cigarette burn away in his hand. Then when it was half-finished, he'd throw it to the ground and trample it with his boot and walk away a few yards. And a hundred men would fling themselves on their knees, punching, scratching, kicking, cursing, to get at the shreds of the tobacco, while the guards laughed at us."

"The magical East," Carroll said. "Some of the things I've seen in Vietnam. . . ."

Rosemary hoped he wouldn't elaborate. She was enjoying her hors d'oeuvres and given half a chance the wine, after all that whiskey, would make her happy to be in Paris. Luckily, Carroll was a taciturn man and didn't go on. All he did was to reach into his pocket and take out a photograph and put it on the table in front of Rosemary. It was the sort of photograph you were used to seeing these days. A woman who looked about eighty years old, in black, squatting against a wall, her hand held out, begging, with a small, starved, almost naked child seated, puppy-eyed, beside her. A slender Eurasian girl, heavily made up, with a bouffant hairdo and a long slit in her silk dress showing a marvelous leg was walking past the old woman without glancing at her. On the wall that filled the background of the picture somebody had scrawled, in large chalk letters, God was here, but He left early.

"I took it for my religious editor," Carroll said, pouring himself some more wine.

Anna picked up the photograph. "That girl," she said. "If I am man I would never look at white women." She handed the photograph to the young Englishman, who studied it for a long time.

"In China," he said, "I understand there are no more beggars." Then he blushed, as though he had said something dirty and put the picture down quickly.

Eldred Harrison tilted his head, birdlike, to peer at the

photograph. "The new art of America," he said. "Graffiti. Wall-to-wall communication." He smiled deprecatingly at his joke.

Carroll put the picture back into his pocket.

"I didn't see a woman for two and a half years," Harrison said, starting on his steak.

Paris, Rosemary thought, the capital of dazzling conversation. Flaubert and his friends. She began to try to think of excuses for leaving before the dessert. The young Englishman poured her some more wine, almost filling the deep glass. "Thank you," she said. He turned his head away, uncomfortable. He had a beautiful long English nose, blond eyelashes, drawn-in pink cheeks, and full, girlish lips. *Alice in Wonderland* in his pocket during the barrage, Rosemary remembered vaguely, from a summer revival of *Journey's End*. All this talk of war. She wondered what he'd do if she quietly said, *Does anybody here know of a reliable abortionist?*

"We had a large group of Gurkhas in the camp, maybe two hundred," Harrison said, slicing his steak. We are in the Far East for the night, Rosemary thought. "Wonderful chaps. Enormous soldiers. The Japs kept working on them to come over to their side. Brothers-in-color, exploited by the white imperialists, that sort of thing. Gave them extra rations, cigarettes. The Gurkhas would carefully divide the rations with all the other prisoners. As for the cigarettes. . . ." Harrison shook his head in wonderment, twenty-five years later. "They'd accept the cigarettes, without a word. Then, as one man, they'd tear them deliberately to bits. Right in front of the guards. The guards would laugh and next day they'd give them more cigarettes and the same thing would happen. It went on like that for more than six months. Inhuman discipline. Marvelous troops, they were. In all that mud and dust, with people dropping dead all around them." Harrison sipped at his wine. All this seemed to be aiding his appetite, distant deprivation edging today's pleasure. "Finally," he said, "their colonel called them together and said it had to stop, it was degrading that the Japs could still think they could buy Gurkhas. He said a gesture was needed, a convincing gesture. The next day a Jap had to be killed—publicly. They were on work details and were issued shovels. He wanted one man to sharpen the rim of a shovel and when the work details were formed up next morning brain the nearest guard." Harrison finished his steak and pushed the plate an inch away from him, reflecting on Asia. "The colonel asked for a volunteer. Every man stepped forward in one moment, as if it were a parade. The colonel didn't hesitate. He picked the man directly in front of him. The man worked on sharpening his shovel all night with a big stone. And in the morning, in the sunlight, he moved over to the guard who was assigning the details and brained him. He himself was shot immediately, of course, and fifty others were beheaded. But the Japs stopped handing out cigarettes to Gurkhas."

"I'm glad I was too young for that war," Carroll said.

"Excuse me," Rosemary said, standing. "I'll be right back." The ladies' room was upstairs and she climbed the steps carefully, holding onto the banister, trying not to weave. In the ladies' room she put cold water on her eyelids, small remedy against all that whiskey and all that wine and the fifty beheaded soldiers. She put on some lipstick, moving her hand very precisely. Her face in the mirror was surprisingly fresh, a nice American lady tourist enjoying a night out in Paris with some of the people you're likely to pick up in a place like Paris. If there had been another door and she could have slipped out unnoticed, she would have gone home.

"Armstead," she said, "Brian Armstead." That was the name of the interior decorator they had found dead in Livorno. He had done Yoga exercises every day, she remembered, and once when she had met him on the beach at Southampton she had noticed that he had a firm brown delicate body with shapely legs and small sunburned feet with polished toenails.

The lights had been turned off outside the ladies' room and the landing was in darkness. Rosemary made her way cautiously toward the glow coming up the stairwell from the restaurant below. She stepped back with a little cry when she felt a hand touch her wrist.

"Mrs. Maclain," a man's voice whispered. "Don't be frightened. I wanted to talk to you alone." It was the young Englishman. He spoke rapidly, nervously. "I saw you were disturbed."

"Not really," she said. She wished she could remember his name. Robert? Ralph? No. She was having trouble with names tonight. "I've been around ex-soldiers before."

"He shouldn't really talk like that," the young man said (Rodney, that was it, Rodney). "Eldred. It's because you're Americans. You and the photographer. He's obsessed with what you're doing in Vietnam, his rooms're cluttered with the most dreadful photographs, he collects them. That's how he got so friendly with Carroll. He's a most peaceful man, Eldred, and he can't bear the thought. But he's too polite to argue with you openly, he's very fond of Americans, so he keeps on about all those other horrors he went through. It's his way of saying, Please stop, no more horror, please."

"Vietnam?" Rosemary said stupidly. She felt foolish talking about things like this in the dark outside the ladies' room with a nervous breathy young man who seemed frightened of her. "I'm not doing anything in Vietnam."

"Of course not," Rodney said hurriedly. "It's just that —well, being American, you see. . . . He really is an extraordinary man, Eldred, it's really worthwhile to get to know him and understand him, you see."

Fags, she thought cruelly. Is that it? But then Rodney said, "May I see you home safely, Mrs. Maclain? That is, whenever you're ready to go home, of course."

"I'm not that drunk," Rosemary said with dignity.

"Of course not," Rodney said. "I do apologize if that's the impression I . . . I think you're a splendidly beautiful woman, Mrs. Maclain."

He wouldn't have been able to say that if the light were on and she could see his face. *Splendidly.* Right out of Trollope.

"That's very kind of you, Rodney," she said. Neither a yes nor a no. "Now I think we'd better get back to our table."

"Of course," Rodney said. He took her arm and guided her toward the stairwell. His hand was trembling. English education, she thought.

"There was this sergeant we called Brother Three-

Iron," Harrison was saying as they came to the table. He stood up as Rosemary sat down. Carroll made a symbolic American move in his chair, theoretically rising. "He was tall for a Jap," Harrison went on, seating himself, "with bulging arms and shoulders and a cigarette dangling all the time from his lips. We called him Brother Three-Iron because he had got himself a golf club somewhere and was never seen without it. When he was displeased, which was often, he beat our people with it. Brother Three-Iron." Harrison spoke fondly, as if the Japanese sergeant and he had many warm memories to share between them. "He was displeased with me more than anyone else in the camp, it seemed, although he had killed several men with the club from time to time. But more or less impersonally. In the rounds of his duty, as it were. But with me, it was a . . . a particular impatience with my existence. When he saw me he would smile and say, 'Are you still alive?' He spoke some English, in that peculiar harmless way Japanese speak the language. I think he must have overheard something I said about him before I knew he could understand. Perhaps I smiled once inadvertently. I lost count of the number of times he beat me senseless. But he was always careful not to finish me off. I believe he was waiting for me to kill myself. That would have satisfied him. It helped keep me alive, the thought of not satisfying him. But if the war had lasted another month or two I doubt that I would have lasted. One last bottle of wine, wouldn't you say?" Harrison gestured toward the only waiter left in the empty restaurant.

"Policemen," Anna said. "They are the same everywhere." She pronounced it "ahverywhere." She seemed

younger than earlier in the evening, much younger. Her
eyes were like the eyes of the child in the photograph.

"What happened to the sonofabitch?" Carroll asked.
He was slumped in his chair, his chin resting on his chest
in ruffles of dark wool from the turtleneck collar, his own
bust in thin bronze. "Do you know?"

"I know," Harrison said offhandedly. "But it's of no
importance. Mrs. Maclain, you must be terribly bored
with these sorry reminiscences. I must really have had
one too many to drink. I'm sure you didn't come to Paris
to hear about a war that took place so far away, when you
were just a little girl learning how to read. If Bert hears
about this evening he'll be furious with me."

If you knew what I came to Paris for, brother, Rosemary thought. She was conscious of Rodney looking at
her almost imploringly. "I would like to know what happened," she said.

She could hear Rodney exhale. Relief, she thought. I
have passed a test.

"The Japanese have an admirable stoicism about death,"
Harrison said, pouring the last bottle of wine. His voice
was light-timbred, unemphatic. "When the war was over
teams came in from our Army to try to round up war
criminals. There was a section among the guards that was
composed of people very much like the German SS. They
were the systematic torturers and interrogators and exter-
minators. There were about twenty of them still in the
camp and when the British team came to their quarters
they were all lined up at attention in their best uniforms.
Before anybody could say a word to them, they went
down on their knees and bowed their heads and their

commanding officer said, in passable English, to the British major in charge of the party, 'Sir, we are war criminals. Kindly execute us immediately.' " Harrison shook his head, almost amused, almost admiring.

"Did you ever see the sergeant again?" Carroll asked.

"Brother Three-Iron? Oh, yes. Only a few days after the camp was liberated. When they let me out of hospital, I was down to ninety-eight pounds. I weighed a hundred and sixty at the beginning of the war. I was a young man then. I was called to the Camp Commandant's office. The major in charge of the war-crimes team was there. Ellsworth, his name was. A sturdy no-nonsense type. He'd been sent out from North Africa when they closed up shop there. Seen all kinds of fighting. I never saw him smile. Brother Three-Iron was standing in front of his desk. And behind Ellsworth's desk there was the golf club."

Rosemary began to feel very warm. She could sense the sweat breaking out on her throat.

"Brother Three-Iron looked the same as usual. Except that there was no cigarette hanging from his lip. It made a different man of him. It deprived him of authority. After our first glance we didn't look at each other. He gave no sign of recognition and I . . . well, to tell the truth, and I can't really understand it, I felt slightly . . . embarrassed. After all those years, the situation seemed . . . well, irregular. Wrong. One falls into patterns of behavior and when they are suddenly upset. . . ." Harrison shrugged. "Ellsworth didn't waste any words. 'I've heard about this fellow,' he said, 'and the way he went for you with that club.' He picked up the club and laid it on his desk, right in front of Brother Three-Iron. Brother Three-Iron looked at it once and something went on behind his eyes, though I couldn't say even to this day what it was. 'Well,' Ellsworth said, 'the club's yours now.' He pushed it a little way toward me. '*He*'s yours.' But I didn't pick it up. 'What're you waiting for, man?' Ellsworth said. 'I'm afraid I don't understand, sir," I said. I was telling the truth. I actually didn't. Then Ellsworth began to curse. I've never seen a man so angry. 'Ah, get out of my sight. There're too many like you. You went under. If I had my way you'd never get back to Britain. You'll always be prisoners. You've got the balls of prisoners.' Forgive me, Mrs. Maclain." Harrison turned apologetically toward Rosemary. "I've never told this part of the story before and my memory has remained uncensored."

"What finally happened?" Rosemary asked, disregarding the apology.

"I got out of Ellsworth's sight. Never saw him again, either. Luckily for me. His contempt was unendurable. I imagine Brother Three-Iron was eventually executed." He looked at his watch. "It *is* getting late." He waved for the bill.

Carroll hunched forward on the wine-stained table-cloth. "I wish I could be sure that I would have acted the same way as you did," he said to Harrison.

"Really?" Harrison sounded mildly surprised. "I keep wondering if Ellsworth wasn't right. I might be an entirely different man today." He made a failure's gesture.

"I wouldn't want you to be different man," Anna said softly.

Harrison patted her hand on the table. "You're a dear young girl, my Anna," he said. "Oh, perhaps it didn't really matter. In the state I was in it would have taken me weeks to kill him." Harrison paid the check and they stood up. "May I suggest a nightcap? I told some friends I'd meet them in St.-Germain-des-Près."

"I have to go back to the office," Carroll said. "They promised the blowups'd be in before midnight."

"It's late for me," Rosemary said. "I have a big day tomorrow."

The lights went out in the restaurant as they closed the door behind them. There was a wind blowing and the street was dark.

"Well, then," Harrison said, "we'll take Mrs. Maclain home."

"There's no need," Rosemary said.

"I've offered to accompany Mrs. Maclain, Eldred," Rodney said. His voice was tentative.

"Ah, then," said Harrison, "you're in safe hands." He kissed Rosemary's hand. He had been in France for years. "I *have* enjoyed this evening. Mrs. Maclain, I hope I may call you again. I must write to Bert and thank him."

They said their good nights. Rosemary said she wanted to walk a bit, to clear her head, and Carroll and Harrison and Anna got into a taxi together, since Carroll's office was on Harrison's way. The taxi dieseled down the dark street into silence. Rosemary allowed Rodney to take her arm and they walked toward the Champs-Elysées without talking.

The cold air hit Rosemary hard and there was an elliptical spin that started at the base of her neck and widened to include the city of Paris. She leaned harder on Rodney's arm.

"I say," he began, "I think a taxi might . . ."

"Sssh," she said. She stopped and kissed him in the last ten yards of darkness before the lights of the boulevard. To create a fixed point. To keep the spin within reasonable limits. His mouth tasted like fresh grapes. He trembled as he kissed her. His face was very warm in the cold spring night wind.

She pulled away, without haste. "Sssh," she said again, although he hadn't said anything.

They walked up the Champs-Elysées. People were coming out of a movie theater. On a giant poster above the entrance, a gigantic girl in a nightgown pointed a pistol the size of a cannon at a thirty-foot-tall man in a dinner jacket. Whores cruised slowly in pairs in sports cars, searching trade. If she were a man, she would try that. At least once. The flesh of Paris spinning against the flesh of Paris. Man and Woman, created He them. At this moment, in the whirling, secret beds of the city, how many were clasped, the world forgot . . . ? Harrison, prisoners' balls, forgetting Asia on the warm young chubby body of the girl from the Warsaw jail? Carroll, with one of those superb fashion models he photographed when he wasn't taking pictures of wars? God was here, but He left early, propped against the mantelpiece, to oversee the exercise?

Jean-Jacques, with his hard, expert body, entwined in legitimate abandon with the wide-eyed wife who didn't like to ski, in the great *lit matrimonial* off the Avenue Foch, and a girl in Strasbourg in reserve and another for the weekend of spring skiing, before he stopped off in Zurich to find an obliging psychiatrist?

The various uses and manifestations of the flesh. To caress, to mangle, to behead, to kill with a karate stroke on a city street, to prepare out of cloth a derisive simulacrum of the instrument of sex in a Polish prison. To cherish and despise. To protect and destroy. To clamor in the womb to become flesh. (A boy does what he has to do, Love.) To lie like Armstead, dead in the Livorno alley, with the polished toenails and shapely Yoga brown legs. To turn into Bert, with a Greek sailor in besieged Athens, the window open and a view of the Parthenon. Or floating face-down in the oily waters of the harbor of Piraeus. The grapey young kiss of the young Englishman.

Two stout, decorously dressed middle-aged men came out of a café. They were discussing interest rates. Tomorrow would they cross swords gingerly in a garden and claim blood's honor while the photographers clicked away?

A man with a turban passed them. A Gurkha with a shovel, honing it down to a knife edge to avenge the insult of the cigarettes. Violence, costumed, pursues us. Rosemary shivered.

"You're cold," Rodney said and they got into a taxi. She huddled against him, as close as she could get. She unbuttoned his shirt and put her hand on his chest. The skin was soft and hairless; the flesh, unscarred, had never known the harshness of uniforms, the death of prisons. Gentle, that fair English skin, gentle the soft hands.

"I don't want to be alone tonight," she whispered in the dark taxi.

Gentle the uncertain, unfamiliar, undemanding kiss. The

winy desires of the Paris night, the torment of the past, the imperious clamor of tomorrow, were made cozy, manageable. Even if she hadn't remembered his name it would have been all right.

They went up to her room together. The night clerk didn't even look up when he handed her the key. They didn't put on the light when they undressed. But then, in bed, it turned out he didn't want to make love to her. He merely wanted to spank her. She repressed the desire to laugh. She allowed him to do whatever he wanted to do. Who was she to be spared?

When he left, toward dawn, he kissed her, gently as ever, and asked if they could meet for lunch. When he had gone through the door she put on the light, went into the bathroom and took off her makeup. Looking into the mirror, she began to laugh, coarse, unstoppable laughter.

Where All Things Wise
and Fair Descend

❖   HE WOKE UP feeling good. There was no reason for
him to wake up feeling anything else.

He was an only child. He was twenty years old. He was
over six feet tall and weighed 180 pounds and had never
been sick in his whole life. He was number two on the
tennis team and back home in his father's study there was
a whole shelf of cups he had won in tournaments since he
was eleven years old. He had a lean, sharply cut face,
topped by straight black hair that he wore just a little long,
which prevented him from looking merely like an athlete.
A girl had once said he looked like Shelley. Another, like
Laurence Olivier. He had smiled noncommittally at both
girls.

He had a retentive memory and classes were easy for
him. He had just been put on the dean's list. His father,
who was doing well up North in an electronics business,
had sent him a check for $100 as a reward. The check
had been in his box the night before.

He had a gift for mathematics and probably could get
a job teaching in the department if he wanted it upon

graduation, but he planned to go into his father's business.

He was not one of the single-minded educational wizards who roamed the science departments. He got A's in English and history and had memorized most of Shakespeare's sonnets and read Roethke and Eliot and Ginsberg. He had tried marijuana. He was invited to all the parties. When he went home, mothers made obvious efforts to throw their daughters at him.

His own mother was beautiful and young and funny. There were no unbroken silver cords in the family. He was having an affair with one of the prettiest girls on the campus and she said she loved him. From time to time he said he loved her. When he said it he meant it. At that moment, anyway.

Nobody he had ever cared for had as yet died and everybody in his family had come home safe from all the wars.

The world saluted him.

He maintained his cool.

No wonder he woke up feeling good.

❖ ❖ ❖

It was nearly December, but the California sun made a summer morning of the season and the girls and boys in corduroys and T-shirts and bright-colored sweaters on their way to their ten-o'clock classes walked over green lawns and in and out of the shadows of trees that had not yet lost their leaves.

He passed the sorority house where Adele lived and waved as she came out. His first class every Tuesday was at ten o'clock and the sorority house was on his route to the arts building in which the classroom was situated.

Adele was a tall girl, her dark, combed head coming well above his shoulder. She had a triangular, blooming, still-childish face. Her walk, even with the books she was carrying in her arms, wasn't childish, though, and he was amused at the envious looks directed at him by some of the other students as Adele paced at his side down the graveled path.

" 'She walks in beauty,' " Steve said, " 'like the night/ Of cloudless climes and starry skies;/And all that's best of dark and bright/Meet in her aspect and her eyes.' "

"What a nice thing to hear at ten o'clock in the morning," Adele said. "Did you bone up on that for me?"

"No," he said. "We're having a test on Byron today."

"Animal," she said.

He laughed.

"Are you taking me to the dance Saturday night?" she asked.

He grimaced. He didn't like to dance. He didn't like the kind of music that was played and he thought the way people danced these days was devoid of grace. "I'll tell you later," he said.

"I have to know today," Adele said. "Two other boys've asked me."

"I'll tell you at lunch," he said.

"What time?"

"One. Can the other aspirants hold back their frenzy to dance until then?"

"Barely," she said. He knew that with or without him, Adele would be at the dance on Saturday night. She loved to dance and he had to admit that a girl had every right to expect the boy she was seeing almost every night in the week to take her dancing at least once on the weekend. He felt very mature, almost fatherly, as he resigned himself to four hours of heat and noise on Saturday night. But he didn't tell Adele that he'd take her. It wouldn't do her any harm to wait until lunch.

He squeezed her hand as they parted and watched for a moment as she swung down the path, conscious of the provocative way she was walking, conscious of the eyes on her. He smiled and continued on his way, waving at people who greeted him.

It was early and Mollison, the English professor, had not yet put in an appearance. The room was only half full as Steve entered it, but there wasn't the usual soprano-tenor tuning-up sound of conversation from the students who were already there. They sat in their chairs quietly, not talking, most of them ostentatiously arranging their books or going through their notes. Occasionally, almost furtively, one or another of them would look up toward the front of the room and the blackboard, where a thin boy with wispy reddish hair was writing swiftly and neatly behind the teacher's desk.

"Oh, weep for Adonais—he is dead!" the red-haired boy had written. "Wake, melancholy Mother, wake and weep!"

> *Yet wherefore? Quench within their burning*
> *bed*
> *Thy fiery tears, and let thy loud heart keep*
> *Like his a mute and uncomplaining sleep;*
> *For he is gone where all things wise and fair*

Descend. Oh, dream not that the amorous
  Deep
Will yet restore him to the vital air;
Death feeds on his mute voice, and laughs
  at our despair.

Then, on a second blackboard, where the boy was finishing the last lines of another stanza, was written:

He has outsoared the shadow of our night;
Envy and calumny and hate and pain,
And that unrest which men miscall delight,
Can touch him not and torture not again;
From the contagion of the world's slow stain
He is secure, and now can never mourn
A heart grown cold, a head grown gray in vain;

Professor Mollison came bustling in with the half-apologetic smile of an absent-minded man who is afraid he is always late. He stopped at the door, sensing by the quiet that this was no ordinary Tuesday morning in his classroom. He peered nearsightedly at Crane writing swiftly in rounded chalk letters on the blackboard.

Mollison took out his glasses and read for a moment, then went over to the window without a word and stood there looking out, a graying, soft-faced, rosy-cheeked old man, the soberness of his expression intensified by the bright sunlight at the window.

"Nor," Crane was writing, the chalk making a dry sound in the silence,

when the spirit's self has ceased to burn,
With sparkless ashes load an unlamented urn.

When Crane had finished, he put the chalk down neatly and stepped back to look at what he had written. A girl's laugh came in on the fragrance of cut grass through the open window and there was a curious hushing little intake of breath all through the room.

The bell rang, abrasively, for the beginning of classes. When the bell stopped, Crane turned around and faced the students seated in rows before him. He was a lanky, skinny boy, only 19, and he was already going bald. He hardly ever spoke in class and when he spoke, it was in a low, harsh whisper.

He didn't seem to have any friends and he never was seen with girls and the time he didn't spend in class he seemed to spend in the library. Crane's brother had played fullback on the football team, but the brothers had rarely been seen together, and the fact that the huge, graceful athlete and the scarecrow bookworm were members of the same family seemed like a freak of eugenics to the students who knew them both.

Steve knew why Crane had come early to write the two verses of Shelley's lament on the clean morning blackboard. The Saturday night before, Crane's brother had been killed in an automobile accident on the way back from the game, which had been played in San Francisco. The funeral had taken place yesterday, Monday. Now it was Tuesday morning and Crane's first class since the death of his brother.

Crane stood there, narrow shoulders hunched in a bright tweed jacket that was too large for him, surveying the class without emotion. He glanced once more at what he had written, as though to make sure the problem he had placed on the board had been correctly solved, then turned again to the group of gigantic, blossoming, rosy California boys and girls, unnaturally serious and a little embarrassed by this unexpected prologue to their class, and began to recite.

He recited flatly, without any emotion in his voice, moving casually back and forth in front of the blackboards, occasionally turning to the text to flick off a little chalk dust, to touch the end of a word with his thumb, to hesitate at a line, as though he had suddenly perceived a new meaning in it.

Mollison, who had long ago given up any hope of making any impression on the sun-washed young California brain with the fragile hammer of nineteenth century Romantic poetry, stood at the window, looking out over the campus, nodding in rhythm from time to time and occasionally whispering a line, almost silently, in unison with Crane.

" '. . . an unlamented urn,' " Crane said, still as flat and unemphatic as ever, as though he had merely gone through the two verses as a feat of memory. The last echo of his voice quiet now in the still room, he looked out at the class through his thick glasses, demanding nothing. Then he went to the back of the room and sat down in his chair and began putting his books together.

Mollison, finally awakened from his absorption with the sunny lawn, the whirling sprinklers, the shadows of the trees speckling in the heat and the wind, turned away from the window and walked slowly to his desk. He peered nearsightedly for a moment at the script crammed on the blackboards, then said, absently, "On the death of Keats. The class is excused."

For once, the students filed out silently, making a point, with youthful good manners, of not looking at Crane, bent over at his chair, pulling books together.

Steve was nearly the last one to leave the room and he waited outside the door for Crane. *Somebody* had to say something, do something, whisper "I'm sorry," shake the boy's hand. Steve didn't want to be the one, but there was nobody else left. When Crane came out, Steve fell into place beside him and they went out of the building together.

"My name is Dennicott," Steve said.

"I know," said Crane.

"Can I ask you a question?"

"Sure." There was no trace of grief in Crane's voice or manner. He blinked through his glasses at the sunshine, but that was all.

"Why did you do that?"

"Did you object?" The question was sharp but the tone was mild, offhand, careless.

"Hell, no," Steve said. "I just want to know why you did it."

"My brother was killed Saturday night," Crane said.

"I know."

" 'The death of Keats. The class is excused.' " Crane chuckled softly but without malice. "He's a nice old man, Mollison. Did you ever read the book he wrote about Marvell?"

"No," Steve said.

"Terrible book," Crane said. "You really want to know?" He peered with sudden sharpness at Steve.

"Yes," Steve said.

"Yes," Crane said absently, brushing at his forehead, "you would be the one who would ask. Out of the whole class. Did you know my brother?"

"Just barely," Steve said. He thought about Crane's brother, the fullback. A gold helmet far below on a green field, a number (what number?), a doll brought out every Saturday to do skillful and violent maneuvers in a great wash of sound, a photograph in a program, a young, brutal face looking out a little scornfully from the page. Scornful of what? Of whom? The inept photographer? The idea that anyone would really be interested in knowing what face was on that numbered doll? The notion that what he was doing was important enough to warrant this attempt to memorialize him, so that somewhere, in somebody's attic fifty years from now, that young face would still be there, in the debris, part of some old man's false memory of his youth?

"He didn't seem much like John Keats to you, did he?" Crane stopped under a tree, in the shade, to rearrange the books under his arm. He seemed oppressed by sunshine and he held his books clumsily and they were always on the verge of falling to the ground.

"To be honest," Steve said, "no, he didn't seem much like John Keats to me."

Crane nodded gently. "But I knew him," he said. "I knew him. And nobody who made those goddamned speeches at the funeral yesterday knew him. And he didn't believe in God or in funerals or those goddamned speeches.

He needed a proper ceremony of farewell," Crane said, "and I tried to give it to him. All it took was a little chalk, and a poet, and none of those liars in black suits. Do you want to take a ride today?"

"Yes," Steve said without hesitation.

"I'll meet you at the library at eleven," Crane said. He waved stiffly and hunched off, gangling, awkward, ill-nourished, thin-haired, laden with books, a discredit to the golden Coastal legend.

❖   ❖   ❖

They drove north in silence. Crane had an old Ford without a top and it rattled so much and the wind made so much noise as they bumped along that conversation would have been almost impossible, even if they had wished to talk. Crane bent over the wheel, driving nervously, with an excess of care, his long pale hands gripping the wheel tightly. Steve hadn't asked where they were going and Crane hadn't told him. Steve hadn't been able to get hold of Adele to tell her he probably wouldn't be back in time to have lunch with her, but there was nothing to be done about that now. He sat back, enjoying the sun and the yellow, burnt-out hills and the long, grayish-blue swells of the Pacific beating lazily into the beaches and against the cliffs of the coast. Without being told, he knew that this ride somehow was a continuation of the ceremony in honor of Crane's brother.

They passed several restaurants alongside the road. Steve was hungry, but he didn't suggest stopping. This was

Crane's expedition and Steve had no intention of inter-
fering with whatever ritual Crane was following.

They rocked along between groves of lemon and orange
and the air was heavy with the perfume of the fruit,
mingled with the smell of salt from the sea.

They went through the flecked shade of avenues of
eucalyptus that the Spanish monks had planted in another
century to make their journeys from mission to mission
bearable in the California summers. Rattling along in the
noisy car, squinting a little when the car spurted out into
bare sunlight, Steve thought of what the road must have
looked like with an old man in a cassock nodding along
it on a sleepy mule, to the sound of distant Spanish bells,
welcoming travelers. There were no bells ringing today.
California, Steve thought, sniffing the diesel oil of a truck
in front of them, has not improved.

The car swerved around a turn, Crane put on the brakes
and they stopped. Then Steve saw what they had stopped
for.

There was a huge tree leaning over a bend of the highway and all the bark at road level on one side of the tree
had been ripped off. The wood beneath, whitish, splintered,
showed in a raw wound.

"This is the place," Crane said, in his harsh whisper.
He stopped the engine and got out of the car. Steve followed him and stood to one side as Crane peered nearsightedly through his glasses at the tree. Crane touched the
tree, just at the edge of the wound.

"Eucalyptus," he said. "From the Greek, meaning well
covered; the flower, before it opens having a sort of cap.

A genus of plants of the N. O. Myrtaceae. If I had been a true brother," he said, "I would have come here Saturday morning and cut this tree down. My brother would be alive today." He ran his hand casually over the torn and splintered wood, and Steve remembered how he had touched the blackboard and flicked chalk dust off the ends of words that morning, unemphatically, in contact with the feel of things, the slate, the chalk mark at the end of the last "s" in Adonais, the gummy, drying wood. "You'd think," Crane said, "that if you loved a brother enough you'd have sense enough to come and cut a tree down, wouldn't you? The Egyptians, I read somewhere," he said, "were believed to have used the oil of the eucalyptus leaf in the embalming process." His long hand flicked once more at the torn bark. "Well, I didn't cut the tree down. Let's go."

He strode back to the car, without looking back at the tree. He got into the car behind the wheel and sat slumped there, squinting through his glasses at the road ahead of him, waiting for Steve to settle himself beside him. "It's terrible for my mother and father," Crane said, after Steve had closed the door behind him. A truck filled with oranges passed them in a thunderous whoosh and a swirl of dust, leaving a fragrance of a hundred weddings on the air. "We live at home, you know. My brother and I were the only children they had, and they look at me and they can't help feeling, If it had to be one of them, why couldn't it have been *him?* and it shows in their eyes and they know it shows in their eyes and they know I agree with them and they feel guilty and I can't help them." He started the engine with a succession of nervous, uncertain gestures, like a man who was just learning how to drive. He turned the car around in the direction of Los Angeles and they started south. Steve looked once more at the tree, but Crane kept his eyes on the road ahead of him.

"I'm hungry," he said. "I know a place where we can get abalone about ten miles from here."

❖   ❖   ❖

They were sitting in the weather-beaten shack with the windows open on the ocean, eating their abalone and drinking beer. The jukebox was playing *Downtown*. It was the third time they were listening to *Downtown*. Crane kept putting dimes into the machine and choosing the same song over and over again.

"I'm crazy about that song," he said. "Saturday night in America. Budweiser Bacchanalia."

"Everything all right, boys?" The waitress, a fat little dyed blonde of about 30, smiled down at them from the end of the table.

"Everything is perfectly splendid," Crane said in a clear, ringing voice.

The waitress giggled. "Why, that sure is nice to hear," she said.

Crane examined her closely. "What do you do when it storms?" he asked.

"What's that?" She frowned uncertainly at him.

"When it storms," Crane said. "When the winds blow. When the sea heaves. Then the young sailors drown in the bottomless deeps."

"My," the waitress said, "and I thought you boys only had one beer."

"I advise anchors," Crane said. "You are badly placed. A turn of the wind, a twist of the tide, and you will be afloat, past the reef, on the way to Japan."

"I'll tell the boss," the waitress said, grinning. "You advise anchors."

"You are in peril, lady," Crane said seriously. "Don't think you're not. Nobody speaks candidly. Nobody tells you the one-hundred-percent honest-to-God truth." He pushed a dime from a pile at his elbow, across the table to the waitress. "Would you be good enough to put this in the box, my dear?" he said formally.

"What do you want to hear?" the waitress asked.

"*Downtown*," Crane said.

"Again?" The waitress grimaced. "It's coming out of my ears."

"I understand it's all the rage," Crane said.

The waitress took the dime and put it in the box and *Downtown* started over again.

"She'll remember me," Crane said, eating fried potatoes covered with ketchup. "Every time it blows and the sea comes up. You must not go through life unremembered."

"You're a queer duck, all right," Steve said, smiling a little, to take the sting out of it, but surprised into saying it.

"Ah, I'm not so queer," Crane said, wiping ketchup off his chin. "I don't behave like this ordinarily. This is the first time I ever flirted with a waitress in my life."

Steve laughed. "Do you call that flirting?"

"Isn't it?" Crane looked annoyed. "What the hell is it if it isn't flirting?" He surveyed Steve appraisingly. "Let me ask you a question," he said. "Do you screw that girl I always see you with around the campus?"

Steve put down his fork. "Now, wait a minute," he said.

"I don't like the way she walks," Crane said. "She walks like a coquette. I prefer whores."

"Let's leave it at that," Steve said.

"Ah, Christ," Crane said, "I thought you wanted to be my friend. You did a friendly, sensitive thing this morning. In the California desert, in the Los Angeles Gobi, in the Camargue of Culture. You put out a hand. You offered the cup."

"I want to be your friend, all right," Steve said, "but there're limits . . ."

"The word friend has no limits," Crane said harshly. He poured some of his beer over the fried potatoes, already covered with ketchup. He forked a potato, put it in his mouth, chewed judiciously. "I've invented a taste thrill," he said. "Let me tell you something, Dennicott, friendship is limitless communication. Ask me anything and I'll answer. The more fundamental the matter, the fuller the answer. What's your idea of friendship? The truth about trivia—and silence and hypocrisy about everything else? God, you could have used a dose of my brother." He poured some more beer over the gobs of ketchup on the fried potatoes. "You want to know why I can say Keats and name my brother in the same breath?" he asked challengingly, hunched over the table. "I'll tell you why. Because he had a sense of elation and a sense of purity." Crane squinted thoughtfully at Steve. "You, too," he said, "that's why I said you would be the one to ask, out of the whole class. You have it, too—the sense of elation. I could tell—listening to you laugh, watching you walk down the library steps holding your girl's elbow. I, too," he said gravely, "am capable of elation. But I reserve it for other things." He made a mysterious inward grimace. "But the purity—" he said. "I don't know. Maybe you don't know yourself. The jury is still out on you. But I knew about my brother. You want to know what I mean by purity?" He was talking compulsively. Silence would have made memory unbearable. "It's having a private set of standards and never compromising them," he said. "Even when it hurts, even when nobody else knows, even when it's just a tiny, formal gesture, that ninety-nine out of a hundred people would make without thinking about it."

Crane cocked his head and listened with pleasure to the chorus of *Downtown,* and he had to speak loudly to be heard over the jukebox. "You know why my brother wasn't elected captain of the football team? He was all set for it, he was the logical choice, everybody expected it. I'll tell you why he wasn't, though. He wouldn't shake the hand of last year's captain, at the end of the season, and last year's captain had a lot of votes he could influence any way he wanted. And do you know why my brother wouldn't shake his hand? Because he thought the man was a coward. He saw him tackle high when a low tackle would've been punishing, and he saw him not go all the way on blocks when they looked too rough. Maybe nobody else saw what my brother saw or maybe they gave the man the benefit of the doubt. Not my brother. So he didn't shake his hand, because he didn't shake cowards' hands, see, and somebody else was elected captain. That's what I mean by purity," Crane said, sipping at his beer and looking out at the deserted beach and the ocean. For the first time, it occurred to Steve that it was perhaps just as well that he had never known Crane's brother, never been measured against that Cromwellian certitude of conduct.

"As for girls," Crane said. "The homeland of compromise, the womb of the second best—" Crane shook his head emphatically. "Not for my brother. Do you know what he did with his first girl? And he thought he was in love with her, too, at the time, but it still didn't make any difference. They only made love in the dark. The girl insisted. That's the way some girls are, you know, darkness excuses all. Well, my brother was crazy about her, and he didn't mind the darkness if it pleased her. But one night he saw her sitting up in bed and the curtains on the window moved in the wind and her silhouette was outlined against the moonlight, and he saw that when she sat like that she had a fat, loose belly. The silhouette, my brother said, was slack and self-indulgent. Of course, when she was lying down it sank in, and when she was dressed she wore a girdle that would've tucked in a beer barrel. And when he saw her silhouette against the curtain, he said to himself, This is the last time, this is not for me. Because it wasn't perfect, and he wouldn't settle for less. Love or no love, desire or not. He, himself, had a body like Michelangelo's David and he knew it and he was proud of it and he kept it that way, why should he settle for imperfection? Are you laughing, Dennicott?"

"Well," Steve said, trying to control his mouth, "the truth is, I'm smiling a little." He was amused, but he couldn't help thinking that it was possible that Crane had loved his brother for all the wrong reasons. And he couldn't help feeling sorry for the unknown girl, deserted, without knowing it, in the dark room, by the implacable athlete who had just made love to her.

"Don't you think I ought to talk about my brother this way?" Crane said.

"Of course," Steve said. "If I were dead, I hope my brother could talk like this about me the day after the funeral."

"It's just those goddamned speeches everybody makes," Crane whispered. "If you're not careful, they can take the whole idea of your brother away from you."

He wiped his glasses. His hands were shaking. "My goddamned hands," he said. He put his glasses back on his head and pressed his hands hard on the table, so they wouldn't shake.

"How about you, Dennicott?" Crane said. "Have you ever done anything in your whole life that was unprofitable, damaging, maybe even ruinous, because it was the pure thing to do, the uncompromising thing, because if you acted otherwise, for the rest of your life you would remember it and feel shame?"

Steve hesitated. He did not have the habit of self-examination and had the feeling that it was vanity that made people speak about their virtues. And their faults. But there was Crane, waiting, himself open, naked. "Well, yes . . ." Steve said.

"What?"

"Well, it was never anything very grandiose . . ." Steve said, embarrassed, but feeling that Crane needed it, that in some way this exchange of intimacies helped relieve the boy's burden of sorrow. And he was intrigued by Crane, by the violence of his views, by the almost comic flood of his reminiscence about his brother, by the importance that Crane assigned to the slightest gesture, by his searching for meaning in trivialities, which gave the dignity of examination to every breath of life. "There was the time on the beach at Santa Monica," Steve said, "I got myself beaten up and I knew I was going to be beaten up . . ."

"That's good," Crane nodded approvingly. "That's always a good beginning."

"Oh, hell," Steve said, "it's too picayune."

"Nothing is picayune," said Crane. "Come on."

"Well, there was a huge guy there who always hung around and made a pest of himself," Steve said. "A physical-culture idiot, with muscles like basketballs. I made fun of him in front of some girls and he said I'd insulted him, and I had, and he said if I didn't apologize, I would have to fight him. And I was wrong, I'd been snotty and superior, and I realized it, and I knew that if I apologized, he'd be disappointed and the girls'd still be laughing at him—so I said I wouldn't apologize and I fought him there on the beach and he must have knocked me down a dozen times and he nearly killed me."

"Right." Crane nodded again, delivering a favorable judgment. "Excellent."

"Then there was this girl I wanted . . ." Steve stopped.

"Well?" Crane said.

"Nothing," Steve said. "I haven't figured it out yet." Until now he had thought that the episode with the girl reflected honorably on him. He had behaved, as his mother would have put it, in a gentlemanly manner. He wasn't sure now that Crane and his mother would see eye to eye. Crane confused him. "Some other time," he said.

"You promise?" Crane said.

"I promise."

"You won't disappoint me, now?"

"No."

"OK." Crane said. "Let's get out of here."

They split the check.

"Come back again sometime, boys," the blonde waitress said. "I'll play that record for you." She laughed, her breasts shaking. She had liked having them there. One of them was very good-looking, and the other one, the queer one with the glasses, she had decided, after thinking about it, was a great joker. It helped pass the long afternoon.

On the way home, Crane no longer drove like a nervous old maid on her third driving lesson. He drove very fast, with one hand, humming *Downtown*, as though he didn't care whether he lived or died.

Then, abruptly, Crane stopped humming and began to drive carefully, timidly, again. "Dennicott," he said, "what are you going to do with your life?"

"Who knows?" Steve said, taken aback by the way Crane's conversation jumped from one enormous question to another. "Go to sea, maybe, build electronic equipment, teach, marry a rich wife . . ."

"What's that about electronics?" Crane asked.

"My father's factory," Steve said. "The ancestral business. No sophisticated missile is complete without a Dennicott supersecret what-do-you-call-it."

"Nah," Crane said, shaking his head, "you won't do that.

And you won't teach school, either. You don't have the soul of a didact. I have the feeling something adventurous is going to happen to you."

"Do you?" Steve said. "Thanks. What're you going to do with *your* life?"

"I have it all planned out," Crane said, "I'm going to join the forestry service. I'm going to live in a hut on the top of a mountain and watch out for fires and fight to preserve the wilderness of America."

That's a hell of an ambition, Steve thought, but he didn't say it. "You're going to be awfully lonesome," he said.

"Good," Crane said. "I expect to get a lot of reading done. I'm not so enthusiastic about my fellow man, anyway. I prefer trees."

"What about women?" Steve asked. "A wife?"

"What sort of woman would choose me?" Crane said harshly. "I look like something left over after a New Year's party on skid row. And I would only take the best, the most beautiful, the most intelligent, the most loving. I'm not going to settle for some poor, drab Saturday-night castaway."

"Well, now," Steve said, "you're not so awful." Although, it was true, you'd be shocked if you saw Crane out with a pretty girl.

"Don't lie to your friends," Crane said. He began to drive recklessly again, as some new wave of feeling, some new conception of himself, took hold of him. Steve sat tight on his side of the car, holding onto the door, wondering if a whole generation of Cranes was going to meet death on the roads of California within a week.

They drove in silence until they reached the university

library. Crane stopped the car and slouched back from the wheel as Steve got out. Steve saw Adele on the library steps, surrounded by three young men, none of whom he knew. Adele saw him as he got out of the car and started coming over to him. Even at that distance, Steve could tell she was angry. He wanted to get rid of Crane before Adele reached him. "Well, so long," Steve said, watching Adele approach. Her walk *was* distasteful, self-conscious, teasing.

Crane sat there, playing with the keys to the ignition, like a man who is always uncertain that the last important word has been said when the time has come to make an exit.

"Dennicott," he began, then stopped, because Adele was standing there, confronting Steve, her face set. She didn't look at Crane.

"Thanks," she said to Steve. "Thanks for the lunch."

"I couldn't help it," Steve said. "I had to go someplace."

"I'm not in the habit of being stood up," Adele said.

"I'll explain later," Steve said, wanting her to get out of there, away from him, away from Crane, watching soberly from behind the wheel.

"You don't have to explain anything," Adele said. She walked away. Steve gave her the benefit of the doubt. Probably she didn't know who Crane was and that it was Crane's brother who had been killed Saturday night. Still . . .

"I'm sorry I made you miss your date," Crane said.

"Forget it," Steve said. "She'll get over it."

For a moment he saw Crane looking after Adele, his face cold, severe, judging. Then Crane shrugged, dismissed the girl.

"Thanks, Dennicott," Crane said. "Thanks for coming

to the tree. You did a good thing this afternoon. You did a friendly thing. You don't know how much you helped me. I have no friends. My brother was the only friend. If you hadn't come with me and let me talk, I don't know how I could've lived through today. Forgive me if I talked too much."

"You didn't talk too much," Steve said.

"Will I see you again?" Crane asked.

"Sure," said Steve. "We have to go back to that restaurant to listen to *Downtown* real soon."

Crane sat up straight, suddenly, smiling shyly, looking pleased, like a child who has just been given a present. If it had been possible, Steve would have put his arms around Crane and embraced him. And with all Crane's anguish and all the loneliness that he knew so clearly was waiting for him, Steve envied him. Crane had the capacity for sorrow and now, after the day Steve had spent with the bereaved boy, he understood that the capacity for sorrow was also the capacity for living.

"*Downtown*," Crane said. He started the motor and drove off, waving gaily, to go toward his parents' house, where his mother and father were waiting, with the guilty look in their eyes, because they felt that if one of their sons had to die, they would have preferred it to be him.

Steve saw Adele coming back toward him from the library steps. He could see that her anger had cooled and that she probably would apologize for her outburst. Seeing Adele suddenly with Crane's eyes, he made a move to turn away. He didn't want to talk to her. He had to think about her. He had to think about everything. Then he remembered the twinge of pity he had felt when he had heard about the fat girl erased from her lover's life by the movement of a curtain on a moonlit night. He turned back and smiled in greeting as Adele came up to him. Crane had taught him a good deal that afternoon, but perhaps not the things Crane had thought he was teaching.

"Hello," Steve said, looking not quite candidly into the young blue eyes on a level with his own. "I was hoping you'd come back."

But he wasn't going to wake up, automatically feeling good, ever again.

PART II

Whispers in Bedlam

❖ HE WAS a typical 235-pound married American boy, rosy-cheeked, broken-nosed, with an excellent five-tooth bridge across the front of his mouth and a sixty-three-stitch scar on his right knee, where the doctors had done some remarkable things with floating cartilage. His father-in-law had a thriving insurance agency and there was a place open in it for him, the sooner, his father-in-law said, the better. He was growing progressively deafer in the left ear, due to something that had happened to him during the course of his work the year before on a cold Sunday afternoon out in Green Bay, Wisconsin. He was a professional football player. He played middle line-backer on defense and a certain amount of physical wear and tear was to be expected, especially in Green Bay.

His name was Hugo Pleiss. He was not famous. He had played on three teams, the sort of teams that are always around the bottom of their division. When coaches said that they were going to rebuild their clubs for next year, the first thing they did was to trade Hugo or declare him a free agent. But with all the new teams coming into the leagues, and the consequent demand for experienced players, Hugo always managed to be on somebody's roster when a new season started. He was large and eager to learn and he liked to play football and he had what coaches called "desire" when talking to sportswriters. While intelligent enough in real life (he had been a B student in college), on the field he was all too easily fooled. Perhaps, fundamentally, he was too honest and trusting of his fellow man. Fake hand-offs sent him crashing to the left when the play went to the right. He covered decoys with religious devotion while receivers whistled past him into the clear. He had an unenviable record of tackling blockers while allowing ball carriers to run over him. He hadn't intercepted a single pass in his entire career. He was doing well enough, though, until the incident of his ear at Green Bay. The man who played left corner back with him, Johnny Smathers, had a quick instinct for reading plays and, as the offense shaped up, would shout to Hugo and warn him where the play was going. Smathers was small, distrustful and crafty, with a strong instinct for self-preservation and more often than not turned out to be right. So Hugo was having a pretty fair season until he began to go deaf in the ear on Smathers' side and could no longer hear the corner back's instructions.

After two games in which Smathers had correctly diagnosed and called dozens of plays, only to see Hugo go hurtling off in the opposite direction, Smathers had stopped talking to Hugo at all, on or off the field. This hurt Hugo, who was a friendly soul. He liked Smathers and was grateful for his help and he wished he could explain about his left ear; but once the word got around that he was deaf, he was sure he'd be dropped from the squad. He wasn't yet ready to sell insurance for his father-in-law.

Luckily, the injury to Hugo's ear came near the end of the season and his ordinary level of play was not so high that the drop in his efficiency had any spectacular effect on the coaches or the public. But Hugo, locked in his auditory half-world, fearful of silent enemies on his left and oblivious to the cheers and jeers of half the stadium, brooded.

Off the field, despite occasional little mishaps, he could do well enough. He learned to sit on the left of the coach at all meetings and convinced his wife that he slept better on the opposite side of the bed than on the one he had always occupied in the three years of their marriage. His wife, Sibyl, was a girl who liked to talk, anyway, mostly in protracted monologues, and an occasional nod of the head satisfied most of her demands for conversational responses. And a slight and almost unnoticeable twist of the head at most gatherings put Hugo's right ear into receiving position and enabled him to get a serviceable fix on the speaker.

With the approach of summer and the imminence of the pre-season training sessions, Hugo brooded more than ever. He was not given to introspection or fanciful similes about himself, but he began to think about the left side of his head as a tightly corked carbonated cider bottle. He poked at his eardrum with pencil points, toothpicks and a nail clipper, to let the fizz out; but aside from starting a slight infection that suppurated for a week, there was no result.

Finally, he made hesitant inquiries, like a man trying to find the address of an abortionist, and found the name of an ear specialist on the other side of town. He waited for Sibyl to go on her annual two-week visit to her parents in Oregon and made an appointment for the next day.

Dr. G. W. Sebastian was a small oval Hungarian who was enthusiastic about his work. He had clean, plump little busy hands and keen, merry eyes. Affliction, especially in his chosen field, pleased him and the prospect of long, complicated and possibly dangerous operations filled him with joy. "Lovely," he kept saying, as he stood on a leather stool to examine Hugo's ear, "Oh, absolutely lovely." He didn't seem to have many patients. "Nobody takes ears seriously enough," he explained, as he poked with lights and curiously shaped instruments into Hugo's ear. "People always think they hear well enough or that other people have suddenly all begun to mumble. Or, if they do realize they're not getting everything, that there's nothing to be done about it. You're a wise young man, very wise, to have come to me in time. What is it you told Miss Cattavi your profession was?"

Miss Cattavi was the nurse. She was a six-foot, 165-pounder who looked as though she shaved twice a day. She had immigrated from northern Italy and was convinced that Hugo played soccer for a living. "That Pele," she had said. "The money he makes!"

Dr. Sebastian had never seen a football game in his life, either, and an impatient look came over his face as Hugo tried to explain what he did on Sundays and about Johnny Smathers and not being able to hear cleats pounding perilously on his left side when he went in to stop a draw over center. Dr. Sebastian also looked a little puzzled when Hugo tried to explain just exactly what had happened at Green Bay. "People do things like that?" he had said incredulously. "Just for money? In America?"

He probed away industriously, clucking to himself and smelling of peppermint and newly invented antiseptics, orating in little bursts that Hugo couldn't quite hear. "We are far behind the animals," was one thing Hugo *did* hear. "A dog responds to a whistle on a wave length that is silence for a human being. He hears a footfall on grass fifty yards away and growls in the darkness of the night. A fish hears the splash of a sardine in the water a mile away from him, and we have not yet begun to understand the aural genius of owls and bats."

Hugo had no desire to hear whistles on dogs' wave lengths or footfalls on grass. He was uninterested in the splash of distant sardines and he was not an admirer of the genius of owls and bats. All he wanted to be able to hear was Johnny Smathers ten yards to his left in a football stadium. But he listened patiently. After what doctors had done for his knee, he had a childlike faith in them; and if Dr. Sebastian, in the course of restoring his hearing, wanted to praise the beasts of the field and the birds of the air, Hugo was prepared to be polite and nod agreement from time to time, just as he did when Sibyl spoke about politics or miniskirts or why she was sure Johnny Smathers' wife was no better than she should be when the team was on the road.

"We have allowed our senses to atrophy." Hugo winced as Dr. Sebastian rose on his toes for leverage and went rather deep with a blunt instrument. "We have lost our animal magic. We are only one third in communication, even the best of us. Whole new fields of understanding are waiting to be explored. When Beethoven's last quartets are played in a concert hall, a thousand people should fall out of their seats and writhe in unbearable ecstasy on the floor. Instead, what do they do? They look at their programs and wonder if there will be a time for a beer before catching the last train home."

Hugo nodded. He had never heard any of Beethoven's last quartets and the floor of a concert hall didn't seem like the place a nice, well-brought-up married American boy should choose to writhe in ecstasy; but now that he had taken the step of going to a doctor, he was going to see it through. Still, with talk like that, about dogs and owls and sardines, he could see why there were no patients waiting in Dr. Sebastian's outer office.

"A crusade," Dr. Sebastian was saying, his eye glued to a lighted chromium funnel whose narrow end seemed to be embedded deep in Hugo's brain. Dr. Sebastian's breath pepperminted warmly on Hugo's bare neck. "A crusade is called for. You have a most unusually arranged collection of bones, Mr. Pleiss. A crusade to lift the curtain of sound, to unmuffle, to recapture our animal heritage, to distinguish whispers in bedlam, to hear the rustle of roses opening in the morning sun, to catch threats before they are really spoken, to recognize promises that are hardly formulated. I never did see a bone structure like this, Mr. Pleiss."

"Well, that feller in Green Bay weighed nearly three hundred pounds and his elbow—"

"Never mind, never mind," Dr. Sebastian finally pulled various bits of machinery out of his ear. "We will operate tomorrow morning, Miss Cattavi."

"OK," Miss Cattavi said. She had been sitting on a bench, looking as though she were ready to go in as soon as her team got the ball. "I'll make the arrangements."

"But—" Hugo began.

"I'll have everything ready." Dr. Sebastian said. "You've got nothing to worry about. Merely present yourself at the Lubenhorn Eye, Ear and Nose Clinic at three P.M. this afternoon."

"But there're one or two things I'd like to—"

"I'm afraid I'm terribly busy, Mr. Pleiss," Dr. Sebastian said. He whisked out of the office, peppermint receding on the aseptic air.

"He'll fix you," Miss Cattavi said, as she showed him to the door.

"I'm sure he will," said Hugo, "but—"

"I wouldn't be surprised," Miss Cattavi said, "if you came back to have the other ear done."

❖   ❖   ❖

When Hugo woke up after the operation, Dr. Sebastian was standing next to his bed, smiling merrily. "Naturally," Dr. Sebastian said, "there is a certain slight discomfort."

The left side of Hugo's head felt as though it were inside the turret of a tank that was firing sixty rounds a minute. It also still felt like a corked cider bottle.

"You have an extraordinary bone structure, Mr. Pleiss." The doctor raised himself on tiptoe, so as to be able to smile approvingly down into Hugo's face. He spent a lot of time on his toes, Dr. Sebastian. In one way, it would have been more sensible if he had specialized in things like knees and ankles, instead of ears. "So extraordinary that I hated to finish the operation. It was like discovering a new continent. What a morning you have given me, Mr. Pleiss! I am even tempted not to charge you a penny."

It turned out later that Dr. Sebastian resisted this temptation. He sent a bill for $500. By the time Hugo received the bill, on the same day that Sibyl came back from Oregon, he was happy to pay it. The hearing in his left ear was restored. Now, if only Johnny Smathers wasn't traded away and if their relationship could be patched up, Hugo was sure he'd be in there at middle linebacker for the whole season.

There was a red scar behind his ear, but Sibyl didn't notice it for four days. She wasn't a very observant girl, Sibyl, except when she was looking at other girls' clothes and hair. When Sibyl finally did notice the scar, Hugo told her he'd cut himself shaving. He'd have had to use a saw-toothed bread knife to shave with to give himself a scar like that, but Sibyl accepted his explanation. He was rock-bottom honest, Hugo, and this was the first time he'd ever lied to his wife. The first lie is easy to get away with.

❖   ❖   ❖

When he reported in to training camp, Hugo immediately patched up his friendship with Johnny Smathers. Johnny was a little cool at first, remembering how many times at the end of last season he had been made to look bad, all alone out there with two and three blockers trampling over him as Hugo was dashing away to the other side of the field, where nothing was happening. But when Hugo went as far as to confide in him that he'd had a little ringing in his left ear after the Green Bay game, a condition that had subsided since, Smathers had been understanding, and they even wound up as roommates.

Pre-season practice was satisfactory. The coach understood about the special relationship between Hugo and Smathers and always played them together and Hugo's performance was respectable, even though nobody was confusing him with Sam Huff or Dick Butkus or people like that.

The exhibition games didn't go badly and while Hugo didn't distinguish himself particularly, he made his fair share of tackles and batted down a few passes, listening carefully to Johnny Smathers' instructions and not being caught out of position too many times. It was a more-or-less normal September for Hugo, like so many Septembers of his life—sweaty, full of aches and bruises and abuse from coaches, not making love on Friday and Saturday, so as not to lose his edge for Sunday, feeling frightened for his life on Sunday morning and delighted to be able to walk out of the stadium on his own two feet in the dusk on Sunday afternoon. For want of a better word, what Hugo felt was happiness.

Then, just a minute before the end of the first regular league game of the season, something peculiar happened. Hugo's team was ahead twenty-one to eighteen, and the other team had the ball on his team's eight-yard line. It was third down and four to go and the crowd was yelling so much, the opposing quarterback, Brabbledoff, kept holding up his arms to get them to quiet down enough so that he could be heard in the huddle. The crowd hushed a bit; but, even so, Hugo was afraid he wouldn't be able to hear Smathers when the play started. He shook his head to clear the sweat from the inside of his helmet and, for a moment, his left ear was parallel to the opposing huddle. Then the peculiar thing happened. He heard what Brabbledoff was saying, just as if he were right there next to him in the huddle. And the huddle was a good fifteen yards away from Hugo, at least, and the crowd was roaring. "I'm going to bootleg it to the weak side," Brabbledoff was saying. "And, for Christ's sake, make it look real!"

The opposing team lined up and just before the snap, Hugo heard Smathers yell, "Around end to the strong side, around end to the strong side, Hugo!"

The two lines leaped into action; the guards pulled out to lead the run to the strong side. Hugo could have sworn he saw Brabbledoff hand off to Frenzdich, the halfback, who churned after the screen of interference, while Brabbledoff sauntered back, as though out of the play. Everybody on Hugo's team scrambled to stop the strong-side thrust. Everybody but Hugo. It was as though a button had been pushed somewhere in his back, making his moves mechanical. Struggling against the tide of traffic, he trailed Brabbledoff, who suddenly, in the clear, with no one near him, began to run like a frightened deer toward the weak-side corner, the ball now pulled out from behind the hip that had been hiding it. Hugo was there on the line of scrimmage, all alone, and he hurled himself at Brabbledoff.

Brabbledoff said something unsportsmanlike as he went down with Hugo on top of him, then fumbled the ball. Hugo kneeled on Brabbledoff's face and recovered the ball.

Hugo's teammates pummeled him in congratulation and they ran out the clock with two line bucks and the game was over, with the score twenty-one to eighteen.

The team voted Hugo the game ball in the locker room and the coach said, "It's about time you read a play correctly, Pleiss," which was high praise, indeed, from that particular coach.

In the shower, Johnny Smathers came over to him. "Man," Johnny said, "I could have killed you when I saw you drifting over to the weak side after I yelled at you. What tipped you off?"

"Nothing," Hugo said, after a moment's hesitation.

"It was a hell of a play," said Smathers.

"It was just a hunch," Hugo said modestly.

He was quieter than usual that Sunday night, especially after a win. He kept thinking about Dr. Sebastian and the sound of roses opening.

❖   ❖   ❖

The next Sunday, Hugo went out onto the field just like every Sunday. He hadn't heard anything all week that a man wouldn't ordinarily hear and he was sure that it had been an acoustical freak that had carried Brabbledoff's voice to him from the huddle. Nothing unusual happened in the first half of the game. Smathers guessed right about half of the time and while there was no danger that Hugo was going to be elected defensive player of the week by the newspapers, he served creditably for the first thirty minutes.

It was a rough game and in the third quarter, he was shaken breaking into a screen and got up a little groggy. Moving around to clear his head while the other team was in the huddle, he happened to turn his left side toward the line of scrimmage. Then it happened again. Just as though he were right there, in the middle of the opposing huddle, he heard the quarterback say, in a hoarse whisper, "Red right! Flood left! Wing square in! R down and out . . . on five!"

Hugo looked around to see if any of his teammates had heard, too. But they looked just the way they always looked—muddy, desperate, edgy, overweight, underpaid and uninformed. As the opposing team came out of the huddle, up to the line of scrimmage, Hugo moved automatically into the defensive formation that had been called by Krkanius, who played in the front four and ran the defense positions. "Red right! Flood left! Wing square in! R down and out . . . on five!" he repeated silently to himself. Since he didn't know the other team's signals, that didn't help him much, except that "on five" almost certainly meant that the ball was going to be snapped on the fifth count.

Smathers yelled, "Pass. On the flank!" and, again, Hugo felt as though a button had been pushed in his back. He was moving on the four count and was across the line of scrimmage, untouched, a fraction of a second after the ball was snapped, and laid the quarterback low before he could take a half step back into the pocket.

"Have you got a brother on this team, you son of a

bitch?" the quarterback asked Hugo as Hugo lay on the quarterback's chest.

After that, for most of the rest of the afternoon, by turning to his right, Hugo heard everything that was said in the opposing huddle. Aside from an occasional commonplace remark, like "Where were you on that play, fat ass, waving to your girl?" or "If that Hunsworth puts his fingers into my eye once more, I'm going to kick him in the balls," the only operational intelligence that came across to Hugo was in the quarterback's coded signals, so there wasn't much advantage to be gained from Hugo's keenness of hearing. He knew *when* the ball was going to be snapped and could move a step sooner than otherwise, but he didn't know where it was going and still had to depend upon Smathers in that department.

Going into the last two minutes of the game, they were ahead, fourteen to ten. The Studs were one of the strongest teams in the league and Hugo's team was a twenty-point underdog on the Las Vegas line and a win would be a major upset. But the Studs were on his team's thirty-eight-yard line, first down and ten to go, and moving. Hugo's teammates were getting up more and more slowly from the pile-ups, like losers, and they all avoided looking over toward the bench, where the coach was giving an imitation of General George S. Patton on a bad day along the Rhine.

The Studs went briskly into their huddle, keyed up and confident. Hugo had been blocked out of the last three plays ("wiped out like my three-year-old daughter" had been the phrase the coach had used) and he was preparing his excuses if he was pulled out of the game. The Studs were talking it up in the huddle. a confused babel of sound, when suddenly Hugo heard one voice, very clearly. It was Dusering, the leading pass catcher in the league. Hugo knew his voice well. Dusering had expressed himself to Hugo with some eloquence after Hugo had pushed him out of bounds in what Dusering considered an ungentlemanly manner after a thirty-yard gain on a pass to the side line.

"Listen," Dusering was saying in the huddle fifteen yards away, "I got Smathers all set up. I can beat him on a button-hook on the inside."

"OK," Hugo heard the quarterback say, and then the signal.

The Studs trotted up to the line of scrimmage. Hugo glanced around at Smathers. Smathers was pulling back deep, worried about Dusering's getting behind him, too busy protecting his area to bother about calling anything to Hugo. Hugo looked at Dusering. He was wide, on the left, looking innocent, giving nothing away.

The ball was snapped and Dusering went straight down the side line, as though for the bomb. A halfback came charging out in front of Hugo, yelling, his arms up, but Hugo ignored him. He cut back to his left, waited for a step, saw Dusering stop, then buttonhook back inside, leaving Smathers hopelessly fooled. The ball came floating out. Just as Dusering set himself to get it at waist height, Hugo flung himself across the trajectory of the pass and gathered it in. He didn't get far with it, as Dusering had him on the first step, but it didn't matter. The game was, to all intents and purposes, over, a stunning victory. It was the first pass Hugo had ever intercepted.

He was voted the game ball that Sunday, too.

In the locker room, the coach came over to Hugo while he was taking off his jockstrap. The coach looked at him curiously. "I really ought to fine you," the coach said. "You left the middle as open as a whore's legs on Saturday night."

"Yes, Coach," Hugo said, modestly wrapping a towel around him. He didn't like rough language.

"What made you cover the buttonhook?" the coach asked.

"I . . ." Hugo looked guiltily down at his bare toes. They were bleeding profusely and one nail looked as though he was going to lose it. "Dusering tipped it off. He does something funny with his head before the buttonhook."

The coach nodded, a new light of respect in his eyes.

It was Hugo's second lie. He didn't like to lie, but if he told the coach he could hear what people were whispering in a huddle fifteen yards away, with 60,000 people screaming in the stands like wild Indians, the coach would send him right over to the doctor to be treated for concussion of the brain.

❖   ❖   ❖

During the week, for the first time, he was interviewed by a sportswriter. The article came out on Friday and there was a picture of him crouching with his hands spread out, looking ferocious. The headline over the article said, "MR. BIG PLAY MAN."

Sibyl cut the article out and sent it to her father, who always kept saying that Hugo would never amount to anything as a football player and ought to quit and start selling insurance before he got his brains knocked out, after which it would be too late to sell anything, even insurance.

Practice that week was no different from any other week, except that Hugo was limping because of his crushed toes. He tested himself, to see if he could hear what people were saying outside of normal range, but even in the comparative silence of the practice field, he didn't hear any better or any worse than he had before his ear was hurt. He didn't sleep as well as he usually did, as he kept thinking about the next Sunday, and Sibyl complained, saying he was making an insomniac out of her, thrashing around like a beached whale. On Thursday and Friday nights, he slept on the couch in the living room. The clock in the living room sounded like Big Ben to him, but he attributed it to his nerves. On Saturday, the whole team went to a hotel for the night, so Sibyl had nothing to complain about. Hugo shared a room with Smathers. Smathers smoked, drank and chased girls. At two in the morning, still awake, Hugo looked over at Johnny, sleeping beatifically, and wondered if perhaps he was making a mistake somewhere in the way he led his life.

❖   ❖   ❖

Even limping from his crushed toes, Sunday was a remarkable day for Hugo. In the middle of the first quarter, after the opposing tackle had given him the knee to the head on a block, Hugo discovered that he not only could hear the signals in the other team's huddle but *knew what they meant*, just as though he had been studying their playbook for months. "Brown right! Draw fifty-five . . . on two!" came through in the quarterback's voice to his left ear, as though on a clear telephone connection, and was somehow instantly translated in Hugo's brain to "Flanker to the right, fake to the fullback over right guard, hand-off to right halfback and cutback inside left end."

Hugo still lined up obediently in the defensive formations called by Krkanius; but once the plays got under way, he disregarded his regular assignments and went where he knew the plays were going. He intercepted two passes, knocked down three more and made more tackles than the rest of the team put together. It was with somber satisfaction mixed with a curious sense of guilt that he heard Gates, the opposing quarterback, snarl in the huddle. "Who let that fish face Pleiss in there again?" It was the first time that he had heard any quarterback in the league mention him by name.

It was only as he was leaving the field that Hugo realized that Smathers hadn't called a play to him once during the whole game. He tried to catch Smathers' eye in the locker room, but Smathers always seemed to be looking the other way.

On Monday morning, when they ran the game films, the coach kept stopping the film on plays in which Hugo figured and rerunning those bits in slow motion over and over again. Hugo began to feel even more uncomfortable than he usually felt at these Monday-morning entertainments. The coach didn't say anything, except, "Let's look at that once more"; but seeing himself over and over again, in the center of plays so many times, embarrassed Hugo, as though he were showboating in front of his teammates. It was also embarrassing to see how often, even though he was right there, he allowed himself to be knocked down by blockers who were primarily going for another man, and how many tackles he had made that should have been clean but that developed into dogged, drag-me-along-with-you-Nellie yard-eating affairs. It was a stern rule with the coach that no comments were allowed by the players at the showings, so Hugo had no notion of what his teammates' estimate of his performance might be.

When the film was finally over, Hugo tried to be the first man out the door, but the coach signaled to him and pointed with his thumb to the office. Leaning heavily on his cane, Hugo hobbled into the office, prepared for the worst. The cane was not merely window dressing. The toes on Hugo's right foot looked like a plate of hamburger and, while he waited for the coach, Hugo thought of ways to introduce his infirmity as an excuse for some of the less glorious moments of his performance as revealed by the movies of the game.

The coach came in, opening the collar of his size-nineteen shirt so that he could express himself freely. He shut the door firmly, sat down and grunted. The grunt meant that Hugo could sit down, too. Hugo seated himself on a straight wooden chair, placing his cane prominently in front of him.

Behind the coach, on the wall, there was a blown-up photograph of a player in a 1940ish uniform. The player's name was Jojo Baines and he had once been voted the dirtiest lineman ever to play in the National Football League. The only time Hugo had ever heard a note of tenderness creep into the coach's voice was when he mentioned Jojo Baines.

"Ever since you joined this club, Pleiss," said the coach, "I have been appalled when I looked down at the starting line-up and seen your name on it—in my own handwriting."

Hugo smiled weakly, hoping to recognize a pleasantry.

"I won't keep it a secret from you, Pleiss," the coach went on. "For two years, I've been trying to get rid of you. I have made the circuit of every city in this league with my hat in hand, eating the bread of humiliation, trying to beg, borrow or steal another middle linebacker. To no avail." The coach had an ear for rhetoric, when he was so inclined. "No avail," he repeated. "They all knew that as long as I had to start you every Sunday, we were never a threat to anybody. I am going to give you an impersonal estimate of your abilities, Pleiss. You're slow, you have a miserable pair of hands, you don't hit hard enough to drive my grandmother out of a rocking chair, you close your eyes on contact, you run like a duck with gout, you wouldn't get angry if a man hit you over the head with an automobile jack and raped your wife in front of your eyes, and you get fooled on plays that would have made a high school cheerleader roar with laughter in 1910. Have I left out anything?"

"Not that I can think of, sir," Hugo said.

"With all that," the coach went on, "you have saved three games in a row for us. You make a mockery out of the holy sport of football, but you have saved three games in a row for us and I am hereby increasing your salary by one thousand dollars for the season. If you tell this to anyone else on the team, I will personally nail you by the hands to the locker-room wall."

"Yes, sir," said Hugo.

"Now, get out of here," the coach said.

"Yes, sir," Hugo said. He stood up.

"Give me that cane," the coach said.

Hugo gave him the cane. The coach broke it in two, without rising from his chair. "I can't stand the sight of cripples," he said.

"Yes, sir," Hugo said. He tried not to limp as he walked out of the office.

❖   ❖   ❖

The next Sunday was unsettling.

It started on an audible.

When the opposing team lined up after the huddle, Hugo knew that the play that had been called in the huddle was a short pass to the right flank. But when the quarterback took his position behind the center, Hugo saw him scanning the defensive setup and frowning. The quarterback's lips didn't move, but Hugo heard, just as though the man were talking directly to him, the word "No." There was a little pause and then, "It won't work, they're overshifting on us."

Hugo didn't have time to wonder at this new extension of his powers, as the quarterback began to call a set of signals aloud, changing the play he'd picked in the huddle. Everybody could hear the signals, of course, but Hugo was the only one on his team who knew that the quarterback was calling for an end around, from left to right. Just before the snap, when it was too late for the quarterback to call any changes, Hugo broke for the left side. He knew, without thinking about why he knew it, that the end would take two steps to his left, hesitate for one beat, then whirl around and streak for the quarterback and the ball on the way around the opposite end. As the ball was snapped, Hugo was knifing in between the end and the tackle, and when the end, after his two steps, came around, Hugo flattened him with a block. The quarterback was left all alone, holding the ball, like a postman delivering a package to the wrong door, and was downed for a five-yard loss.

But it was an expensive exploit for Hugo. The end's knee caught him in the head as they went down together and he was stretched out unconscious when the whistle blew.

When he woke up some minutes later, he was lying behind the bench, with the doctor kneeling over him, prodding the back of his neck, for broken vertebrae, and the trainer jamming spirits of ammonia under his nostrils. The jolt had been so severe that when the coach asked him at half time how he had been able to nip the end-around play in the bud, Hugo had to confess that he didn't remember anything about the play. In fact, he didn't remember leaving the hotel that morning, and it took him a good ten minutes after the coach had spoken to him to remember the coach's name.

The doctor wouldn't let him go back into the game and his value to the team was neatly demonstrated to the coach by the fact that they lost by three touchdowns and a field goal.

The plane was quiet on the flight home. The coach did not appreciate a show of youthful high spirits or resilience in adversity by teams of his when they had lost by three touchdowns and a field goal. And, as usual on such occasions, he had forbidden any drinks to be served, since he didn't believe the fine, full flavor of defeat should be adulterated by alcohol. So the plane sped through the night sky in a long funereal hush.

Hugo himself was feeling better, although he still didn't remember anything about the game that afternoon. He had a nagging sensation that something peculiar and fundamentally unwholesome had occurred *before* his injury, but he couldn't bring it up to the level of consciousness. There was a small poker game going on up front in low whispers and Hugo decided to sit in, to stop himself from profitless probing into the afternoon's events. He usually lost in these games, since one glance at his open face by any normally acquisitive poker player showed whether Hugo had a pair, two pairs or was buying to a straight.

Either because it was too dark in the plane for the other players to get a clear look at Hugo's face or because the head injury had hurt some nerve and rendered him expressionless, Hugo kept winning a fair proportion of the pots. He was a careless player and didn't keep track of his winnings and merely felt that it was about time that luck was turning his way.

After about an hour of play, he had a sizable stack of chips in front of him. He was sitting with three aces in his hand, having gotten two of them on a four-card draw, and he was about to raise the man on his left, Krkanius, who had drawn three cards, when somehow, just as though Krkanius had nudged him and whispered the news into his ear, he knew that Krkanius had a full house, jacks and fours. He didn't raise Krkanius but threw his cards in.

Someone else saw Krkanius and Krkanius put his cards down. Full house. Jacks and fours.

"I'm not feeling so well," Hugo said. "I'm cashing in." He stood up and went back to his seat.

It was a miserable night and the plane was bucking through thick cloud and Hugo sat at the window, looking out and feeling horrible. He was a cheat. He could make all sorts of excuses to himself, he could say he had acted out of surprise, without thinking, that it was the first time anything like that had ever happened to him, but he knew that if that weird message hadn't come through to him from Krkanius, on his left, he'd have raised Krkanius $10 and Krkanius would have raised him and Krkanius would be at least $20 or $30 richer right now. No matter how he tried to wriggle out of it, his conscience told him he was just as guilty as if he had taken $30 out of Krkanius' wallet.

Then, in a flash, he remembered the afternoon—the moment on the field when he was sure that he knew what the quarterback was thinking on the end-around play and his automatic reaction to it and his blotting out the end. It was another form of cheating, but he didn't know what to do about it. He could keep from playing poker, but he made his living out of playing football.

He groaned. He came from a deeply religious family, with a stern sense of morality. He didn't smoke or drink and he believed in hell.

After the plane landed, Hugo didn't go right home. Sibyl was away in Chicago, attending the wedding of one of her sisters, and he didn't feel like rattling around in an empty house. Krkanius, who had emerged from the poker game the big winner, invited him and a couple of the other boys to join him for a drink and, while Hugo didn't drink, he went along for the company.

The bar Krkanius took them to was crowded and noisy. There was a group of men with some girls at the bar, and as Hugo followed Krkanius to the back room, he heard a woman's voice say, "Uh-huh. That's for me. That big innocent-looking one."

Hugo looked around. A round blonde at the bar was staring directly at him, a sweet small smile on her full lips. If you didn't know what went on in her head, she looked like somebody's pure young daughter. "I'm going to teach you a few things tonight, baby," Hugo heard, staring, frozen, at the girl. The girl's mouth had never shown the slightest tremor of movement.

Hugo wheeled and hurried into the back room. When the waiter asked him what he wanted to drink, he ordered bourbon.

"Man," Krkanius said, surprised, "you really must've got shaken up today." Nobody had ever seen Hugo drink anything stronger than ginger ale before.

Hugo drank his bourbon quickly. He didn't like the taste, but it seemed to help his nerves. The blonde girl came into the back room and leaned over a table nearby to talk to somebody she knew. Remembering what she had been thinking as he passed her on the way in, Hugo ordered another bourbon. She glanced, as though by accident, at the table of football players. The way her sweater fit around her bosom made a peculiar ache come up in Hugo's throat.

"What're you waiting for, sweets?" he heard her think

as her glance swept over him. "The night's not getting any younger."

He drank the second bourbon even more quickly than the first. "Oh, God," he thought, "I'm becoming a drunkard." The bourbon didn't seem to do anything for his nerves this time.

"It's time to go home," he said, standing up. His voice didn't sound like his. "I'm not feeling so well."

"Get a good night's sleep," Krkanius said.

"Yeah." If Krkanius knew that he'd had $30 stolen from him that evening, he wouldn't have been so solicitous.

Hugo walked quickly past the bar, making sure not to look at the girl. It was raining outside now and all the taxis were taken. He was just about to start walking when he heard the door open behind him. He couldn't help but turn. The girl was standing there, alone, with her coat on. She was scanning the street for a taxi, too. Then she looked at him. "Your move, baby," he heard, in a voice that was surprisingly harsh for a girl so young.

Hugo felt himself blush. Just then, a taxi drove up. Both he and the girl started for it.

"Can I give you a lift?" Hugo heard himself saying.

"How kind of you," the girl said, demurely.

❖   ❖   ❖

On the way home, in the dawn, many hours later, Hugo wished for the first time in his life that he had been born a Catholic. Then he could have gone directly to a priest, confessed, accepted penance and been absolved of sin.

Sibyl called in the morning to tell him that her parents, who had come East for the wedding, were taking a trip to New York and wanted her to go along with them. Ordinarily, he wouldn't have been able to keep the disappointment at news like that out of his voice. He loved Sibyl dearly and usually felt lost without her. But now a wave of relief swept over him. The moment of confrontation, the moment when he would have to tell his innocent and trusting young wife about his appalling lapse from grace or, even worse, lie to her, was postponed.

"That's all right, honey," he said, "you just go along with your mother and dad and have a good time. You deserve a holiday. Stay as long as you like."

"Hugo," Sibyl said, "I just could break down and cry, you're so good to me."

There was the sound of a kiss over the telephone and Hugo kissed back. When he hung up, he leaned his head against the wall and closed his eyes in pain. One thing he was sure of, he wasn't going to see that girl, that Sylvia, again. Sylvia. Almost the same name as Sibyl. How rotten could a man be?

❖   ❖   ❖

Passion spent for the moment, he lay in the largest double bed he had ever seen, next to the dazzling body that had opened undreamed-of utopias of pleasure for him. Ashamed of himself even for thinking about it, he was sure that if Sibyl lived to the age of ninety, she wouldn't know one tenth as much as Sylvia must have known the day she was born.

In the soft glow of a distant lamp, he looked at the bed-side clock. It was past four o'clock. He had to report for practice, dressed, at ten o'clock. After a losing game, the coach gave them wind sprints for forty-five minutes every day for a week. He groaned inwardly as he thought of what he was going to feel like at 10:45 that morning. Still, for some reason, he was loath to go.

An hour later, he was finally dressed. He leaned over Sylvia to kiss her good-bye. She lay there, fresh as the morning, smiling, breathing placidly. He wished he were in as good condition as she was. "G'night, sweets," she said, an arm around his neck. "Don't let those rough boys hurt you today. And bring Baby a little giftie tonight. Try Myer's, on Sanford Street. They're full of goodies."

Walking home along the dark streets, Hugo thought, "Of course. Girls like little tokens of affection. Flowers, candy. Sentimental creatures." He didn't remember any store called Myer's on Sanford Street, but he supposed it was a confectionery shop that had some specialties that Sylvia had a taste for. He resolved to get her the best five-pound box of candy money could buy.

That afternoon, feeling a little light-headed from lack of sleep and the wind sprints, he walked along Sanford Street, searching for a shop called Myer's. He stopped short. MYER, the thin lettering read on the window. But instead of boxes of candy displayed behind the glass, there was a blaze of gold and diamonds. Myer's sold jewelry. Expensive jewelry.

Hugo did not go in. Thrift was another of the virtues his excellent family had instilled in him as a boy. He walked along Sanford Street until he found a candyshop and bought a five-pound box of chocolates. It cost $15 and Hugo felt a twinge at his extravagance as the clerk wrapped the box in festive paper.

That night, he didn't stay more than ten minutes in Sylvia's apartment. She had a headache, she said. She didn't bother to unwrap the candy.

The next night, he stayed longer. He had visited Myer's during the afternoon and bought a gold bracelet for $300. "I do like a generous man," Sylvia said.

The pain Hugo had felt in handing over the $300 to the clerk in Myer's was considerably mitigated by the fact that the night before, when he had left Sylvia with her headache, he had remembered that every Tuesday there was a poker game at Krkanius' apartment. Hugo had sat in for three hours and had won $416, the record for a single night's winnings since the inception of the game. During the course of the evening, by twisting his head a little now and then to get a fix with his left ear, he had been warned of lurking straights, one flush and several full houses. He had discarded a nine-high full house himself because Croker, of the taxi squad, was sitting in the hole with a jack-high full house; and Hugo had won with a pair of sevens after Krkanius had bluffed wildly through a hand with a pair of fives. Somehow, he told himself piously, as he stuffed bills and checks into his wallet when the game broke up, he would make it up to his teammates. But not just now. Just now, he couldn't bear the thought of Sylvia having any more headaches.

❖   ❖   ❖

Luckily, Sibyl didn't return until Friday. On Friday nights during the season, Hugo slept on the living-room couch, so as not to be tempted to impair his energies for Sundays' games, so *that* problem was postponed. He was afraid that Sibyl's woman's intuition would lead her to discover a fateful change in her husband, but Sibyl was so grateful for her holiday that her intuition lay dormant. She merely tucked him in and kissed him chastely on the forehead and said, "Get a good night's sleep, honey."

When she appeared with his breakfast on a tray the next morning, his conscience stirred uneasily; and after the light Saturday-morning practice, he went into Myer's and bought Sibyl a string of cultured pearls for $85.

Sunday was triumphal. Before the game, suiting up, Hugo decided that the best way he could make up to his teammates for taking $416 away from them was by doing everything he could to win the game for them. His conscience clear, obeying the voices within his head, he was in on half the tackles. When he intercepted a pass in the last quarter and ran for a touchdown, the first of his life, to put the game on ice, the entire stadium stood and cheered him. The coach even shook his hand when he came off the field. He felt dainty footed and powerful and as though he could play forever without fatigue. The blood coursing through his veins felt like a new and exhilarating liquid, full of dancing bubbles.

After the game, he was dragged off to a television interview in a little make-shift studio under the stands. He had never been on television before, but he got through it all right and later that night, somebody told him he was photogenic.

His life entered a new phase. It was as definite as opening and going through a door and closing it behind him, like leaving a small, shabby corridor and with one step emerging into a brilliantly lit ballroom.

His photograph was in the papers every week, with laudatory articles. Newspapermen sought him out and quoted him faithfully when he said, "The trick is to study your opponents. The National Football League is no place for guesswork."

He posed for advertising stills, his hair combed with greaseless products. He modeled sweaters and flowered bathing trunks and was amazed at how simple it was to earn large sums of money in America merely by smiling.

His picture was on the cover of *Sports Illustrated* and small boys waited for him at the players' entrance after practice. He autographed footballs, and taxi drivers recognized him and sometimes refused to take payment for their fares. He took to eating out in restaurants with Sibyl, because the managers more often than not tore up the check when he asked for it. He learned to eat caviar and developed a taste for champagne.

He was invited to parties at the home of Bruce Fallon, the quarterback, who had been paid $200,000 to sign and who was called a superstar by the sportswriters. Until then, Fallon, who only went around with the famous old-timers and the upper-bracket players on the club, had never even said hello to him when they passed on the street. "Do you play bridge, Hugo?" Fallon asked.

They played bridge, Fallon and Fallon's wife, Nora, and Hugo and Sibyl, in the huge living room of the Fallons' apartment, which had been decorated by an imported Norwegian. "Isn't this cozy?" Nora Fallon said, as the four of them sat around the pale wood table before the fire, playing for ten cents a point. Hugo's left ear worked for bridge as well as poker and Hugo wound up the first evening with an $800 profit, and Fallon said, "I've heard about your poker from the boys, Hugo. I've never met anybody with a card sense like yours."   ,

Fallon discussed the coach with him. "If Bert would really let me call my own game," Fallon said, pouring whiskeys for himself and Hugo, "we'd be twenty points better a Sunday."

"He's a little primitive, Bert, that's true," Hugo said, "but he's not a bad guy at heart." He had never heard anybody criticize the coach before and had never even thought of him by his first name. Even now, with the coach a good seven miles away across town and safely in bed, Hugo felt a curious little tickling in the small of his back as he realized that he had actually said, "Bert."

When they left that night, with Fallon's check for $800 in his pocket, Nora Fallon put up her cheek to be kissed. She had gone to school in Lausanne. She said, "We have to make this a weekly affair," as Hugo kissed her, and he knew she was thinking, "Wouldn't it be nice if we could have a little quiet tête-à-tête, you and I, sometime soon?"

That night, when Hugo got home, he wrote the Fallon telephone number in his little pocket address book. He wondered what it could be like, making love to a woman who thought in French.

❖   ❖   ❖

The trainer took a fussy interest in him now and, when he came up with a small bruise on his knee, insisted on giving him whirlpool baths for six days. The coach let him off a half hour early one day to make a speech at a local high school. Brenatskis, the publicity man, rewrote his biography for the programs and said that he had made Phi Beta Kappa in college. When Hugo protested, mildly, Brenatskis said, "Who'll know?" and, "It's good for your image." He also arranged for a national magazine to have Hugo photographed at home for a feature article. Sibyl insisted on buying a pair of gold-lamé pajamas if she was going to be photographed for a national magazine, and on having new curtains in the living room and new slip-covers made. When the article came out, there was only one picture accompanying it—Hugo in an apron, cooking in the kitchen. He was supposed to be making a compli-cated French dish. He never actually even made coffee for himself.

He bought three loud checked sports jackets for him-self and a $400 brooch for Sylvia, who was still subject to headaches. He couldn't tear himself away from Sylvia, al-though he was beginning to find her rather common, especially compared with Nora Fallon. He bought a $100 pair of earrings for Sibyl.

On Sundays, he raged over all the fields in the league, and at the end of home games, he had to get to the locker room fast to keep from being mobbed by fans. He began to receive love letters from girls, who sometimes included photographs taken in surprising positions. He knew that these letters disturbed Sibyl, but the mails were free, after all. By now, everybody agreed that he was photogenic.

Sibyl one day announced that she was pregnant. Until then, although Hugo had wanted children from the beginning of their marriage, she had insisted that she was too young. Now, for some reason, she had decided that she was no longer too young. Hugo was very happy, but he was so occupied with other things that he didn't have quite the time to show it completely. Still, he bought her a turquoise necklace.

Fallon, who was a born gambler, said that it was a shame to waste Hugo's card sense on penny-ante poker games and ten-cent-a-point family bridge. There was a big poker game in town that Fallon played in once a week. In the game, there were a stockbroker, a newspaper publisher, the president of an agricultural-machinery firm, an automobile distributor and a man who owned, among other things, a string of race horses. When Fallon brought Hugo into the hotel suite where the game was held, there was a haze of money in the room as palpable as the cigar smoke that eddied over the green table and against the drawn curtains. Hugo and Fallon had made a private deal that they would split their winnings and their losses. Hugo wasn't sure about the morality of this, since they weren't letting the others know that they were up against a partnership, but Fallon said, "What the hell, Huge, they're only civilians." Anybody who wasn't in some way involved in professional football was a civilian in Fallon's eyes. "Huge" was Fallon's friendly corruption of Hugo's name and it had caught on with the other men on the team and with the newspapermen who followed the club. When the offensive team trotted off the field, passing the defensive team coming in, Fallon had taken to calling out, "Get the ball back for me, Huge." A sportswriter had picked it up and had written a piece on Hugo using that as the title, and now, whenever the defensive team went in, the home crowd chanted, "Get the ball back for me, Huge." Sometimes, listening to all that love and faith come roaring through the autumn air at him, Hugo felt like crying for joy out there.

❖   ❖   ❖

The men around the green table all stood up when Fallon and Hugo came into the room. The game hadn't started yet and they were still making up the piles of chips. They were all big men, with hearty, authoritative faces. They shook hands with the two football players as Fallon introduced Hugo. One of them said, "It's an honor," and another man said, "Get the ball back for me, Huge," as he shook Hugo's hand and they all roared with kindly laughter. Hugo smiled boyishly. Because of the five-tooth bridge in the front of his mouth, Hugo for years had smiled as little as possible: but in the past few weeks, since he had become photogenic, he smiled readily. He practiced grinning boyishly from time to time in front of the mirror at home. People, he knew, were pleased to be able to say about him, "Huge? He looks rough, but when he smiles, he's just a nice big kid." Civilians.

They played until two o'clock in the morning. Hugo had won $6020 and Fallon had won $1175. "You two fellers are just as tough off the field as on," said the automobile distributor admiringly as he signed a check, and the other men laughed jovially. Losing money seemed to please them.

"Beginner's luck," Hugo said. Later on, the automobile distributor would tell his wife that Huge didn't look it, but he was witty.

They hailed a taxi outside the hotel. Fallon hadn't brought his Lincoln Continental, because there was no sense in taking a chance that somebody would spot it parked outside the hotel and tell the coach his quarterback stayed out till two o'clock in the morning. In the taxi, Fallon asked, "You got a safe-deposit box, Huge?"

"No," Hugo said.

"Get one tomorrow."

"Why?"

"Income tax," Fallon said. In the light of a street lamp, he saw that Hugo looked puzzled. "What Uncle Sam doesn't know," Fallon said lightly, "won't hurt him. We'll cash these checks tomorrow, divvy up and stash the loot away in nice dark little boxes. Don't use your regular bank, either."

"I see," Hugo said. There was no doubt about it; Fallon was a brainy man. For a moment, he felt a pang of regret that he had taken Nora Fallon to a motel the week before. He hadn't regretted it at the time, though. Quite the contrary. He had just thought that if the child Sibyl was carrying turned out to be a girl, he wouldn't send her to school in Lausanne.

Sibyl awoke when he came into the bedroom. "You win, honey?" she asked sleepily.

"A couple of bucks," Hugo said.

"That's nice," she said.

❖   ❖   ❖

By now, Hugo was free of doubt. If God gave you a special gift, He obviously meant you to use it. A man who could run the hundred in nine flat would be a fool to allow himself to be beaten by a man who could do only nine, five. If it was God's will that Hugo should have the good things of life—fame, success, wealth, beautiful women —well, that was God's will. Hugo was a devout man, even though, in the season, he was busy on Sunday and couldn't go to church.

During next week's poker game, Hugo saw to it that he didn't win too much. He let himself get caught bluffing several times and deliberately bet into hands that he knew were stronger than his. There was no sense in being greedy and killing the goose that laid the golden eggs. Even so, he came out almost $2000 ahead. Fallon lost nearly $500, so nobody had reason for complaint.

When the game broke up, Connors, the automobile distributor, told Hugo he'd like to talk to him for a minute. They went downstairs and sat in a deserted corner of the lobby. Connors was opening a sports-car agency and he wanted Hugo to lend his name to it. "There's nothing to it," Connors said. "Hang around the showroom a couple of afternoons a week and have your picture taken sitting in a Porsche once in a while. I'll give you ten thousand a year for it."

Hugo scratched his head boyishly, turning his left ear slightly toward Connors. The figure $25,000 came through loud and clear. "I'll take twenty-five thousand dollars and ten percent of the profits," Hugo said.

Connors laughed, delighted with his new employee's astuteness. "You must have read my mind," he said. They shook on the deal. Hugo was to go on the payroll the next day.

"He's got a head on his shoulders, old Huge," Connors told his wife. "He'll sell cars."

Another of the poker players, Hartwright, the race-horse owner, called Hugo and, after swearing him to secrecy, told him that he and what he called "a few of the boys" were buying up land for a supermarket in a suburb of the city. There was inside information that a superhighway was being built out that way by the city. "It'll be a gold mine," Hartwright said. "I've talked it over with the boys and they think it'd be a nice idea to let you in on it. If you don't have the cash, we can swing a loan. . . ."

Hugo got a loan for $50,000. He was learning that nothing pleases people more than helping a success. Even his father-in-law, who had until then never been guilty of wild feats of generosity, was moved enough by the combination of Hugo's new-found fame and the announcement that he was soon to be a grandfather to buy Hugo and Sibyl an eight-room house with a swimming pool in a good suburb of the city.

So the season went on, weeks during which Hugo heard nothing, spoken or unspoken, that was not for his pleasure or profit, the golden autumn coming to a rhythmic climax once every seven days in two hours of Sunday violence and huzzas.

The newspapers were even beginning to talk about the possibility of "The Cinderella Boys," as Fallon and Hugo and their teammates were called, going all the way to the showdown with Green Bay for the championship. But

on the same day, both Fallon and Hugo were hurt—Fallon
with a cleverly dislocated elbow and Hugo with a head
injury that gave him a severe attack of vertigo that made
it seem to him that the whole world was built on a slant.
They lost that game and they were out of the running
for the championship of their division and the dream was
over.

Before being injured, Hugo had had a good day; and
in the plane flying home, even though it seemed to Hugo
that it was flying standing on its right wing, he did not
feel too bad. All that money in the bank had made him
philosophic about communal misfortunes. The team doctor,
a hearty fellow who would have been full of cheer at
the fall of the Alamo, had assured him that he would
be fine in a couple of days and had regaled him with
stories of men who had been in a coma for days and had
gained more than 100 yards on the ground the following
Sunday.

An arctic hush of defeat filled the plane, broken only
by the soft complaints of the wounded, of which there
were many. Amidships sat the coach, with the owner,
forming glaciers of pessimism that flowed inexorably down
the aisle. The weather was bad and the plane bumped
uncomfortably through soupy black cloud and Hugo,
seated next to Johnny Smathers, who was groaning like
a dying stag from what the doctor had diagnosed as a
superficial contusion of the ribs, was impatient for the
trip to end, so that he could be freed from this atmosphere
of Waterloo and return to his abundant private world.
He remembered that next Sunday was an open date and
he was grateful for it. The season had been rewarding,

but the tensions had been building up. He could stand a week off.

Then something happened that made him forget about football.

There was a crackling in his left ear, like static. Then he heard a man's voice saying, "VHF one is out." Immediately afterward he heard another man's voice saying, "VHF two is out, too. We've lost radio contact." Hugo looked around, sure that everybody else must have heard it, too, that it had come over the public-address system. But everybody was doing just what he had been doing before, talking in low voices, reading, napping.

"That's a hell of a note." Hugo recognized the captain's voice. "There's forty thousand feet of soup from here to Newfoundland."

Hugo looked out the window. It was black and thick out there. The red light on the tip of the wing was a minute blood-colored blur that seemed to wink out for seconds at a time in the darkness. Hugo closed the curtain and put on his seat belt.

"Well, kiddies," the captain's voice said in Hugo's ear, "happy news. We're lost. If anybody sees the United States down below, tap me on the shoulder."

Nothing unusual happened in the passenger section.

The door to the cockpit opened and the stewardess came out. She had a funny smile on her face that looked as though it had been painted on sideways. She walked down the aisle, not changing her expression, and went to the tail of the plane and sat down there. When she was sure nobody was looking, she hooked the seat belt around her.

The plane bucked a bit and people began to look at their watches. They were due to land in about ten minutes and they weren't losing any altitude. There was a warning squawk from the public-address system and the captain said, "This is your captain speaking. I'm afraid we're going to be a little late. We're running into head winds. I suggest you attach your seat belts."

There was the click of metal all over the plane. It was the last sound Hugo heard for a long time, because he fainted.

He was awakened by a sharp pain in one ear. The right one. The plane was coming down for a landing. Hugo pulled the curtain back and looked out. They were under the cloud now, perhaps 400 feet off the ground and there were lights below. He looked at his watch. They were nearly three hours late.

"You better make it a good one," he heard a man's voice say, and he knew the voice came from the cockpit. "We don't have enough gas for another thousand yards."

Hugo tried to clear his throat. Something dry and furry seemed to be lodged there. Everybody else had already gathered up his belongings, placidly waiting to disembark. They don't know how lucky they are, Hugo thought bitterly as he peered out the window, hungry for the ground.

The plane came in nicely and as it taxied to a halt, the captain said cheerily, "I hope you enjoyed your trip, folks. Sorry about the little delay. See you soon."

The ground hit his feet at a peculiar angle when he debarked from the plane, but he had told Sylvia he would look in at her place when he got back to town. Sibyl was away in Florida with her parents for the week, visiting relatives.

Going over in the taxi, fleeing the harsh world of bruised and defeated men and the memory of his brush with death in the fogbound plane, he thought yearningly of the warm bed awaiting him and the expert, expensive girl.

Sylvia took a long time answering the bell and when she appeared, she was in a bathrobe and had her headache face on. She didn't let Hugo in, but opened the door only enough to speak to him. "I'm in bed, I took two pills," she said, "I have a splitting—"

"Ah, honey," Hugo pleaded. There was a delicious odor coming from her nightgown and robe. He leaned gently against the door.

"It's late," she said sharply. "You look awful. Go home and get some sleep." She clicked the door shut decisively. He heard her putting the chain in place.

On the way back down the dimly lit staircase from Sylvia's apartment, Hugo resolved always to have a small emergency piece of jewelry in his pocket for moments like this. Outside in the street, he looked up longingly at Sylvia's window. It was on the fourth floor and a crack of light, cozy and tantalizing, came through the curtains. Then, on the cold night air, he heard a laugh. It was warm and sensual in his left ear and he remembered, with a pang that took his breath away, the other occasions when he had heard that laugh. He staggered down the street under the pale lampposts, carrying his valise, feeling like Willy Loman coming toward the end of his career in *Death of a Salesman*. He had the impression that he was being followed slowly by a black car, but he was too distracted to pay it much attention.

When he got home, he took out a pencil and paper and noted down every piece of jewelry he had bought Sylvia that fall, with its price. The total came to $3468.30, tax included. He tore up the piece of paper and went to bed. He slept badly, hearing in his sleep the sound of faltering airplane engines mingled with a woman's laughter four stories above his head.

It rained during practice the next day and as he slid miserably around in the icy, tilted mud, Hugo wondered why he had ever chosen football as a profession. In the showers later, wearily scraping mud off his beard, Hugo became conscious that he was being stared at. Croker, the taxi-squad fullback, was in the next shower, soaping his hair and looking at Hugo with a peculiar small smile on his face. Then, coming from Croker's direction, Hugo heard the long, low, disturbing laugh he had heard the night before. It was as though Croker had it on tape inside his head and was playing it over and over again, like a favorite piece of music. Croker, Hugo thought murderously, Croker! A taxi-squadder! Didn't even get to make the trips with the team. Off every Sunday, treacherously making every minute count while his teammates were fighting for their lives.

Hugo heard the laugh again over the sound of splashing water. The next time there was an intrasquad scrimmage, he was going to maim the son of a bitch.

He wanted to get away from the locker room fast, but when he was dressed and almost out the door, the trainer called to him.

"The coach wants to see you, Pleiss," the trainer said, "Pronto."

Hugo didn't like the "pronto." The trainer had a disagreeable habit of editorializing.

The coach was sitting with his back to the door, looking up at the photograph of Jojo Baines. "Close the door, Pleiss," the coach said, without turning around.

Hugo closed the door.

"Sit down," the coach said, still with his back to Hugo, still staring at the photograph of what the coach had once said was the only 100 percent football player he had ever seen.

Hugo sat down.

The coach said, "I'm fining you two hundred and fifty dollars, Pleiss."

"Yes, sir," Hugo said.

The coach finally swung around. He loosened his collar. "Pleiss," he said, "what in the name of Knut Rockne are you up to?"

"I don't know, sir," Hugo said.

"What the hell are you doing staying up until dawn night after night?"

Staying up was not quite an accurate description of what Hugo had been doing, but he didn't challenge the coach's choice of words.

"Don't you know you've been followed, you dummy?" the coach bellowed.

The black car on the empty street. Hugo hung his head. He was disappointed in Sibyl. How could she be so suspicious? And where did she get the money to pay for detectives?

The coach's large hands twitched on the desk. "What are you, a sex maniac?"

"No, sir," Hugo said.

"Shut up!" the coach said.

"Yes, sir," said Hugo.

"And don't think it was me that put a tail on you," the coach said. "It's a lot worse than that. The tail came from the commissioner's office."

Hugo let out his breath, relieved. It wasn't Sibyl. How could he have misjudged her?

"I'll lay my cards on the table, Pleiss," the coach said. "The commissioner's office has been interested in you for a long time now. It's their job to keep this game clean, Pleiss, and I'm with them all the way on that, and make no mistake about it. If there's one thing I won't stand for on my club, it's a crooked ballplayer."

Hugo knew that there were at least 100 things that the coach had from time to time declared he wouldn't stand for on his club, but he didn't think it was the moment to refresh the coach's memory.

"Coach," Hugo began.

"Shut up! When a ballplayer as stupid as you suddenly begins to act as though he has a ouija board under his helmet and is in the middle of one goddamn play after another, naturally they begin to suspect something." The coach opened a drawer in his desk and took out a dark-blue folder from which he extracted several closely typewritten sheets of paper. He put on his glasses to read. "This is the report from the commissioner's office." He ran his eyes over some of the items and shook his head in wonder. "Modesty forbids me from reading to you the account of your sexual exploits, Pleiss," the coach said, "but I must remark that your ability even to trot out onto the field on Sunday after some of the weeks you've spent leaves me openmouthed in awe."

There was nothing Hugo could say to this, so he said nothing.

"So far, you've been lucky," the coach said. "The papers haven't latched onto it yet. But if one word of this comes out, I'll throw you to the wolves so fast you'll pull out of your cleats as you go through the door. Have you heard me?"

"I've heard you, Coach," Hugo said.

The coach fingered the papers on his desk and squinted through his bifocals. "In your sudden career as a lady's man, you also seem to have developed a sense of largess in the bestowal of jewelry. In one shop in this town alone, you have spent well over three thousand dollars in less than two months. At the same time, you buy an eight-room house with a swimming pool, you send your wife on expensive vacations all over the country, you invest fifty thousand dollars in a real-estate deal that is barely legal, you are known to be playing cards for high stakes with the biggest gamblers in the city and you rent a safe-deposit box and are observed stuffing unknown sums of cash into it every week. I know what your salary is, Pleiss. Is it unmannerly of me to inquire whether or not you have fallen upon some large outside source of income recently?"

The coach closed the folder and took off his glasses and sat back. Hugo would have liked to explain, but the words strangled in his throat. All the things that had seemed to him like the smiling gifts of fate now, in that cold blue folder, were arranged against him as the criminal profits of corruption. Hugo liked everyone to like him and he had become used to everyone wishing him well. Now the realization that there were men, the coach among them, who were ready to believe the worst of him and ruin him forever because of it, left him speechless. He waved his hands helplessly.

"Pleiss," the coach said, "I want you to answer one question, and if I ever find out you're lying. . . ." He stopped, significantly. He didn't add the usual coda, "I'll personally nail you by the hands to the locker-room wall." This omission terrified Hugo as he waited numbly for the question.

"Pleiss," the coach said, "are you getting information from gamblers?"

A wave of shame engulfed Hugo. He couldn't remember ever having felt so awful. He began to sob, all 235 pounds of him.

The coach looked at him, appalled. "Use your handkerchief, man," he said.

Hugo used his handkerchief. Damply he said, "Coach, I swear on the head of my mother, I never talked to a gambler in my life."

"I don't want the head of your mother," the coach snarled. But he seemed reassured. He waited for Hugo's sobs to subside. "All right. Get out of here. And be careful. Remember, you're being watched at all times."

Drying his eyes, Hugo dragged himself out of the office. The public-relations man, Brenatskis, was having a beer in the locker room with a small, gray-haired man with cigarette ash on his vest. Hugo recognized the man. It was Vincent Haley, the sports columnist. Hugo tried to get out without being seen. This was no day to be interviewed by a writer. But Brenatskis spotted him and called, "Hey, Hugo, come over here for a minute."

Flight would be damning. Hugo was sure that the whole world knew by now that he was a man under suspicion. So he tried to compose his face as he went over to the two men. He even managed an innocent, deceitful, country boy's smile.

"Hello, Mr. Haley," he said.

"Glad to see you, Pleiss," said Haley. "How's your head?"

"Fine, fine," Hugo said hurriedly.

"You're having quite a season, Pleiss," Haley said. His voice was hoarse and whiskeyish and full of contempt for athletes, and his pale eyes were like laser beams. "Yeah, quite a season. I don't think I've ever seen a linebacker improve so much from one game to another."

Hugo began to sweat. "Some years you're lucky," he said. "Things fall into place." He waited, cowering inwardly, for the next doomful inquiry. But Haley merely asked him some routine questions, like who was the toughest man in the league going down the middle and what he thought about the comparative abilities of various passers he had played against. "Thanks, Pleiss," Haley said, "that's about all. Good luck with your head." He held out his hand and Hugo shook it gratefully, glad that in another moment he was going to be out of range of those bone-dissolving eyes.

With his hand still in the writer's hand, Hugo heard the whiskeyish voice, but different, as though in some distant echo chamber, saying, in his left ear, "Look at him—two hundred and thirty-five pounds of bone and muscle, twenty-five years old, and he's back here raking in the dough, while my kid, nineteen years old, a hundred and thirty pounds dripping wet, is lying out in the mud and jungle in Vietnam, getting his head shot off. Who did *he* pay off?"

Haley gave Hugo's hand another shake. He even smiled, showing jagged, cynical, tar-stained teeth. "Nice talking to you, Pleiss." he said. "Keep up the good work."

"Thanks, Mr. Haley," Hugo said earnestly. "I'll try."

He went out of the stadium, not watching or caring where he was going, surrounded by enemies.

He kept hearing that rasping, disdainful "Who did *he* pay off?" over and over again as he walked blindly through the streets. At one moment, he stopped, on the verge of going back to the stadium and explaining to the writer about the sixty-three stitches in his knee and what the Army doctor had said about them. But Haley hadn't said anything aloud and it would be a plunge into the abyss if Hugo had to acknowledge that there were certain moments when he could read minds.

So he continued to walk toward the center of the city, trying to forget the coach and the gamblers, trying to forget Vincent Haley and Haley's nineteen-year-old son, weight 130 pounds, getting his head shot off in the jungle. Hugo didn't bother much about politics. He had enough to think about trying to keep from being killed every Sunday without worrying about disturbances 10,000 miles away in small

Oriental countries. If the United States Army had felt that he wasn't fit for service, that was their business.

But he couldn't help thinking about that kid out there, with the mortars bursting around him or stepping on poisoned bamboo stakes or being surrounded by grinning little yellow men with machine guns in their hands.

Hugo groaned in complicated agony. He had walked a long way and he was in the middle of the city, with the bustle of the business section all around him, but he couldn't walk away from that picture of Haley's kid lying torn apart under the burned trees whose names he would never know.

Slowly, he became aware that the activity around him was not just the ordinary traffic of the weekday city. He seemed to be in a parade of some kind and he realized, coming out of his private torment, that people were yelling loudly all around him. They also seemed to be carrying signs. He listened attentively now. "Hell, no, we won't go," they were yelling, and, "U.S. go home," and other short phrases of the same general import. And, reading the signs, he saw, BURN YOUR DRAFT CARDS and DOWN WITH AMERICAN FASCISM. Interested, he looked carefully at the hundreds of people who were carrying him along with them. There were quite a few young men with long hair and beards, barefooted in sandals, and rather soiled young girls in blue jeans, carrying large flowers, all intermingled with determined-looking suburban matrons and middle-aged, grim-looking men with glasses, who might have been college professors. My, he thought, this is worse than a football crowd.

Then he was suddenly on the steps of the city hall and

there were a lot of police, and one boy burned his draft card and a loud cheer went up from the crowd, and Hugo was sorry he didn't have his draft card on him, because he would have liked to burn it, too, as a sort of blind gesture of friendship to Haley's soldier son. He was too shy to shout anything, but he didn't try to get away from the city-hall steps; and when the police started to use their clubs, naturally, he was one of the first to get hit, because he stood head and shoulders above everybody else and was a target that no self-respecting cop would dream of missing.

❖   ❖   ❖

Standing in front of the magistrate's bench a good many hours later, with a bloody bandage around his head, Hugo was grateful for Brenatskis' presence beside him, although he didn't know how Brenatskis had heard about the little run-in with the police so soon. But if Brenatskis hadn't come, Hugo would have had to spend the night in jail, where there was no bed large enough to accommodate him.

When his name was called, Hugo looked up at the magistrate. The American flag seemed to be waving vigorously on the wall behind the magistrate's head, although it was tacked to the plaster. Everything had a bad habit of waving after the policeman's club.

The magistrate had a small, scooping kind of face that made him look as though he would be useful in going into small holes to search for vermin. The magistrate looked at him with distaste. In his left ear, Hugo heard the magistrate's voice—"What are you, a fag or a Jew or something?" This seemed to Hugo like a clear invasion of his rights, and he raised his hand as if to say something, but Brenatskis knocked it down, just in time.

"Case dismissed," the magistrate said, sounding like a ferret who could talk. "Next."

A lady who looked like somebody's grandmother stepped up belligerently.

Five minutes later, Hugo was going down the night-court steps with Brenatskis. "Holy man," Brenatskis said, "what came over you? It's a lucky thing they got hold of me or you'd be all over the front page tomorrow. And it cost plenty, I don't mind telling you."

Bribery, too, Hugo recorded in his book of sorrows. Corruption of the press and the judiciary.

"And the coach—" Brenatskis waved his arm hopelessly, as though describing the state of the coach's psyche at this juncture were beyond the powers of literature. "He wants to see you. Right now."

"Can't he wait till morning?" Hugo wanted to go home and lie down. It had been an exhausting day.

"He can't wait until morning. He was very definite. The minute you got out, he said, and he didn't care what time it was."

"Doesn't he ever sleep?" Hugo asked forlornly.

"Not tonight, he's not sleeping," said Brenatskis. "He's waiting in his office."

A stalactite formed in the region of Hugo's liver as he thought of facing the coach, the two of them alone at midnight in naked confrontation in a stadium that could accommodate 60,000 people. "Don't you want to come along with me?" he asked Brenatskis.

"No," said Brenatskis. He got into his car and drove off.

Hugo thought of moving immediately to Canada. But he hailed a cab and said "The stadium" to the driver. Perhaps there would be a fatal accident on the way.

There was one forty-watt bulb burning over the players' entrance and the shadows thrown by its feeble glare made it look as though a good part of the stadium had disappeared centuries before, like the ruins of a Roman amphitheater. Hugo wished it *were* the ruins of a Roman amphitheater as he pushed the door open. The night watchman, awakened from his doze on a chair tilted back against the wall, looked up at him. "They don't give a man no rest, none of them," Hugo heard the watchman think as he passed him. "God-damned prima donnas. I hope they all break their fat necks."

"Evenin', Mr. Pleiss. Nice evenin'," the watchman said.

"Yeah," said Hugo. He walked through the shadows under the stands toward the locker room. The ghosts of hundreds of poor, aching, wounded, lame, contract-haunted football players seemed to accompany him, and the wind sighing through the gangways carried on it the echoes of a billion boos. Hugo wondered how he had ever thought a stadium was a place in which you enjoyed yourself.

His hand on the locker-room door, Hugo hesitated. He had never discussed politics with the coach, but he knew that the coach cried on the field every time the band played *The Star-Spangled Banner* and had refused to vote for Barry Goldwater because he thought Goldwater was a Communist.

Resolutely, Hugo pushed the door open and went into the deserted locker room. He passed his locker. His name was still on it. He didn't know whether it was a good or a bad sign.

The door to the coach's office was closed. After one last look around him at the locker room, Hugo rapped on it.

"Come in," the coach said.

Hugo opened the door and went in. The coach was dressed in a dark suit and his collar was closed and he had a black tie on, as though he were en route to a funeral. His face was ravaged by his vigil, his cheeks sunk, his eyes peered out of purplish caverns. He looked worse than Hugo had ever seen him, even worse than the time they lost 45 to 0 to a first-year expansion club.

"My boy," the coach said in a small, racked voice, "I am glad you came late. It has given me time to think, to take a proper perspective. An hour ago, I was ready to destroy you in righteous anger with my bare hands. But I am happy to say that the light of understanding has been vouchsafed me in the watches of this painful night." The coach was in one of his Biblical periods. "Luckily," he said, "after Brenatskis called me to tell me that he had managed to persuade the judge to dismiss the case against you for a hundred dollars—naturally, your pay will be docked—and that the story would be kept out of the papers for another hundred and fifty—that will make two hundred and fifty, in all—I had time to consider. After all, the millions of small boys throughout America who look up to you and your fellows as the noblest expression of clean, aggressive American spirit, who model themselves with innocent hero worship after you and your teammates, are now going to be spared the shock and disillusionment of learning that a player of mine so far forgot himself as to be publicly associated with the enemies of his country—Are you following me, Pleiss?"

"Perfectly, Coach," said Hugo. He felt himself inching back toward the door. This new, gentle-voiced, understanding aspect of the coach was infinitely disturbing, like seeing water suddenly start running uphill, or watching the lights of a great city go out all at once.

"As I was saying, as long as no harm has been done to this multitude of undeveloped souls who are, in a manner of speaking, our responsibility, I can search within me for Christian forbearance." The coach came around the desk and put his hand on Hugo's shoulder. "Pleiss, you're not a bad boy—you're a stupid boy, but not a bad boy. It was my fault that you got involved in that sordid exhibition. Yes, my fault. You received a terrible blow on the head on Sunday—I should have spotted the symptoms. Instead of brutally making you do wind sprints and hit the dummy for two hours, I should have said, 'Hugo, my boy, go home and lie down and stay in bed for a week, until your poor head has recovered.' Yes, that's what I should have done. I ask your forgiveness, Hugo, for my shortness of vision."

"Sure, Coach," Hugo said.

"And now," said the coach, "before you go home to your loving wife and a good long rest, I want you to do one thing for me."

"Anything you say, Coach."

"I want you to join me in singing one verse—just one small verse—of *The Star-Spangled Banner*. Will you do that for me?"

"Yes, sir," Hugo said, sure that he was going to forget what came after "the rockets' red glare."

The coach gripped his shoulder hard, then said, "One, two, three. . . ."

They sang *The Star-Spangled Banner* together. The coach was weeping after the first line.

When they had finished and the echoes had died down under the grandstand, the coach said, "Good. Now go home. I'd drive you home myself, but I'm working on some new plays I want to give the boys tomorrow. Don't you worry. You won't miss them. I'll send them along to you by messenger and you can glance at them when you feel like it. And don't worry about missing practice. When you feel ready, just drop around. God bless you, my boy." The coach patted Hugo a last time on the shoulder and turned to gaze at Jojo Baines, his eyes still wet from the anthem.

Hugo went out softly.

❖   ❖   ❖

He stayed close to home all the rest of the week, living off canned goods and watching television. Nothing much could happen to him, he figured, in the privacy of his own apartment. But even there, he had his moments of distress.

He was sitting watching a quiz show for housewives at nine o'clock in the morning when he heard the key in the door and the cleaning woman, Mrs. Fitzgerald, came in. Mrs. Fitzgerald was a gray-haired lady who smelled of other people's dust. "I hope you're not feeling poorly, Mr. Pleiss," she said solicitously. "It's a beautiful day. It's a shame to spend it indoors."

"I'm going out later," Hugo lied.

Behind his back, he heard Mrs. Fitzgerald think. "Lazy, hulking slob. Never did an honest day's work in his life. Comes the revolution, they'll take care of the likes of him.

He'll find himself with a pick in his hands, on the roads. I hope I live to see the day."

Hugo wondered if he shouldn't report Mrs. Fitzgerald to the FBI, but then decided against it. He certainly didn't want to get involved with *them*.

He listened to a speech by the President and was favorably impressed by the President's command of the situation, both at home and abroad. The President explained that although things at the moment did not seem 100 percent perfect, vigorous steps were being taken, at home and abroad, to eliminate poverty, ill health, misguided criticism by irresponsible demagogues, disturbances in the streets and the unfavorable balance of payments. Hugo was also pleased, as he touched the bump on his head caused by the policeman's club, when he heard the President explain how well the war was going and why we could expect the imminent collapse of the enemy. The President peered out of the television set, masterly, persuasive, confident, including all the citizens of the country in his friendly, fatherly smile. Then, while the President was silent for a moment before going on to other matters, Hugo heard the President's voice, though in quite a different tone, saying, "Ladies and gentlemen, if you really knew what was going on here, you'd *piss*."

Hugo turned the television set off.

Then, the next day, the television set broke down, and as he watched the repairman fiddle with it, humming mournfully down in his chest somewhere, Hugo heard the television repairman think, "Stupid jerk. All he had to do was take a look and he'd see the only thing wrong is this loose wire. Slap it into the jack and turn a screw and the job's done." But when the television man turned around, he was shaking his head sadly. "I'm afraid you got trouble, mister," the television repairman said. "There's danger of implosion. I'll have to take the set with me. And there's the expense of a new tube."

"What's it going to cost?" Hugo asked.

"Thirty, thirty-five dollars, if we're lucky," said the television repairman.

Hugo let him take the set. Now he knew he was a moral coward, along with everything else.

He was cheered up, though, when his mother and father telephoned, collect, from Maine, to see how he was. They had a nice chat. "And how's my darling Sibyl?" Hugo's mother said. "Can I say hello to her?"

"She's not here," Hugo said. He explained about the trip to Florida with her parents.

"Fine people, fine people," Hugo's mother said. She had met Sibyl's parents once, at the wedding. "I do hope they're all enjoying themselves down South. Well, take care of yourself, Hooey. . . ." Hooey was a family pet name for him. "Don't let them hit you in the face with the ball." His mother's grasp of the game was fairly primitive. "And give my love to Sibyl when she gets home."

Hugo hung up. Then, very clearly, he heard his mother say to his father, 1000 miles away in northern Maine, "With her parents. I bet."

Hugo didn't answer the phone the rest of the week.

Sibyl arrived from Florida late Saturday afternoon. She looked beautiful as she got off the plane and she had a new fur coat that her father had bought her. Hugo had bought a hat to keep Sibyl from noticing the scalp wound inflicted by the policeman's club, at least at the airport, with people around. He had never owned a hat and he hoped Sibyl wouldn't notice this abrupt change in his style of dressing. She didn't notice it. And back in their apartment, she didn't notice the wound, although it was nearly four inches long and could be seen quite clearly through his hair, if you looked at all closely. She chattered gaily on about Florida, the beaches, the color of the water, the flamingos at the race track. Hugo told her how glad he was that she had had such a good time and admired her new coat.

Sibyl said she was tired from the trip and wanted to have a simple dinner at home and get to bed early. Hugo said he thought that was a good idea. He didn't want to see anybody he knew, or anybody he didn't know.

By nine o'clock, Sibyl was yawning and went in to get undressed. Hugo had had three bourbons to keep Sibyl from worrying about his seeming a bit distracted. He started to make up a bed on the living-room couch. From time to time during the week, he had remembered the sound of the low laugh from Sylvia's window and it had made the thought of sex distasteful to him. He had even noticed a certain deadness in his lower regions and he doubted whether he ever could make love to a woman again. "I bet," he thought, "I'm the first man in the history of the world to be castrated by a laugh."

Sibyl came out of the bedroom just as he was fluffing up a pillow. She was wearing a black nightgown that concealed nothing. "Sweetie," Sibyl said reproachfully.

"It's Saturday night," Hugo said, giving a final extra jab at the pillow.

"So?" You'd never guess that she was pregnant as she stood there at the doorway in her nightgown.

"Well, Saturday night, during the season," Hugo said. "I guess I've gotten into the rhythm, you might say, of sleeping alone."

"But there's no game tomorrow, Hugo." There was a tone of impatience in Sibyl's voice.

The logic was unassailable. "That's true," Hugo said. He followed Sibyl into the bedroom. If he was impotent, Sibyl might just as well find it out now as later.

It turned out that his fears were groundless. The three bourbons, perhaps.

As they approached the climax of their lovemaking, Hugo was afraid Sibyl was going to have a heart attack, she was breathing so fast. Then, through the turbulence, he heard what she was thinking. "I should have bought that green dress at Bonwit's," Sibyl's thoughtful, calm voice echoed just below his eardrum. "I could do without the belt, though. And then I just might try cutting up that old mink hat of mine and using it for cuffs on that dingy old brown rag I got last Christmas. Maybe my wrists wouldn't look so skinny with fur around them."

Hugo finished his task and Sibyl said "Ah" happily and kissed him and went to sleep, snoring a little. Hugo stayed awake for a long time, occasionally glancing over at his wife's wrists and then staring at the ceiling and thinking about married life.

Sibyl was still asleep when he woke up. He didn't waken her. A church bell was ringing in the distance, inviting, uncomplicated and pure, promising peace to tormented souls. Hugo got out of bed and dressed swiftly but carefully and hurried to the comforts of religion. He sat in the rear, on the aisle, soothed by the organ and the prayers and the upright Sunday-morning atmosphere of belief and remittance from sin.

The sermon was on sex and violence in the modern world and Hugo appreciated it. After what he had gone through, a holy examination of those aspects of today's society was just what he needed.

The minister was a big red-faced man, forthright and vigorous. Violence actually got only a fleeting and rather cursory condemnation. The Supreme Court was admonished to mend its ways and to refrain from turning loose on a Christian society a horde of pornographers, rioters, dope addicts and other sinners because of the present atheistic conception of what the minister scornfully called civil rights, and that was about it.

But when it came to sex, the minister hit his stride. The church resounded to his denunciation of naked and leering girls on magazine stands, of sex education for children, of an unhealthy interest in birth control, of dating and premarital lasciviousness, of Swedish and French moving pictures, of mixed bathing in revealing swimsuits, of petting in parked cars, of all novels that had been written since 1910, of coeducational schools, of the new math, which, the minister explained, was a subtle means of undermining the moral code. Unchaperoned picnics were mentioned, miniskirts got a full two minutes, and even the wearing of wigs, designed to lure the all-too-susceptible American male into lewd and unsocial behavior, came in for its share of condemnation. The way the minister was going on, it would not have surprised some members of the congregation if he finished up with an edict against cross-pollination.

Hugo sat at the rear of the church, feeling chastened. It was a good feeling. That was what he had come to church for, and he almost said "Amen" aloud after one or two of the more spiritedly presented items on the minister's list.

Then, gradually, he became aware of a curious cooing voice in his left ear. "Ah, you, fourth seat to the left in the third row," he heard, "you with that little pink cleft just peeping out, why don't you come around late one weekday afternoon for a little spiritual consolation, ha-ha." Aghast, Hugo realized it was the minister's voice he was hearing.

Aloud, the minister was moving on to a rather unconvincing endorsement of the advantages of celibacy. "And you, the plump one in the fifth row, with the tight brassiere, Mrs. What's-your-name, looking down at your hymnbook as though you were planning to go into a nunnery," Hugo heard, mixed with loud advice on holy thoughts and vigorous, innocent exercise, "I can guess what you're up to when your husband goes out of town. I wouldn't mind if you had *my* private telephone number in your little black book, ha-ha."

Hugo sat rigid in his pew. This was going just a little bit too far.

The minister had swung into chastity. He wanted to end on a note of uplift. His head was tilted back, heavenward, but through slitted eyes, he scanned his Sunday-best parishioners. The minister had a vested interest in chastity and his voice took on a special solemn intonation as he described how particularly pleasing this virtue was in the eyes of God and His angels. "And little Miss Crewes, with your white gloves and white socks," Hugo heard, "ripening away like a tasty little Georgia persimmon, trembling on the luscious brink of womanhood, nobody has to tell me what you do behind the stands on the way home from school. The rectory is only two blocks from school, baby, and it's on your way home. Just one timid knock on the door will suffice, ha-ha. There's always tea and little cakes for little girls like you at the rectory, ha-ha."

If Hugo hadn't been afraid of making a scene, he would have got up and run out of the church. Instead, he rapped himself sharply across the left ear. The consequent ringing kept him from hearing anything else. Several people turned around at the sound of the blow and stared disapprovingly at Hugo, but he didn't care. By the time the ringing stopped, the sermon was over and the minister was announcing the number of the hymn.

It was *Rock of Ages*. Hugo wasn't sure of the words, but he hummed, so as not to draw any more attention to himself.

The organ swelled, the sopranos, altos, tenors and bassos joined in, musical and faithful.

> "*Rock of Ages, cleft for me,*
> *Let me hide myself in Thee.*
> *Let the water and the blood,*
> *From Thy side, a healing flood,*
> *Be of sin the double cure . . .*"

Hugo was swept along on the tide of sound. He didn't have much of an ear for music and the only things he played on the phonograph at home were some old 78-rpm Wayne King records that his mother had collected when she was a girl and had given him as a wedding present. But now the diapason of the organ, the pure flutelike tones of the women and young girls addressing God, the deep cello support of the men, combined to give him a feeling of lightness, of floating on spring airs, of being lost in endless fragrant gardens. Virgins caressed his forehead with petaled fingers, waters sang in mountain streams, strong men embraced him in everlasting brotherhood. By the time the congregation reached "Thou must save, and Thou alone," Hugo was out of his pew and writhing in ecstasy on the floor.

It was lucky he was in the last row, and on the aisle.

The hymn was never finished. It started to falter at "While I draw this fleeting breath," as people turned around to see what was happening and came to a final stop on "When I rise to worlds unknown." By that time, everybody in the church was standing up and looking at Hugo, trembling, sprawled on his back, in the middle of the aisle.

The last notes of the organ came to a halt discordantly, at a signal from the minister. Hugo lay still for an instant, conscious of 300 pairs of eyes on him. Then he leaped up and fled.

❖   ❖   ❖

He rang the bell a long time, but it was only when he roared, "I know you're in there. Open up or I'll break it down," and began to buck at the door with his shoulder that it opened.

"What's going on here?" Miss Cattavi asked, blocking his way. "There are no visiting hours on Sunday."

"There will be this Sunday," Hugo said hoarsely. He pushed roughly past Miss Cattavi. She was all muscle. It was the first time he had ever been rude to a lady.

"He's in Romania," Miss Cattavi said, trying to hold on to him.

"I'll show him Romania," Hugo cried, throwing open doors and dragging Miss Cattavi after him like a junior high school guard.

Dr. Sebastian was behind the fourth door, in a room like a library, practicing dry-fly casting. He was wearing hip-length rubber boots.

"Oh, Mr. Pleiss," Dr. Sebastian said merrily, "you came back."

"I sure did come back," Hugo said. He had difficulty talking.

"You want your other ear done, I wager," said Dr. Sebastian, reeling in delicately.

Hugo grabbed Dr. Sebastian by the lapels and lifted him off the floor so that they were eye to eye. Dr. Sebastian weighed only 140 pounds, although he was quite fat. "I don't want the other ear done," Hugo said loudly.

"Should I call the police?" Miss Cattavi had her hand on the phone.

Hugo dropped Dr. Sebastian, who went down on one knee but made a creditable recovery. Hugo ripped the phone out of the wall. He had always been very careful of other people's property. It was something his father had taught him as a boy.

"Don't tell me," Dr. Sebastian said solicitously, "that

the ear has filled up again. It's unusual, but not unheard of. Don't worry about it. The treatment is simple. A little twirl of an instrument and—"

Hugo grabbed the doctor's throat with one hand and kept Miss Cattavi off with the other. "Now, listen to this," Hugo said, "listen to what you did to me."

"Cawlsnhnd on my goddamn windpipe," the doctor said. Hugo let him go.

"Now, my dear young man," Dr. Sebastian said, "if you'll only tell me what little thing is bothering you...."

"Get her out of the room." Hugo gestured toward Miss Cattavi. The things he had to tell Dr. Sebastian could not be said in front of a woman.

"Miss Cattavi, please..." Dr. Sebastian said.

"Animal," Miss Cattavi said, but she went out of the room and closed the door behind her.

Moving out of range, Dr. Sebastian went behind a desk. He remained standing. "I could have sworn that your ear was in superb condition," he said.

"Superb!" Hugo was sorry he had taken his hand off the doctor's throat.

"Well, you can hear your team's signals now, can't you?" Dr. Sebastian said.

"If that's all I could hear," Hugo moaned.

"Ah." Dr. Sebastian brightened. "Your hearing is better than normal. I told you you had an extraordinary aural arrangement. It only took a little cutting, a bold clearing away of certain extraneous matter.... You must be having a very good season."

"I am having a season in hell," Hugo said, unconscious that he was now paying tribute to a French poet.

"I'm terribly confused," the doctor said petulantly. "I do better for you than you ever hoped for and what is my reward—you come in here and try to strangle me. I do think you owe me an explanation, Mr. Pleiss."

"I owe you a lot more than that," Hugo said. "Where did you learn your medicine—in the Congo?"

Dr. Sebastian drew himself to his full height. "Cornell Medical School," he said with quiet pride. "Now, if you'll only tell me—"

"I'll tell you, all right," Hugo said. He paced up and down the room. It was an old house and the timbers creaked. The sound was like a thousand sea gulls in Hugo's ear.

"First," said Dr. Sebastian, "just what is it that you want me to do for you?"

"I want you to put my ear back the way it was when I came to you," Hugo said.

"You want to be deaf again?" the doctor asked incredulously.

"Exactly."

Dr. Sebastian shook his head. "My dear fellow," he said, "I can't do that. It's against all medical ethics. If it ever got out, I'd be barred forever from practicing medicine anyplace in the United States. A graduate of Cornell—"

"I don't care where you graduated from. You're going to do it."

"You're overwrought, Mr. Pleiss," the doctor said. He sat down at his desk and drew a piece of paper to him and took out a pen. "Now, if you'll only attempt, in a calm and orderly way, to describe the symptoms...."

Hugo paced up and down some more, trying to be calm and orderly. Deep down, he still had a great respect for doctors. "It started," he began, "with hearing the other team's signals."

Dr. Sebastian nodded approvingly and jotted something down.

"In the huddle," Hugo said.

"What's a huddle?"

Hugo explained, as best he could, what a huddle was. "And it's fifteen yards away and they whisper and 60,000 people are yelling at the top of their lungs all around you."

"I knew it was a successful operation," Dr. Sebastian said, beaming in self-appreciation, "but I had no idea it was *that* successful. It must be very helpful in your profession. Congratulations. It will make a most interesting paper for the next congress of—"

"Shut up," Hugo said. He then went on to describe how he began understanding what the signals meant. Dr. Sebastian's face got a little graver as he asked Hugo to kindly repeat what he had just said and to explain exactly what was the significance of "Brown right! Draw fifty-five . . . on two!" When he finally got it straight and noted that it was a secret code, different for each team, and that the codes were as jealously guarded from opposing teams as the crown jewels, he stopped jotting anything down. And when Hugo went on to the moment when he knew that the opposing quarterback was thinking, "No. . . . It won't work, they're overshifting on us," in just those words, Dr. Sebastian put his pen down altogther and a look of concern came into his eyes.

The description of the poker game only made the doctor

shrug. "These days," he said, "we are just beginning to catch a glimmer of the powers of extrasensory perception, my dear fellow. Why, down at Duke University—"

"Keep quiet," Hugo said, and described, with a reminiscent thrill of terror, the radio breakdown in the cockpit of the airplane and hearing the conversation between the pilots.

"I'm sure that could be explained," the doctor said. "A freak electronic phenomenon that—"

Hugo cut in. "I want you to hear what happened to me with a girl," Hugo said. "There was nothing electronic about that."

Dr. Sebastian listened with interest as Hugo relived the experience with Sylvia. Dr. Sebastian licked his lips from time to time but said nothing. He clucked sympathetically, though, when Hugo described the laughter four stories up and Croker's replay in the shower.

Hugo didn't say anything about his conversations with the coach. There were certain things too painful to recall.

In a rush, Hugo let all the rest of it out—Vietnam, the clubbing by the policeman, the interior sneer of the magistrate, Mrs. Fitzgerald's dangerous radical leanings, the President's speech, the television repairman's chicanery, his mother's judgment of his wife.

Dr. Sebastian sat there without saying a word, shaking his head pityingly from time to time.

Hugo went on, without mercy for himself, about the green dress and the mink cuffs at a time when you'd bet for sure a woman would be thinking about other things. "Well," he demanded, "what've you got to say about that?"

"Unfortunately," Dr. Sebastian said, "I've never been married. A man my size." He shrugged regretfully. "But there are well-documented cases on record of loving couples who have spent long years together, who are very close together, who have a telepathic sympathy with each other's thoughts. . . ."

"Let me tell you what happened in church this morning," Hugo said desperately. The doctor's scientific ammunition was beginning to take its toll. The fearful thought occurred to him that he wasn't going to shake the doctor and that he was going to walk out of the door no different from the way he had entered.

"It is nice to hear that a big, famous, attractive young man like you still goes to church on Sunday morning," the doctor murmured.

"I've gone to my last church," Hugo said and gave him the gist of what he had heard the minister think while he was delivering his sermon on sex and violence.

The doctor smiled tolerantly. "The men of the cloth are just like us other poor mortals," he said. "It's very probable that it was merely the transference of your own desires and—"

"Then the last thing," Hugo said, knowing he *had* to convince the doctor somehow. He told him about writhing on the floor of the church, the spring breezes, the smell of flowers, the unutterable ecstasy during *Rock of Ages*.

The doctor made an amused little *moue*. "A common experience," he said, "for simple and susceptible religious natures. It does no harm."

"Three hundred people watching a two-hundred-and-thirty-five-pound man jerking around on the floor like a hooked tuna!" Hugo shouted. "That does no harm? And you yourself told me that if people could *really* hear, they'd writhe on the floor in ecstasy when they listened to Beethoven."

"Beethoven, yes," the doctor said. "But *Rock of Ages?*" He was a musical snob, Dr. Sebastian. "Tum-tum-tah-dee, tum-tum-dah," he sang contemptuously. Then he became professional. He leaned across the desk and patted Hugo's hand and spoke quietly. "My dear young man, I believe every word you say. You undoubtedly think you have gone through these experiences. The incidents on the playing field can easily be explained. You are highly trained in the intricacies of a certain game, you are coming into your full powers, your understanding of your profession leads you into certain instantaneous practical insights. Be grateful for them. I've already explained the cards, the minister, your wife. The passage with the lady you call Sylvia is a concretization of your sense of guilt, combined with a certain natural young man's sexual appetite. Everything else, I'm afraid, is hallucination. I suggest you see a psychiatrist. I have the name of a good man and I'll give him a call and—"

Hugo growled.

"What did you say?" the doctor asked.

Hugo growled again and went over to the window. The doctor followed him, worried now, and looked out the window. Fifty yards away, on the soft, leaf-covered lawn, a five-year-old boy in sneakers was crossing over toward the garageway of the next house.

The two men stood in silence for a moment.

The doctor sighed. "If you'll come into my operating room," he said.

❧　　　　　❧　　　　　❧

When he left the doctor's house an hour later, Hugo had a small bandage behind his left ear, but he was happy. The left side of his head felt like a corked-up cider bottle.

Hugo didn't intercept another pass all the rest of the season. He was fooled by the simplest hand-offs and dashed to the left when the play went to the right, and he couldn't hear Johnny Smathers' shouts of warning as the other teams lined up. Johnny Smathers stopped talking to him after two games and moved in with another roommate on road trips. At the end of the season, Hugo's contract was not renewed. The official reason the coach gave to the newspapers was that Hugo's head injury had turned out to be so severe that he would be risking permanent disablement if he ever got hit again.

Dr. Sebastian charged him $500 for the operation and, what with the fine and making up the bribes to the magistrate and the newspapers, that took care of the $1000 raise the coach had promised him. But Hugo was glad to pay for it.

By January tenth, he was contentedly and monogamously selling insurance for his father-in-law, although he had to make sure to sit on the left side of prospects to be able to hear what they were saying.

The Mannichon Solution

✣   ONE LIGHT shone late in the dark bulk of the Vogel-Paulson Research Laboratories. Mice of all colors and genetic backgrounds slept in their cages. Monkeys dozed, dogs dreamed, classified albino rats waited predictably for the morning's scalpels and injections. Computers hummed quietly, preparing gigantic responses on shadowed floors for the morrow. Cultures spread like geometric flowers in shrouded test tubes; city-states of bacteria vanished in aseptic dishes washed by scientific night; surprising serums precipitated obscurely to dash or reward the hopes of daylight. Chemicals secretly traded molecules behind pulled blinds, atoms whirled unobserved, cures and poisons formed in locked rooms. Electromagnetic tumblers guarded a million formulas in safes that reflected a gleam of steel in stray rays of moonlight.

In the one brightly lit, scrubbed room, a figure in white moved from table to table, pouring a liquid into a shallow glass receptacle, adding a puce-colored powder to the contents of a beaker, making notes on a baby-blue work pad. This was Collier Mannichon. He was medium-sized,

plump, his face was melon-round, melon-smooth (he had
to shave only twice a week), his high forehead, melon-
bulged. Looking at him, it was impossible not to be reminded of a smooth-skinned cantaloupe, ripe, but not
particularly tasty, and equipped with thick glasses. He had
teapot-blue eyes, with the expectant expression of an
infant whose diapers have been wet for some time. There
was a blondish fuzz on top of the melony forehead and
a small watermelon of a paunch. Collier Mannichon did
not look like a Nobel Prize winner. He was not a Nobel
Prize winner. He was twenty-nine years and three months
old. He knew that statistics showed that the majority of
great scientific discoveries had been made by men before
they reached their thirty-second birthday. He had two
years and nine months to go.

His chances of making a great scientific discovery in
the Vogel-Paulson Laboratories were remote. He was in
the Detergents and Solvents department. He was assigned
to the task of searching for a detergent that would eventually break down in water, as there had been several unpleasant articles in national magazines recently about
frothing sewers and running brooks covered with layers
of suds in which trout died. Mannichon knew that nobody
had ever won the Nobel Prize for inventing a new detergent, even one that did not kill trout. In one week,
he would be twenty-nine years and four months old.

Other men in the laboratory, younger men, were working on leukemia and cancer of the cervix and compounds
that showed promise in the treatment of schizophrenia.
There was even a twenty-year-old prodigy who was as-

signed to do something absolutely secret with free hy-
drogen. All possible roads to Stockholm. They were called
in to high-level staff meetings, and Mr. Paulson invited
them to the country club and to his home and they drove
around in sports cars with pretty, lascivious girls, almost
like movie actors. Mr. Paulson never came into the detergent department, and when he passed Mannichon in
the corridors, he called him Jones. Somehow, six years
ago, Mr. Paulson had got the idea that Mannichon's name
was Jones.

Mannichon was married to a woman who looked like
a casaba melon and he had two children, a boy and a girl,
who looked like what you might expect them to look like,
and he drove a 1959 Plymouth. His wife made no ob-
jections to his working at night. Quite the opposite.

Still, it was better than teaching chemistry in a high
school.

He was working at night because he had been confronted by a puzzling reaction that afternoon. He had
taken the company's standard detergent, Floxo, and added,
more or less at random, some of the puce-colored powder,
a comparatively simple mixture known familiarly as dioxotetramercphenoferrogene 14, which was known to
combine freely with certain stearates. It was an expensive
chemical and he had had some unpleasant moments with
the auditing department about his budget, so he had used
only one gram to a pound of Floxo, which cost $1.80 a
ton to produce and was sold at all your better super-
markets for forty-seven cents the convenient household
economy-size giant package, with Green Stamps.

He had put in a piece of white cotton waste, stained with

catsup from his luncheon lettuce-and-tomato sandwich
and had been disappointed to see that while his control
solution of pure Floxo had completely removed the stain
from a similarly prepared piece of cotton waste, the solution with dioxotetramercphenoferrogene 14 had left a
clearly defined ring on the cloth, which looked just like
what it was, catsup.

He had tried a solution with one milligram of dioxotetramercphenoferrogene 14, but the result had been exactly the same. He had been working on the project for
16 months and he was understandably a little discouraged
and was about to throw both samples out when he saw
that while the pure Floxo was sudsing away in its usual
national-magazine-disapproved manner, the treated mixture
now looked like the most limpid mountain spring water.

When he realized the enormity of his discovery, he
had to sit down, his knees too weak to carry him. Before
his eyes danced a vision of sewers that looked just like
sewers in 1890 and trout leaping at the very mouths of
conduits leading from thickly settled housing develop-
ments. Mr. Paulson would no longer call him Jones. He
would buy a Triumph. He would get a divorce and get
fitted for contact lenses. He would be promoted to Cancer.

All that remained to be done was to find the right proportion of dioxotetramercphenoferrogene 14 to Floxo, the
exact ratio that would not produce post-operational suds
and at the same time not leave rings and his future would
be assured.

Trained researcher as he was, he set about methodically,
though with quick-beating heart, making one mixture after
another. He was lavish with the dioxotetramercphenofer-

rogene 14. This was no moment for penny-pinching. He ran out of catsup and used tobacco tar from his pipe instead. But all through the afternoon, all through the lonely vigils of the night (he had called his wife and told her not to wait for dinner), the results were always the same. The telltale ring remained. It remained on cotton. It remained on linoleum. It remained on plastic. It remained on leatherette. It remained on the back of his hand.

He did not despair. Erlich had tried 605 combinations before the magic 606th. Science was long, time nothing.

He ran out of inanimate testing materials. He took out two white mice from a batch that had been given to him because they obstinately refused to grow tumors. Vogel-Paulson was running a campaign to induce dog owners to wash their animals' coats with Floxo, because Floxo was lagging in the household field behind its greatest competitor, Wondro, and new avenues of exploitation were being called for. The results on the mice were the same as on everything else. One mouse came out as white as the day it was born and the solution it had been washed in frothed normally. The other mouse looked as though it had been branded, but the solution Mannichon had used on it clarified within five minutes.

He killed the two mice. He was a conscientious man. He didn't use second-run mice. In killing the second mouse, he had the impression of being bitten. He prepared a new solution, this time with a millionth of a gram of dioxo-tetramercphenoferrogene 14, and went to the cages and reached in for two more mice. He had a mixed lot in the cages. Since he got the mice that were considered scientifically useless everywhere else in the laboratories, he had mice that suffered from gigantism, blind mice, black mice, piebald mice, mice that ate their young, freakish yellow mice, gray mice with magenta spots and mice that dashed themselves to death against the bars of their cages upon hearing the note A-flat on a tuning fork.

Gingerly avoiding their fangs, he extracted two mice from their cages. The room in which the cages were kept was in darkness, in deference to the auditing department's views on the extravagant use of electric current in Detergents and Solvents, so Mannichon didn't see the color of the mice until he brought them into his laboratory. They were yellowish in tone, almost like an off-breed golden Labrador or an unwell Chinese laundryman. He stained the mice carefully with tobacco tar. He had been smoking furiously to produce enough tobacco tar and his tongue was raw, but this was no time to balk at sacrifice.

He put one mouse in an inch of Floxo and distilled water and washed it carefully, after running alcohol over his hands. The mouse splashed brightly, seeming to enjoy its bath, as the stain vanished and the suds fizzed. He put the other mouse into a similar mixture and added a millionth of a gram of dioxotetramercphenoferrogene 14. He washed his hands again in alcohol. When he turned back to the second mouse, he saw that it had fallen over on its side into the solution. He bent over and peered at the mouse. It was not breathing. It was dead. He had seen enough dead mice to know a dead mouse when he saw one. He felt a wave of irritation with the organization of the laboratory. How did they expect him to get any serious work done when they gave him mice that collapsed at the first touch of the human hand?

He disposed of the dead mouse and went into the next room for a fresh one. This time, he turned on the light. The hell with those bastards in Audit.

Moved by one of those flashes of inspiration that reason cannot explain but which have made for such leaps forward in the sciences, he picked out another yellowish mouse, a sister of the one that had died. Defiantly, he left the light on in the mouse room, which began to tweak at about eight decibels.

Back in the laboratory, he carefully anointed the new mouse with tobacco tar, noticing meanwhile that the first mouse was still happily frisking in its invigorating suds. He put the mouse he was carrying down in an empty glass dish, its sides just a little too high for jumping. Then he poured some of the mixture with dioxotetramercphenoferrogene 14 in it over the new mouse. For a moment, nothing happened. He watched closely, his face six inches from the glass pan. The mouse sighed and lay down quietly and died.

Mannichon sat up. He stood up. He lit a new pipe. He went to the window. He looked out the window. The moon was sinking behind a chimney. He puffed on his pipe. Somewhere here, he sensed with his scientist's trained intuition, there was a cause and there was an effect. The effect was fairly evident. Two dead mice. But the first mouse, the white mouse, that he had put into practically the same solution, had not died, even though the stain had remained in its fur. White mouse, yellow mouse, yellow mouse, white mouse. Mannichon's head began to ache. The moon disappeared behind the chimney.

Mannichon went back to the table. The dead yellow

mouse in one pan was already stiffening, looking peaceful in the clear, clean-looking liquid. In the other pan, the other yellow mouse was surfing on the pure Floxo suds. Mannichon removed the dead mouse and put it into the refrigerator for future reference.

He went back into the mouse room, now tweaking at eleven decibels. He brought back with him a gray mouse, a black mouse and a piebald mouse. Without bothering to stain them, he put them one by one into the solution in which the two yellow mice had died. They all seemed to relish the immersion and the piebald mouse was so frisky after it that it attempted to mate with the black mouse, even though they were both males. Mannichon put all three control mice back into portable cages and then stared hard and long at the yellow mouse, still basking in its miniature Mediterranean of foamy, never-failing Floxo.

Mannichon gently lifted the yellow mouse out of the suds. He dried it thoroughly, which seemed to irritate the beast. Somehow, Mannichon got the impression that he had been bitten again. Then he carefully let the yellow mouse down into the pan in which his two yellow brethren had died and in which the three varicolored control mice had sported.

For a moment, nothing happened. Then, in his turn, the yellow mouse in the middle of the pan sighed and lay down and died.

Mannichon's headache made him close his eyes for 60 seconds. When he opened them, the yellow mouse was still dead, lying as it had fallen in the crystal-clear liquid.

Mannichon was assailed by a great weariness. Nothing like this had ever occurred to him in all the years he had been serving the cause of science. He was too tired to try to figure out what had been happening, whether it was for the better or for the worse, whether it advanced detergents or put them back 100 years, whether it moved him, Mannichon, closer to Cancer or back to Floor Wax and Glues, or even to severance pay. His brain refused to cope with the problem any longer that night and he mechanically put the dead mouse next to its mate in the refrigerator, tabbed the gray mouse, the black mouse and the piebald mouse, cleaned up, wrote his notes, put out the lights and started for home.

He didn't have the Plymouth tonight, because his wife had needed it to go to play bridge and all the buses had long since stopped running and he couldn't afford a taxi, even if he could have found one at that hour, so he walked home. On his way, he passed the Plymouth, parked in front of a darkened house on Sennett Street, more than a mile away from his home. Mannichon's wife had not told him whose home she was playing bridge in and he didn't recognize the house and he was surprised that people would still be playing bridge at two o'clock in the morning and with the curtains so tightly drawn that no beam of light shone through. But he didn't go in. His presence when she was playing bridge, his wife said, upset her bidding.

❖   ❖   ❖

"Collect your notes," Samuel Crockett was saying, "and put them in your briefcase and lock it. And lock the refrigerator." There were now 18 dead yellow mice in the refrigerator. "I think we'd better talk about this someplace where we won't be disturbed."

It was the next afternoon. Mannichon had called in Crockett, who worked in the laboratory next door, at 11 A.M. Mannichon had arrived at the lab at 6:30 A.M., unable to sleep. and had spent the morning dipping everything yellow he could find into the solution, which Crockett had begun calling the Mannichon solution at 2:17 P.M. It was the first time anything had been called after Mannichon (his two children had been named after his father-in-law and his mother-in-law) and Mannichon was beginning, dimly to see himself as a Figure in the World of Science. He had already decided to get himself fitted for contact lenses before they came to photograph him for the national magazines.

Crockett, or "Crock," as he was called, was one of the young men who drove around in an open sports car with lascivious girls. It was only a Lancia, but it was open. He had been top man in his class at MIT and was only twenty-five years and three months old and he was working on voluntary crystals and complex protein molecules, which was, in the Vogel-Paulson hierarchy, like being a marshal on Napoleon's staff. He was a lean, wiry Yankee who knew which side his experimental bread was buttered on. After the long morning of dipping bits of yellow everything (yellow silk, yellow cotton, yellow blotting paper) into the solution, with no reaction whatsoever, and executing more than a dozen yellow mice, Mannichon had felt the need for another mind and had gone next door, where Crockett had been sitting with his feet up on a stainless-steel laboratory table, chewing on a cube of sugar soaked in LSD and listening to Thelonious Monk on a portable phonograph.

There had been an initial burst of irritation. "What the hell do you want, Flox?" Crockett had said. Some of the younger men called Mannichon "Flox" as a form of professional banter. But then Crockett had consented to come along, after Mannichon had sketched out the nature of his visit. Enlisting Crockett's help had already paid off handsomely. He had had the dazzling idea at 1:57 P.M. of introducing drops of the solution orally to various colored mice, ending up with a yellow mouse, nearly the last of the batch in Mannichon's cages. The white mice, the gray mice, the black mice, the piebald mice, had reacted with vigor after a few drops of the solution, becoming gay and belligerent. The yellow mouse had quietly died twenty-eight minutes after its drink. So now they knew the solution worked internally as well as externally. However, Crockett had not yet come up with any ideas on how to erase the telltale ring that remained after the solution was used to take out stains. He didn't seem to be too interested in that aspect of the problem. But he had been impressed by the way even the smallest proportion of dioxotetra-mercphenoferrogene 14 had reduced the stubborn Floxo suds and had complimented Mannichon in his terse Yankee way. "You've got something there," he had said, sucking on an LSD sugar cube.

"Why can't we talk here?" Mannichon said, as Crockett made preliminary moves to get out of the laboratory. Mannichon punched in and punched out and he didn't want the personnel department coming asking him why he had taken half a Thursday afternoon off.

"Don't be naïve, Flox," was all Crockett said by way of explanation. So Mannichon put all his notes in his briefcase, arranged on shelves all the apparatus and supplies they had been using, locked the refrigerator and followed Crockett out into the corridor.

They met Mr. Paulson near the front gate. "Crock, old Crock," Mr. Paulson said, putting his arm fondly around Crockett's shoulder. "My boy. Hello, Jones. Where the hell are you going?"

"I—" Mannichon began, knowing he was going to stutter.

"Appointment at an optician's," Crockett said crisply. "I'm driving him."

"Aha," said Mr. Paulson. "Science has a million eyes. Good old Crock."

They went out the front gate.

"Aren't you taking your car, Mr. Jones?" the parking-lot attendant asked Mannichon. Four years before, he had heard Mr. Paulson call Mannichon "Jones."

"Here," Crockett cut in. He gave the parking-lot attendant a cube of LSD sugar as a tip. "Suck it."

"Thanks, Mr. Crockett." The parking-lot attendant popped the cube into his mouth and began to suck it. The Lancia swooped out of the lot onto the highway, Italian, the Via Veneto, national magazines, the Affluent Society, open to the sun, wind and rain. Ah, God, Mannichon thought, this is the way to live.

❊   ❊   ❊

"Now," said Crockett, "let's add up the pluses and the minuses."

They were sitting in a dark bar, decorated like an English coaching inn, curled brass horns, whips, hunting prints. At carefully spaced intervals along the mahogany bar, three married ladies sat in miniskirts, waiting for gentlemen who were not their husbands. Crockett was drinking Jack Daniel's and water. Mannichon sipped at an Alexander, the only alcoholic drink he could get down, because it reminded him of a milk shake.

"Plus one," Crockett said. "No suds. Enormous advantage. The polluted rivers of the world. You will be hailed as a Culture Hero."

Mannichon began to sweat, pleasurably.

"Minus one," Crockett went on, waving for another Jack Daniel's. He drank fast. "Minus one—residual rings. Not an insuperable obstacle, perhaps."

"Question of time," Mannichon murmured. "With different catalysts, we might—"

"Perhaps," Crockett said. "Plus two. Distinct affinity, as yet unclear, to yellow living organisms, so far essentially confined to mice. Further experiment clearly indicated along this line. Still, a breakthrough. All specific chemical affinities with diverse particularized organisms eagerly sought after. Definitely a breakthrough. You will be praised."

"Well, Mr. Crockett," Mannichon said, sweating with even more pleasure, hearing language like that from a man who had been first in his year at MIT, "it certainly is—"

"Call me Crock," Crockett said. "We're in this together."

"Crock," Mannichon said gratefully, thinking of the Lancia.

"Minus two," Crockett said, accepting the fresh Jack

Daniel's from the waiter. "Solution seems to be fatal to organisms for which it shows affinity. Question—is it really a minus?"

"It's . . . well . . . unsettling," Mannichon said, thinking of the eighteen rigid mice in the locked refrigerator.

"Negative reactions sometimes positive reactions in disguise. Depends upon point of view," Crockett said. "Natural cycle one of repair *and* destruction. Each at its own time in its own place. Mustn't lose sight."

"No," said Mannichon humbly, determined not to lose sight.

"Commercially," Crockett said. "Look at DDT. Myxomatosis. Invaluable in Australia. Overrun by rabbits. I didn't like that goldfish, though."

They had borrowed a goldfish off the desk of a receptionist and at 12:56 P.M. had put it first in pure Floxo and then in the Mannichon solution. It couldn't be said that the goldfish had seemed to *enjoy* the Floxo—it had stood on its head at the bottom of the pan and shuddered every thirty-six seconds—but it had lived. After twenty seconds in the Mannichon solution, it had expired. It was in the refrigerator now, with the eighteen mice.

"No." Crockett repeated. "I didn't like the goldfish. Not at all."

They sat in silence, regretting the goldfish.

"Recapitulation," Crockett said. "We are in possession of formula with unusual qualities. Breaks down tensile balance of otherwise cohesive liquid molecules at normal temperatures. Laughably cheap to manufacture. Mineral traces in minute quantities almost impossible to identify. Highly toxic to certain, specific organisms, benevolent to others. I don't know how—yet—but somewhere here, there's a dollar to be made. I have a hunch . . . a hunch. There may be a place we can. . . ." He stopped, almost as if he couldn't trust Mannichon with his thoughts. "Yellow, yellow, yellow. What the hell is yellow that we are overrun with, like rabbits in Australia? We answer that question, we can clean up."

"Well," said Mannichon, "I suppose we would be in for a raise at the end of the year from Mr. Paulson. At least a bonus at Christmas."

"A bonus?" Crockett's voice rose for the first time. "A raise? Are you mad, man?"

"Well, my contract says that everything I develop is the property of Vogel-Paulson. In exchange for— Doesn't your contract read the same?"

"What are you, man?" Crockett asked disgustedly. "A Presbyterian?"

"Baptist," Mannichon said.

"Now you see why we had to get out of the laboratory to talk?" Crockett demanded.

"Well," said Mannichon, looking around at the bar and at the three wives in miniskirts, "I suppose this atmosphere is cozier than—"

"Cozier!" Crockett said. Then he used a rude word. "Don't you have a company, man?"

"A company?" Mannichon said, puzzled. "What would I do with a company? I make seventy-eight hundred dollars a year and what with withholding taxes and child psychiatrists and insurance. . . . Do you have a company?"

"Four, five. Maybe seven," Crockett said. "Who keeps track? One in Liechtenstein, two in the Bahamas, one in the name of a divorced nymphomaniac aunt with a legal residence in Ischia. Do I have a company!"

"At your age," Mannichon said admiringly. "At the age of twenty-five and three months. But what are they *for?*"

"Oh, I throw Paulson a bone from time to time," Crockett said. "A low-temperature treatment for polyesters, a crystallization process for storing unstable amino acids, bagatelles like that. Paulson slobbers in gratitude. But for anything big, man, you don't think I go trotting up to the front office, wagging my tail like a bird dog with a quail in its jaws. Christ, man, where've you been? Man, I have four patents in a company's name for the hardening of glass fibers in Germany alone. And as for low-grade bauxite. . . ."

"You don't have to go into detail," Mannichon said, not wishing to seem inquisitive. He was beginning to understand where the Lancias and Corvettes and Mercedes in the laboratory parking lot came from.

"We'll set up a company in Guernsey," Crockett said. "You and I, and whoever else we need. I'm well placed in Guernsey and the bastards speak English. And for any subcompanies that come along, we can use my aunt in Ischia."

"Do you think we'll need anybody else?" Mannichon asked anxiously. In the space of ten minutes, he had acquired the first healthy instinct of a capitalist, not to share wealth unnecessarily.

"I'm afraid so." said Crockett, brooding. "We'll need a first-rate pathologist to tell us just how the Mannichon solution links up with the nuclear material of whatever cells it has an affinity for and how it penetrates the cell wall. We'll need a crackerjack biochemist. And an expert fieldworker to examine how the product behaves in a free environment. This is big, man. No use wasting time on bums. And then, of course, the angel."

"The angel?" Mannichon was at sea. Up to then, religion hadn't seemed to be an integral part of the operation.

"The moneybags," Crockett said impatiently. "All this is going to cost a packet. We can use the laboratory for a lot of things, but finally, we have to set up on our own."

"Of course," Mannichon said, his vocabulary as well as his vision enlarged.

"First, the pathologist," Crockett said. "The best man in the country is right in the shop. Good old Tageka Kyh."

Mannichon nodded. Tageka Kyh had been top man in his year at Kyoto and then top man at Berkeley. He drove a Jaguar XK-E. Tageka Kyh had spoken to him. Once. In a movie. Tageka Kyh had said, "Is this seat taken?" Mannichon had said, "No." He remembered the exchange.

"OK," Crockett said. "Let's go catch Khy before he goes home. No sense in wasting time." He left a ten-dollar bill on the table and Mannichon followed him toward the door, feeling the attractiveness of wealth. He passed the three wives at the bar. One day soon, he thought, a woman like that will be waiting for me at a bar. He shivered deliciously.

On the way to the laboratory, they bought a goldfish for the receptionist. They had promised to bring her fish back. She was attached to it, she said.

"Interesting, interesting," Tageka Kyh was saying. He had riffled quickly through Mannichon's notes and taken a flat, Oriental glance at the eighteen mice in the refrigerator. They were in Mannichon's lab. Crockett was sure that his room and Tageka Kyh's were bugged and that Paulson ran the tapes every night. They all agreed that nobody would bother bugging Detergents and Solvents, so they could speak freely, although in lowered voices.

"Interesting," Tageka Khy repeated. He spoke perfect English, with a Texas accent. He had put on "Nō" plays in San Francisco and was an authority on tobacco mosaic. "The cut is as follows. If there ever *is* a cut. All partners share equally and I have exclusive rights to Guatemala and Costa Rica."

"Kyh," Crockett protested.

"I have certain connections in the Caribbean I have to consider," Tageka Kyh said. "Take it or leave it, pardner."

"OK," Crockett said. Tageka was a lot closer to the Nobel Prize than Crockett and had companies in Panama, Nigeria and Zurich.

Tageka Kyh offhandedly slipped the tray of dead mice out of the refrigerator and the single goldfish on a flat aluminum shovel.

"Excuse me," Mannichon said. A thought had just occurred to him. "I don't like to interfere, but they're yellow —the mice, I mean—" He was sweating now, and not pleasurably. "What I'm trying to say is that up to now, at least, the . . . uh . . . the solution. . . ." Later, he would be able to say the Mannichon solution without blushing, but he wasn't up to that yet. "That is," he went on, stuttering, "the solution so far has been toxic only to . . . uh . . . organisms whose dominant, as it were, pigment, in a manner of speaking, might be described as . . . well . . . yellowish."

"What are you trying to say, pardner?" Tageka Kyh said, wintry-Texas and pre-Perry samurai at one and the same time.

"It's just that, well," Mannichon stammered, sorry he had started this, "well, there might be certain dangers. Rubber gloves, at the very least. Complete asepsis, if I might presume to advise. I'm the last man in the world to dwell on racial . . . uh . . . characteristics, but I'd feel guilty if anything . . . well, you know, if anything *happened*, as it were. . . ."

"Don't you worry about your little yellow brother, pardner," Tageka Kyh said evenly. He went out carrying the tray and the aluminum shovel debonairly, like an old judo trophy.

"Grasping bastard," Crockett said bitterly, as the door closed behind the pathologist. "Exclusive rights to Guatemala *and* Costa Rica. The Rising Sun. March into Manchuria. Just like the last time."

As he drove home, Mannichon had the impression that Crockett and Tageka Kyh, though confronted with the same data as himself, somehow were leaping to conclusions still very much hidden from him. That's why they drive Lancias and Jaguars, he thought.

❖ ❖ ❖

The telephone rang at three in the morning. Mrs. Mannichon groaned as Mannichon reached blearily over her to pick it up. She didn't like him to touch her without warning.

"Crockett here," said the voice on the phone. "I'm at Tageka's. Get over here." He barked out the address. "Pronto."

Mannichon hung up and staggered out of bed and started to dress. He had heartburn from the Alexander.

"Where going?" Mrs. Mannichon said, in a non-melony voice.

"Conference."

"At three in the morning?" She didn't open her eyes, but her mouth certainly moved.

"I haven't looked at the time," Mannichon said, thinking, Not for long, oh, Lord, not for long.

"Good night, Romeo," Mrs. Mannichon said, her eyes still closed.

"That was Samuel Crockett," Mannichon said, fumbling with his pants.

"Fag," Mrs. Mannichon said. "I always knew it."

"Now, Lulu. . . ."After all, Crockett was his partner.

"Bring home some LSD," Mrs. Mannichon said, falling asleep.

Now, that was a funny thing for her to say, Mannichon thought, as he softly closed the door of the split-level behind him, so as not to awaken the children. Both of the children had a deeply rooted fear of sudden noises, the child psychiatrist had told him.

❖   ❖   ❖

Tageka Kyh lived downtown in the penthouse apartment of a thirteen-story building. His Jaguar was parked in front, and Crockett's Lancia. Mannichon parked the

Plymouth behind his partners' cars, thinking, Maybe a Ferrari.

Mannichon had to admit to himself that he was surprised when he was let into the apartment by a Negro butler in a yellow striped vest and immaculate white shirt sleeves with large gold cuff links. Mannichon had expected a severe modern decor, perhaps with a Japanese touch—bamboo mats, ebony headrests, washy prints of rainy bridges on the walls. But it was all done in pure Cape Cod—chintz, cobbler's benches, captain's chairs, scrubbed pine tables, lamps made out of ships' binnacles. Poor man, Mannichon thought, he is trying to assimilate.

Crockett was waiting in the living room, drinking beer and standing looking at a full-rigged clipper ship in a bottle on the mantel.

"Hi," Crockett said. "Have a nice trip?"

"Well," Mannichon said, rubbing at his red eyes behind his glasses, "I must confess I'm not completely on the *qui vive*. I'm used to eight hours' sleep and—"

"Got to learn to cut it down," Crockett said. "I do on two." He drank some beer. "Good old Tageka'll be ready for us any minute. He's in his lab."

A door opened and a lascivious girl in tight silk off-mauve pants came in with some more beer and a plate of chocolate marshmallow cookies. She smiled lasciviously at Mannichon as she offered him the tray. He took a beer and two cookies for her sake.

"His," Crockett said.

"You bet," said the girl.

Oh, to be a Japanese pathologist, Mannichon thought.

A buzzer rang dimly. "Captain Ahab," said the girl. "He's ready for you. You know the way, Sammy."

"This way, Flox," Crockett said, starting out of the room.

"Got some, Sammy?" the girl asked.

Crockett tossed her a sugar cube. She was lying down, with her off-mauve legs high over the back of a ten-foot-long chintz couch and nibbling on the sugar with small white teeth before they were out of the room.

Tageka Kyh's laboratory was bigger and more elaborately equipped than any at Vogel-Paulson. There was a large operating table that could be rotated to any position, powerful lamps on pulleys and swivels, banks of instrument cases, sterilizers, refrigerators with glass doors, a gigantic X-ray machine, stainless-steel sinks and tables and basins, strobomicroscopes, the lot.

"Wow!" Mannichon said, standing at the door, taking it in.

"Ford," Tageka said. He was dressed in a surgeon's apron and he was pulling off a surgeon's mask and cap. Under his apron, Mannichon could see the rolled-up ends of blue jeans and high-heeled, silver-worked cowboy boots. "Well," Tageka said, "I've been teasing away at our problem." He poured himself a tumbler of California sherry from a gallon jug in a corner and drank thirstily. "I've dissected the eighteen mice. Yellow." He smiled at Mannichon with a gleam of samurai teeth. "I've looked at the slides. It's too early to say anything definite yet, Mannichon; all I can offer is an educated guess, but you've hit on something brand-new."

"Have I?" Mannichon said eagerly. "What is it?"

Tageka Kyh and Crockett exchanged significant glances, the born big-leaguers noting with pity and understanding the entrance of the born bush leaguer into the locker room. "I'm not quite sure yet, pardner," Tageka Kyh said gently. "All I'm sure of is that whatever it is, it's new. And we live in an age in which being new is enough. Remember Man Tan, remember the hula hoop, remember No-Cal, remember the stereoscope glasses for three-dimensional films. Fortunes were made. In the space of months." Mannichon began to pant. Tageka shed his apron. Under it he was wearing a Hawaiian shirt. "My preliminary conclusions," he said briskly. "A nontoxic substance, to be designated, for the sake of convenience, as Floxo, combined with another known nontoxic substance, dioxotetramercphenoferrogene 14, shows a demonstrable swift affinity for the pigment material of eighteen yellowish mice and one goldfish—"

"Nineteen," Manichon said, remembering the first yellow mouse he had thrown into the incinerator.

"Eighteen," Tageka said. "I do not work on hearsay."

"I'm sorry," said Mannichon.

"Examination of cells," Tageka went on, "and other organs leads to the observation that in a manner as yet undiscovered, the solution unites with the pigmental matter in the cells, whose chemical formula I shall not at this moment trouble you with, to produce a new compound, formula to be ascertained, that attacks, with great speed and violence, the sympathetic nervous system, leading to almost immediate nonfunctioning of that system and subsequent stoppage of breathing, movement and heartbeat." He poured himself another tumbler of sherry. "Why are your eyes so red, pardner?"

"Well, I'm used to eight hours of sleep a night and—" Mannichon said.

"Learn to cut down," Tageka said. "I do on one."

"Yes, sir," Mannichon said.

"What practical use can be made of this interesting relationship between our solution and certain organic pigments is not within my province," Tageka said. "I'm merely a pathologist. But I am sure a bright young man can come up with a suggestion. Nothing is useless in the halls of science. After all, the Curies discovered the properties of radium because a key left overnight in a darkened room with a lump of refined pitchblende allowed its photograph to be taken. After all, nobody is much interested in taking photographs of keys, are they, pardner?" He giggled unexpectedly.

Japanese are funny, Mannichon thought. They are not like us.

Tageka grew serious again. "Further exhaustive investigation, carefully controlled, will perhaps enlighten us. Experiments with at least five hundred other yellow mice, to begin with, with five hundred controls. A thousand goldfish, similar procedure. Naturally yellow organisms, such as daffodils, parrots, squash, corn, etc., similar procedure. Higher vertebrates, dogs, a certain yellow-bottomed baboon, to be found in the rain forests of New Guinea, unfortunately rare, two horses, roans will do—"

"How can I get two horses into Detergents and Solvents?" Mannichon asked, his head reeling. "Especially if we have to keep this quiet?"

"This laboratory"—Tageka made a courteous east-wind gesture of his hand at the gleam around them—"is at the service of my honorable friends. And we must show a certain amount of initiative in conducting some of our experiments in other localities. All I need is a few correctly prepared tissue slides, stained as I direct."

"But I can't put in request forms for baboons and horses," Mannichon said, sweating again.

"I had thought it understood that we would undertake this privately," Tageka said frostily, looking at Crockett.

"That's right," Crockett said.

"But where's the money going to come from? Yellow-bottomed baboons, for God's sake," Mannichon cried.

"I am merely a pathologist," Tageka said. He drank some more sherry.

"I'm in," Crockett said.

"You can be in," Mannichon said, near tears. "You have companies all over the world. Liechtenstein, Ischia. . . . I make seven thousand, eight hundred dollars a—"

"We know what you make, pardner," Tageka said. "I will absorb your share of the preliminary expenses, along with my own."

Mannichon breathed heavily with gratitude. There was no doubt about it, he was finally in with Class.

"I hardly know what to say. . . ." he began.

"There is no need to say anything," said Tageka. "As partial reimbursement for funds laid out, I shall take the exclusive rights of your share of all of northern Europe for the first ten years, on a line drawn from London to Berlin."

"Yes, sir," said Mannichon. He would have liked to say something else, but what came out was, "Yes, sir."

"I reckon that's about it for the night, pardners," Tageka said. "I don't like to rush you, but I have some work to do before I go to sleep."

He escorted Crockett and Mannichon politely to the door of the laboratory. They heard it lock behind them.

"The Oriental mind," Crockett said. "Always suspicious."

The girl in the off-mauve pants was still lying on the couch. Her eyes were open, but she didn't seem to see anything.

There's no doubt of it, Mannichon thought, taking a last devouring look at the girl, this is the age of specialization.

❖   ❖   ❖

The next weeks were frantic. Mannichon spent his days in Detergents and Solvents writing up reports on nonexistent experiments to indicate on the weekly reviews that he was earning his salary and loyally advancing the interests of Vogel-Paulson. The nights were spent in Tageka Kyh's laboratory. Mannichon had got his sleep down to three hours. The tests went on methodically. The 500 yellow mice duly succumbed. A yellow Afghan with an illustrious pedigree, bought at great expense, lasted less than an hour after lapping up several drops of Mannichon's solution in a bowl of milk, while a black-and-white mongrel liberated from the pound for three dollars barked happily for two days after sharing the same meal. Dead goldfish lay by the hundreds in Tageka's refrigerators and the yellow-bottomed baboon, after showing deep affection for Tageka, tolerance for Crockett and a desire to murder Mannichon, was laid to rest only ten minutes after its relevant parts had been laved in a purposely weakened variant of the solution.

During this period, Mannichon's domestic situation was not all that it might have been. His nightly absences had begun to annoy Mrs. Mannichon. He could not tell her what he was doing, except that he was working with Crockett and Tageka. Because of the community-property laws, he was planning to divorce her before the company showed any profit.

"What have you fellows got going up there every night?" Mrs. Mannichon demanded. "A rainbow-colored daisy chain?"

One more cross to bear, Mannichon thought. Temporarily.

❖   ❖   ❖

Flowers and vegetables had not been affected by the solution and they had not yet tried horses. And despite some ingenious manipulations of the solution by Crockett (he had managed to subtract two hydrocarbon molecules from Floxo and had bombarded dioxotetramercphenoferrogene 14 with a large variety of radioactive isotopes), the residual rings always remained on whatever materials they tried, even after exhaustive scrubbing. While the two other men worked on serenely, checking all leads meticulously night after night and producing dazzling results for Vogel-Paulson day after day, Mannichon, vertiginous from lack of sleep, was beginning to despair of ever finding any practical use for the Mannichon solution. He would write a little paper that might or might not get published, two or three biochemists throughout the country might thumb through the pages offhandedly and another curious little dead end of research would be closed out and forgotten. He would drive the 1959 Plymouth for the rest of his life and he would never see the inside of a divorce court.

He didn't communicate his fears to Crockett and Tageka Kyh. It was hard to communicate *anything* to them. In the beginning, they rarely listened when he talked and after a couple of weeks, they didn't listen at all. He did his work in silence. His work finally consisted of washing up, taking dictation and filing slides. He was having his troubles at Vogel-Paulson, too. His weekly running digests of non-existent experiments were not being received with enthusiasm and an ominous memo had come to him in a baby-blue envelope from Mr. Paulson himself. "Well?" Mr. Paulson had scrawled on a large piece of paper. Just that. It was not promising.

He had decided to quit. He had to quit. He needed at least one night's sleep. He wanted to announce it to his partners, but it was difficult to find the appropriate time. He knew he couldn't say it in front of Tageka Kyh, who was a remote man, but there was a chance that if he got Crockett alone for a minute or two, he could get it out. After all, Crockett was white.

So he took to tagging after Crockett and lying in wait for him whenever he could. But it took nearly another week before his opportunity presented itself. He was waiting in front of the restaurant where Crockett often lunched, usually with a lascivious girl or several lascivious girls. The restaurant was called La Belle Provençale and a meal there never cost less than ten dollars. That is, if you didn't order wine. Mannichon had never eaten there, of course. He took his lunch at the Vogel-Paulson commissary. You could eat there for eight-five cents. That was one good thing about Vogel-Paulson.

It was a hot day and there was no shade. Because of his vertigo, Mannichon rocked from side to side as he waited, as though he were on the deck of a heaving ship. Then he saw the Lancia drive up. For once, Crockett was alone. He left the motor running as he stepped out and turned the car over to the attendant to park. He didn't notice Mannichon as he strode toward the door of La Belle Provençale, although he passed within three feet of him.

"Crock," Mannichon said.

Crockett stopped and looked around. A look of displeasure angled across the Yankee angles of his face. "What the hell are you doing here?" he said.

"Crock," Mannichon said, "I have to talk to you—"

"What the hell're you rocking for?" Crockett asked. "Are you drunk?"

"That's one of the things I wanted to—"

A funny expression, intense and cold, came over Crockett's face. He was staring past Mannichon, over Mannichon's shoulder. "Look!" he said.

"You fellers've been great and all that," Mannichon said, lurching closer to Crockett, "but I have to—"

Crockett grabbed him by the shoulders and swung him around. "I said, 'Look.' "

Mannichon sighed and looked. There was nothing much to look at. Across the street, in front of a bar, there was a broken-down old wagon full of empty ginger-ale bottles and an old horse, its head drooping in the heat.

"Look at what, Crock?" Mannichon said. He was now seeing double, but he didn't want to burden Crockett with his troubles.

"The horse, man, the horse."

"What about the horse, Crock?"

"What color is it, man?"

"They're yellow. I mean, *it's* yellow," Mannichon said, correcting for his double vision.

"Everything comes to him who waits," Crockett said. He took out a small bottle of the Mannichon solution. He never went anyplace without it. He was a dedicated scientist, not one of those timeservers who lock their minds when they lock their office doors. Swiftly, Crockett poured some of the solution on his right hand. He gave Mannichon the bottle to hold, in case the police ever asked any questions. Then he sauntered across the street toward the old yellow horse and the wagon full of empty ginger-ale bottles. It was the first time Mannichon had seen Crockett saunter anywhere.

Crockett went up to the horse. The driver was nowhere in sight. A Buick passed with a colored man at the wheel; but aside from that, the street was empty.

"Good old dobbin," Crockett said. He patted the horse kindly on the muzzle with his wet hand. Then he sauntered back toward Mannichon. "Put that goddamn bottle in your pocket, man," he whispered. He took Mannichon's arm, wiping the last drops of the liquid off on Mannichon's sleeve. It looked friendly, but the fingers felt like steel hooks. Mannichon put the bottle of the solution in his pocket and, side by side, he and Crockett went into the restaurant.

The bar of La Belle Provençale was parallel to the front window and the bottles were arranged on glass shelves up against the window. With the light from the street coming in from behind them, the bottles looked like jewelry. It was an artistic effect. There were quite a few people eating ten-dollar lunches in the dark interior of the restaurant, in a hush of expensive French food, but there was nobody else at the bar. The room was air conditioned and Mannichon shivered uncontrollably as he sat on the bar stool, looking out at the street through the bottles. He could see the yellow horse between a bottle of Chartreuse and a bottle of Noilly-Prat. The yellow horse hadn't moved. He was still there in the heat with his head down.

"What'll it be, Mr. Crockett?" the bartender said. "The usual?" Everybody always knew Crockett's name.

"The usual, Benny," Crockett said. "And an Alexander for my friend." Crockett never forgot anything.

They watched the horse through the bottles while Benny prepared the Jack Daniel's and the Alexander. The horse didn't do anything.

The bartender served the drinks and Crockett drank half of his in one gulp. Mannichon sipped at his Alexander. "Crock," he said, "I really do have to talk to you. This whole thing is getting me—"

"Sssh," Crockett said. The driver of the wagon was coming out of the bar across the street. He climbed up onto the seat of the wagon and picked up the reins. The horse slowly went down on its knees and then all the way down between the traces. The horse didn't move anymore.

"Send two more drinks to the table, Benny," Crockett said. "Come on, Flox, I'll buy you lunch."

Crockett ordered *tripes à la mode de Caen* for lunch and a bottle of hard cider. Crockett certainly wasn't a typical Yankee. As soon as Mannichon saw and smelled the dish, he knew his stomach was going to make some peculiar claims on his attention that afternoon. He never did manage to tell Crockett that he wanted to quit.

❖ ❖ ❖

"Now for the next step," Tageka Kyh was saying. All three of them were in his laboratory in the penthouse. It was comparatively early, only 2:30 A.M. Tageka had taken the news about the horse without surprise, although he did say that it was too bad they hadn't gotten any slides. "We've gone just about as far as necessary with the lower vertebrates," Tageka Kyh said. "The next experiment suggests itself inevitably."

It didn't suggest itself inevitably to Mannichon. "What's that?" he said.

For once, Tageka Kyh answered one of Mannichon's questions. "Man," he said simply.

Mannichon opened his mouth and kept it open. He didn't close it for some time.

Crockett had his face squeezed up into lines of concentration. "I foresee certain complications," he said.

"Nothing serious," Tageka Kyh said. "All it needs is

access to a hospital with a decent selection of pigmented subjects."

"Well, I know everybody at Lakeview General downtown, of course," Crockett said, "but I don't think we'd find the proper range. After all, we're in the Midwest. I doubt if you'd even find more than two or three Indians in a year."

Mannichon still had his mouth open.

"I don't trust those fellows at General," Tageka Kyh said. "They're sloppy. And whatever man we pick we'll have to bring in as a full partner, of course, and I don't like anyone down at General enough to dump a fortune in his lap."

Mannichon would have liked to interrupt at this point. Tageka Kyh's use of the word fortune seemed careless, to say the least. Everything they had done up to now, as far as Mannichon was concerned, had been rigorously devoid of all possibility of profit. But Tageka Kyh was caught up in his planning, speaking smoothly, articulating well, pronouncing every syllable.

"I think all indications point to the West Coast. San Francisco comes to mind," Tageka Kyh said. "A sizable non-white population, well-run hospitals with large non-segregated charity wards. . . ."

"Chinatown," Mannichon said. He had been there on his honeymoon. He had had shark's-fin soup. You only get married once, he had said to Lulu.

"I have a friend on the staff of Mercy and Cancer," Tageka Kyh said. "Ludwig Qvelch."

"Of course," Crockett nodded. "Qvelch. Prostate. Top-notch." Crockett had heard of everybody.

"He was first in his class at Berkeley three years before me," Tageka Kyh said. "I think I'll give him a tinkle." He reached for the phone.

"Wait a minute, please, Mr. Tageka," Mannichon said hoarsely. "Do you mean to say you are going to experiment on living human beings? Maybe kill them?"

"Crock," Tageka Kyh said, "you brought this fellow in on this. You handle him."

"Flox," Crockett said, with evident irritation, "it boils down to this—are you a scientist or aren't you a scientist?"

Tageka Kyh was already dialing San Francisco.

❖　　　　　　❖　　　　　　❖

"Let me see, now," Ludwig Qvelch was saying. "what have we got on hand? I'm thinking of the Blumstein wing. That would seem to be the place to begin, don't you agree, Tageka?"

Tageka Kyh nodded. "The Blumstein wing. Ideal," he said.

Qvelch had arrived only 14 hours after the call to San Francisco. He had closeted himself with Tageka Kyh and Crockett all afternoon and evening. It was midnight now and Mannichon had been admitted to the conference, which was taking place in the Cape Cod living room. Ludwig Qvelch was a huge, tall man, with wonderful white teeth and a hearty Western manner. He wore $300 suits with light ties and he was a man you would instinctively trust anywhere. He had made some marvelously eloquent speeches on national television against Medicare.

Qvelch took out a small black alligator notebook and

thumbed through it. "At the moment," he said, "we have thirty-three Caucasians, twelve Negroes, three indeterminate, one Hindu, one Berber and seven Orientals, six presumably of Chinese extraction, one definitely Japanese. All male, of course." He laughed heartily at this allusion to his specialty, the prostate gland. "I would call that a fair enough sampling, wouldn't you?"

"It'll do," Tageka Kyh said.

"All terminal?" Crockett asked.

"I would say roughly eighty percent," Qvelch said. "Why do you ask?"

"For *his* sake." Crockett gestured toward Mannichon. "He was worried."

"I'm glad to see that the rarefied air of research hasn't wiped out your admirable youthful scruples," Qvelch said, putting a large Western hand on Mannichon's shoulder. "Have no fear. No life will be shortened—appreciably."

"Thanks, doctor," Mannichon mumbled.

Qvelch looked at his watch. "Well, I've got to be tootling back," he said. "I'll keep in touch." He put a liter bottle, usually reserved for carrying volatile acids and encased in lead, into his valise. "You'll be hearing from me." He started briskly toward the door, Tageka Kyh accompanying him. Qvelch stopped before he reached the door. "What is it again? One quarter of all proceeds to each partner, with Guatemala and Costa Rica exclusive to Kyh and Mannichon's share of northern Europe for ten years . . . ?"

"It's all in the memorandum I gave you this afternoon," Tageka Kyh said.

"Yes, of course," Qvelch said. "I just wanted to be able to clear up any little points with my lawyers when the incorporation papers come through. Nice meeting you fellers." He waved to Crockett and Mannichon and was gone.

"I'm afraid we'll have to break it up early tonight, pardners," Tageka Kyh said. "I have some work to do."

Mannichon went right home, looking forward to his first good night's sleep in months. His wife was out playing bridge, so he should have been able to sleep like a baby; but for some reason, he couldn't close his eyes until dawn.

❖   ❖   ❖

"Qvelch called this afternoon," Tageka Kyh said. "He reports results."

Mannichon's eyelids began to twitch in little spasms and he found that his lungs had suddenly begun to reject air. "Do you mind if I sit down?" he said. He had just rung the bell of Tageka's apartment and Tageka himself had come to the door. Supporting himself with his hands against the wall, he made his way into the living room and sat unsteadily in a captain's chair. Crockett was sprawled on the couch, a glass of whiskey on his breastbone. Mannichon couldn't tell from the expression on Crockett's face whether he was sad or happy or drunk.

Tageka followed Mannichon into the room. "Can I get you anything?" Tageka asked, being a host. "A beer? A juice?"

"Nothing, thank you," Mannichon said. This was the first time since they had met that Tageka had been polite to him. He was being prepared for something horrible, he was sure. "What did Dr. Qvelch have to say?"

"He asked to be remembered to you," Tageka said, sitting between Crockett and Mannichon on a cobbler's bench and taking in a hole on the chased-silver buckle of the belt of his jeans.

"What else?" Mannichon asked.

"The first experiment has been concluded. Qvelch himself administered the solution epidermally to eight subjects, five white, two black and one yellow. Seven of the subjects have registered no reaction. The autopsy on the eighth—"

"Autopsy!" Mannichon's lungs were rejecting air in jets. "We've killed a man!"

"Oh, be reasonable, Flox." It was Crockett talking, wearily, the whiskey glass going up and down evenly on his chest. "It happened in San Francisco. Two thousand miles away from here."

"But it's my solution. I—"

"*Our* solution, Mannichon," Tageka said evenly. "With Qvelch, we number four."

"Mine, ours, what's the difference? There's a poor dead Chinaman lying on a slab in—"

"With your temperament, Mannichon," Tageka said, "I don't understand how you happened to go into research instead of psychiatry. If you're going to do business with us, you'll have to restrain yourself."

"Business!" Mannichon staggered to his feet. "What kind of business do you call this? Killing off Chinamen with cancer in San Francisco! Boy," he said with unaccustomed irony, "if ever I heard of a money-maker, this is it."

"Do you want to listen or do you want to make an

oration?" Tageka said. "I have many interesting and valuable things to tell you. But I have work to do and I can't waste my time. That's better. Sit down."

Mannichon sat down.

"And stay down," Crockett said.

"The autopsy, as I was saying," Tageka went on, "indicated that the subject died a natural death. No traces of any unusual matter in any of the organs. Death occurred quietly, due, by inference, to a secondary flash reaction to cancerous material in the region of the prostate gland. We know better, of course."

"I'm a murderer," Mannichon said, putting his head between his hands.

"I really can't tolerate language like that in my house, Crock," Tageka said. "Perhaps we had better let him disassociate."

"If you want to go back to Detergents and Solvents, Flox," Crockett said, without moving from the couch, "you know where the door is."

"That's exactly what I want to do," Mannichon said. He stood up and started toward the door.

"You're walking out on the best part of a million dollars, man," Crockett said calmly.

Mannichon stopped walking toward the door. He turned. He went back to the captain's chair. He sat down. "I might as well hear the worst," he said.

"I was down in Washington three days ago," Crockett said. "I dropped in on an old friend. Simon Bunswanger. I went to school with him at Boston Latin. You haven't heard of him. Nobody's heard of him. He's in the CIA. Big man in the CIA. Big, *big* man. I gave him a little run-

down on our project. He was titillated. He promised to call
a meeting of some of the boys in his shop for briefing and
proposals." Crockett looked at his watch. "He's due here
any minute."

"The CIA?" Mannichon now felt completely adrift.
"What'd you do that for? They'll put us all in jail."

"Quite the opposite," Crockett said. "Quite the opposite. I'll bet you two Alexanders he comes in here with
a nice, fat proposition. . . ."

"For what?" Mannichon asked. Now he was sure that
all those companies and all that lack of sleep had made
irreparable inroads on Crockett's reason. "What would
they want with the Mannichon solution?"

"Remember the first day you came to me, Flox?"
Crockett finally got to his feet. He was in his socks and
he padded over to the bar to pour himself a fresh Jack
Daniel's. "I said, we answer one question, we can clean
up. Remember that?"

"More or less," Mannichon said.

"Do you remember what that one question was?"
Crockett said, drinking, sounding liquid. "I'll refresh your
little old memory cells, reactivate the old nerve patterns.
The question was, 'What the hell is yellow that we are
overrun with, like rabbits in Australia?' Remember that?"

"Yes," Mannichon said. "But what has the CIA got
to . . . ?"

"The CIA, man," said Crockett, "knows exactly what
is yellow and what we are overrun with." He paused,
dropped a piece of ice into his drink and stirred with his
finger. "Chinamen, man."

The doorbell rang. "That must be Bunswanger," Crockett said. "I'll go."

"This is the last time I'll do any work with anybody like you, Mannichon," Tageka said icily. "You're psychically unstable."

Crockett came back into the room with a man who looked as though he could have made a good living as a female impersonator in the old days of vaudeville. He was willowy, had fine blond hair and a small bow mouth and a blushing complexion.

"Si," Crockett said, "I want you to meet my partners." He introduced Tageka, who bowed, and Mannichon, who couldn't look into Bunswanger's eyes as they shook hands. Bunswanger's grip was not that of a female impersonator.

"I'll have a Jack Daniel's, Crock," Bunswanger said. It must have been the campus drink at old Boston Latin. Bunswanger had a voice that reminded Mannichon of Carborundum.

Glass in hand, Bunswanger sat on one of the scrubbed pine tables, his legs crossed in a fetching manner. "Well, the boys in the shop think you fellows have done a dandy little piece of creative research," Bunswanger began. "We had some tests run and they bear your papers out one hundred percent. Did you hear from Qvelch?"

"This afternoon," Tageka said. "Results positive."

Bunswanger nodded. "The boys in the shop said they would be. Well, no use beating around the bush. We want it. The solution. We've already set up preliminary target zones. The source of the Yangtze, three or four lakes in the north, two of the tributaries of the Yellow River, places like that. You don't happen to have a map of China handy, do you?"

"Sorry," said Tageka.

"Pity," Bunswanger said. "It would clear up the picture for you fellows." He looked around. "Nice place you have here. You'd be surprised what they ask for a decent place to live in Washington. Of course, the Russians will help us. We've sounded them out already. Makes it more comfy, reduces the risks. That long border with Siberia and all those delegations. Of course, that's the beauty of the stuff. No bang. We've been searching for something without a bang for years. Nothing satisfactory's come up, until this. Did you fellows test all the way down? I didn't see it in your papers. I was in a hurry, of course, but I wondered."

"Test what down?" Mannichon asked.

"Flox," Crockett said wearily.

"Mannichon," Tageka said warningly.

"Down to effective reaction at lowest possible percentage of solution in H Two O," Bunswanger said.

"We didn't push to the limit, Si," Crockett said. "We only worked nights."

"Amazing efficiency," Bunswanger said. He took a delicate sip of his whiskey. "We ran a few trials. One two-billionth of a part in fresh water. One three-billionth of a part in salt water." He laughed, sounding girlish, remembering something. "There's a curious side effect. It cures jaundice. You could set up a company, pharmaceutical only, and make a wad just on that. Only on a doctor's prescription, of course. You'd have to make sure nobody used it on Orientals or there'd be hell to pay. Well, just a

detail. Now"—he uncrossed his legs—"practical matters.
We'll pay you two million cold for it. Out of unvouchered
funds. So you don't have to pay the tax boys anything on
it. No record. Nothing in writing. It's a great shop to do
business for. No niggling."

Mannichon was panting again.

"Are you all right, sir?" Bunswanger asked, real concern
in his voice.

"Fine," Mannichon said, continuing to pant.

"Of course," Bunswanger said, still looking concernedly
at Mannichon, "if we ever use it, it swings over on a royalty
basis. But we can't guarantee that it will ever go operational. Though the way things look right now. . . ." He
left the sentence unfinished.

Mannichon thought of Ferrari after Ferrari, dozens of
girls in off-mauve pants.

"One more little thing and I'm off," Bunswanger said.
"I have a visit to make in Venezuela tomorrow. Hear this,"
his voice was as precise as a gun sight. "I'm in for twenty
percent. One fifth. For services rendered." He looked
around.

Crockett nodded.

Tageka nodded.

Mannichon nodded, slowly.

"I'm off to Caracas," Bunswanger said gaily. He finished
his drink. They shook hands all around. "There'll be a
fellow here in the morning." Bunswanger said, "with the
loot. In cash, naturally. What time is convenient?"

"Six A.M., Tageka said.

"Done and done," Bunswanger said, making a quick

entry in a small alligator-bound notebook. "Glad you dropped in the other day, Crock. Don't bother seeing me to the door." And he was gone.

There was little more to be done. Since they were going to be paid in cash, they had to figure out what compensation Tageka was to get for his Caribbean rights and his ten-year share of Mannichon's portion of the rights for northern Europe. It didn't take long. Tageka was just as good a mathematician as a pathologist.

Crockett and Mannichon left the apartment together. Crockett had a date at a bar nearby with Mr. Paulson's third and present wife and he was in a hurry to be off. "So long, Flox," he said as he got into his Lancia. "Not a bad day's work." He was humming as he spurted off.

Mannichon got into the Plymouth. He sat there for a while, trying to decide what to do first. He finally decided that first things came first. He drove home at sixty miles an hour to tell Mrs. Mannichon he was going to get a divorce.

❖   ❖   ❖

Up in the apartment, Tageka was sitting on the cobbler's bench, making neat ideograms with a brush and ink on a scratch-pad. After a while, he pressed a buzzer. The Negro butler came in, dressed in his yellow striped vest and white shirt sleeves with heavy gold cuff links.

"James," Tageka Kyh said to the butler, "tomorrow I want you to order five hundred grams each of dioxotetra-mercphenoferrogene, 14, 15 and 17. And five hundred white mice. No—on second thought, better make it a thousand."

"Yes, sir," said James.

"Oh, and James"—Tageka Kyh waved the brush negligently at the butler. "Will you be good enough to put in a call to the Japanese embassy in Washington. I'll speak to the ambassador personally."

"Yes, sir," James said and picked up the phone.

Small Saturday

❖   His sleep had been troubled for weeks. Girls came in and out of the misty edges of dreams to smile at him, beckon him, leer at him, invite him, almost embrace him. He was on city streets, on the decks of great ships, in satiny bedrooms, on high bridges, accompanied and not quite accompanied by the phantom figures whom he always seemed on the verge of recognizing and never recognized, as they slipped away beyond the confines of dream, to leave him lying awake in his single bed, disturbed, sleepless, knowing only that the figures that haunted him were sisters in a single respect—they were all much taller than he—and that when they vanished, it was upward, toward unreachable heights.

Christopher Bagshot woke up remembering that just a moment before he opened his eyes, he had heard a voice saying, "You must make love to a woman at least five feet, eight inches tall tonight." It was the first time in weeks of dreaming that a voice had spoken. He recognized a breakthrough.

He looked at the clock on the bedside table. Twelve

minutes to eight. The alarm would go off on the hour. He stared at the ceiling, searching for significance. He remembered it was Saturday.

He got out of bed and took off the top of his pajamas and did his exercises. Fifteen push-ups, twenty-five sit-ups. He was a small man, five feet, six, but fit. He had beautiful dark eyes, like a Moroccan burro's, with long lashes. His hair was straight and black and girls liked to muss it. Small girls. In another age, before everybody looked as though he or she had been brought up in Texas or California, his size would not have bothered him. He could have fitted into *Henri Quatre*'s armor. And *Henri Quatre* was large enough to say that Paris was worth a Mass. How the centuries slide by.

❖   ❖   ❖

"I had this dream," he said. They were standing on the corner, waiting for the 79th Street crosstown bus. Stanley Hovington, five feet, ten inches tall, neighbor and friend, was waiting for the bus with him. It was a cool, sunny, New York October. Two boys, aged no more than fifteen, one of them carrying a football, slouched into Central Park. Each of them was nearly six feet tall. Autumn Saturday. All over the country, long-legged girls wearing chrysanthemums, cheering for Princeton, Ohio State, Southern California. Large, fearsome men, swift on green turf.

"I had a dream last night, too," Stanley said. "I was caught in an ambush in the jungle. It's the damned television."

"In my dream . . ." Christopher said, uninterested in

Stanley's nighttime problems. Stanley, too, had to work on Saturdays. He had a big job at Bloomingdale's, but the thing was, he had to work on Saturdays. "In my dream," Christopher persisted, "a voice said to me, 'You must make love to a woman at least five feet, eight inches tall tonight.'"

"Did you recognize the voice?"

"No. Anyway, that isn't the point."

"It would seem to me," Stanley said, "that's just the point. Who said it, I mean. And why." He was a good friend, Stanley, but argumentative. "Five feet, eight inches. There might be a clue there."

"What I think it means," Christopher said, "is that my subconscious was telling me it had a message for me."

The bus came along and they mounted and found seats at the rear, because it was Saturday.

"What sort of message?" Stanley asked.

"It was telling me that deep in my soul I feel deprived," Christopher said.

"Of a five-foot-eight girl?"

"It stands to reason," Christopher said earnestly in the rocking bus. "All my life"—he was twenty-five—"all my life, I've been short. But I'm proud, so to speak. I can't bear the thought of looking foolish."

"Stalin wasn't any taller than you," Stanley said. "He wasn't worried about looking foolish."

"That's the other danger," Christopher said, "the Napoleonic complex. Even worse."

"What are you deprived of?" Stanley asked. "What's her name—that girl—she's crazy about you."

"June," Christopher said.

"That's it, June. Damn nice girl."

"I'm not saying anything against June," Christopher said. "Far from it. But do you know how tall she is?"

"I think you're obsessive on the subject," Stanley said, "to tell the truth."

"Five feet, three. And she's the *tallest* girl I ever had."

"So what? You don't play basketball with her." Stanley laughed, appreciating himself.

"It's no laughing matter," Christopher said gravely, disappointed in Stanley. "Look—you have to figure it this way—in this day and age in America, for some goddamn reason, almost all the *great* girls, I mean the *really* great ones, the ones you see in the movies, in the fashion magazines, with their pictures in the papers at all the parties, almost all of them are suddenly *big*."

"Maybe you've got something there," Stanley said thoughtfully. "I hadn't correlated before."

"It's like a new natural resource of America," Christopher said. "A new discovery or a new invention or something. It's part of our patrimony, if you want to talk fancy. Only I'm not getting any of it. I'm being *gypped*. It's like the blacks. They see all these terrific things on television and in the magazines, sports cars, hi-fis, cruises to the Caribbean, only they can't get in on them. I tell you, it teaches you sympathy."

"They're pretty tall," Stanley said. "I mean, look at Wilt Chamberlain."

Christopher made an impatient gesture. "You don't get my point."

"Yeah, yeah," Stanley said, "actually, I do. Though maybe it's more in your imagination than anything else.

After all, it doesn't go by *volume,* for God's sake. I mean, I've had girls all sizes; and once it comes down to the crunch, in bed, I mean, size is no criterion."

"You can say that, Stanley," Christopher said, "you have a choice. And I'm not only talking about in bed. It's the whole attitude. It stands to reason. They're the darlings of our time, the big ones, I mean the marvelous big ones, and they know it, and it gives them something extra, something a lot extra. They feel they're superior and they have to live up to it. If they're naturally funny, they're funnier. If they're sexy, they're sexier. If they're sad, they're sadder. If there're two parties that night, they get invited to the better one. If there're two guys who want to take them to dinner, they go out with the handsomer, richer one. And it's bound to rub off on the guy. *He* feels superior. He knows every other man in the place envies him, he's way up there with the privileged classes. But if a small guy walks somewhere with one of the big beautiful ones, he knows that every cat in the place who's two inches taller than he is is thinking to himself, 'I can take that big mother away from that shrimp any time,' and they're just waiting for the small guy to go to the john or turn his head to talk to the headwaiter, to give his date the signal."

"Jesus," Stanley said, "you've got it bad."

"Have I ever," Christopher said.

Stanley brightened. "I have an idea," he said. "I know some pretty smashing tall girls—"

"I bet you do," Christopher said, loathing his friend momentarily.

"What the hell," Stanley said. "I'll give a party. Just

you and me and maybe two or three fellers even shorter than you and four or five girls, five feet, eight and over. . . . A quiet party, where everybody is just sitting or lying around, no dancing or charades or anything embarrassing like that."

"What're you doing tonight?" Christopher asked eagerly.

"The thing is," Stanley said, "tonight I'm busy. But for next Saturday—"

"The voice said tonight," Christopher said.

They sat in silence, listening to the echo of that ghostly imperative in the back of the cross-town bus.

"Well," Stanley began, his tone dubious, "maybe I could fix you up with a blind date."

"It's Saturday," Christopher reminded him. "What sort of girl five feet, eight or over would be available to go out on a blind date on a Saturday night in New York in October?"

"You can never tell," Stanley said, but without conviction.

"I can just see it," Christopher said bitterly, "I'm sitting in a bar waiting, and this big girl comes in, looking around for me, and I get off the stool and I say, 'You must be Jane' or Matilda or whatever, and she takes one look and that expression comes over her face."

"What expression?"

"That 'What the hell did I let myself in for tonight?' expression," Christopher said. "That 'I should've worn flat heels' expression."

"Maybe you're too sensitive, Chris."

"Maybe I am. Only I'll never know until I've tried. Look, I want to get married, it's about time. I want to marry some great girl and be happy with her and have kids, the whole deal. But I don't want to be nagged all my life by the feeling that I did my shopping only in the bargain basement, in a manner of speaking." Christopher felt that this was an apt and convincing phrase, considering that Stanley worked in Bloomingdale's. "I want to feel I had a pick from every goddamn floor in the place. And I don't want my kids to look at me when they're nineteen and they're five feet, six, and say, 'Is this as high as I go?' the way I look at my father and mother." Christopher's father was even shorter than he was and there was just no use in measuring his mother.

"Do you *know* any big girls?" Stanley asked as Christopher stood up, because they were approaching Madison Avenue. "At least to talk to?"

"Sure," Christopher said. "Plenty of them come into the store." He was the manager of a book-and-record store, one of a chain his father owned. There was a section devoted to greeting cards. Christopher found this demeaning, but his father was profit-minded. When his father retired, Christopher would wipe out the greeting-card section the first week. His father had no complexes about being small. If he had been running the Soviet Union, he would have run it very much along the same lines as Joseph Stalin, only more drastically. Still, Christopher couldn't complain. He was more or less his own boss and he liked being around books and his father was so busy with the more important shops in the chain that he made only flying, unexpected visits to the comparatively minor enterprise over which Christopher presided.

"I *know* plenty of tall girls," he said. "I encourage

charge accounts, so I have plenty of addresses." When a tall girl came into the shop, Christopher tried to be on a library ladder, reaching for a book on an upper shelf. "And telephone numbers. That's no problem."

"Have you tried any yet?"

"No."

"Try," Stanley said. "My advice is, try. Today."

"Yeah," Christopher said dully.

The bus stopped and the door opened and Christopher stepped down onto the curb, with a wintry wave of his hand.

❖   ❖   ❖

Might as well start with the A's, he thought. He was alone in the store. It was impossible to get a decent clerk who would work on Saturdays. He had tried college boys and girls for the one-day-a-week stint, but they stole more than they sold and they mixed up the stock so that it took three days to get it straight again after they had gone. For once, he did not pity himself for working on Saturday and being alone. God knew how many calls he would have to put in and it would have been embarrassing to have someone listening in, male or female. There was no danger of his father's dropping in, because he played golf all day Saturday and Sunday in Westchester County.

*Anderson. Paulette***, he read in his pocket address book. He had a system of drawing stars next to the names of girls. One star meant that she was tall and at least pretty. Two stars meant that she was tall and pretty or even beautiful and that, for one reason or another, she seemed to be a girl who might be free with her favors.

Anderson, Paulette**, had large and excellently shaped breasts, which she took no pains to hide. June had once told Christopher that in her experience, girls with voluptuous bosoms were always jumping into bed with men, out of vanity and exhibitionism. Treacherously, after his conversation with June, Christopher had added a second star to *Anderson, Paulette**.

He didn't have her home address or telephone number, because she worked as an assistant to a dentist in the neighborhood and came around at lunch hour and after work. She wore a womanly chignon and was at least five feet, ten inches tall. Although usually provocatively dressed in cashmere sweaters, she was a serious girl, interested in psychology and politics and prison reform. She bought the works of Erich Fromm and copies of *The Lonely Crowd* as birthday presents for her friends. She and Christopher engaged in deep discussions over the appropriate counters. She sometimes worked on Saturdays, she had told Christopher, because the dentist remade mouths for movie actors and television performers and people like that, who were always pressed for time and had to have their mouths remade on weekends, when they were free.

Anderson, Paulette** wasn't really one of those *marvelous* girls—she wasn't a model and she didn't get her picture in the paper or anything like that—but if she were to do her hair differently and take off her glasses, and didn't tell anybody she was a dental assistant, you certainly would look at her more than once when she came into a room. For the first one, Christopher thought, might as well start modestly. Get the feel.

He sat down at the desk next to the cash register toward the rear of the shop and dialed the number of *Anderson, Paulette***.

❖   ❖   ❖

Omar Gadsden sat in the chair, his mouth open, the chromium tube for saliva bubbling away under his tongue. Occasionally, Paulette, comely in white, would reach over and wipe away the drool from his chin. Gadsden was a news commentator on Educational Television, and even before he had started to come to Dr. Levinson's office to have his upper jaw remade, Paulette had watched him faithfully, impressed by his silvering hair, his well-bred baritone, his weary contempt for the fools in Washington, his trick of curling the corners of his thin lips to one side to express more than the network's policy would otherwise have permitted him.

Right now, with the saliva tube gurgling over his lower lip and all his upper teeth mere little pointed stumps, waiting for the carefully sculpted bridge that Dr. Levinson was preparing to put permanently into place, Omar Gadsden did not resemble the assured and eloquent early-evening father figure of Educational Television. He had suffered almost every day for weeks while Dr. Levinson meticulously ground down his teeth and his dark, noble eyes reflected the protracted pain of his ordeal. He watched Dr. Levinson fearfully as the dentist scraped away with a hooked instrument at the gleaming arc of caps that lay on a mold on the marble top of the high chest of drawers against the wall of the small office.

He was a sight for his enemies' eyes at that moment, Paulette thought; the Vice-President would enjoy seeing him now, and she felt a motherly twinge of pity, although she was only twenty-four. She had become very friendly with the commentator during the last month of preparing hypodermics of Novocain for him and adjusting the rubber apron around his neck and watching him spit blood into the basin at the side of the chair. Before and after the sessions, in which he had shown exemplary courage, they had had short but informative conversations about affairs of the day and he had let drop various hints about scandals among the mighty and prophecies of disaster, political, financial and ecological, that lay ahead for America. She had gained a new respect from her friends in retelling, in the most guarded terms, of course, some of the more dire items that Omar Gadsden vouchsafed her.

She was sure that Mr. Gadsden liked her. He addressed her by her first name and when he telephoned to postpone an appointment, he always asked her how she was doing and called her his Angel of Hygeia. One day, after a grueling two hours, after Dr. Levinson had put in his temporary upper bridge, he had said, "Paulette, when this is over, I'm going to treat you to the best lunch in town."

Today it was all going to be over and Paulette was wondering if Mr. Gadsden was going to remember his promise, when the telephone rang.

"Excuse me," she said and went out of the office, in a starchy, bosomy white bustle, to her desk in the small reception room, where the telephone was.

"Dr. Levinson's office," she said. "Good morning."

She had a high, babyish voice, incongruous for her size and womanly dimensions. She knew it, but there was nothing she could do about it. When she tried to pitch it lower, she sounded like a female impersonator.

"Miss Anderson?"

"Yes." She had the feeling she had heard the voice before, but she couldn't quite place it.

"This is Christopher Bagshot."

"Yes?" She waited. The name meant something, but, like the voice, it was just beyond the boundaries of recognition.

"From the Browsing Corner."

"Oh, yes, of course," Paulette said. She began to riffle through Dr. Levinson's appointment book, looking for open half hours on the schedule for the next week. Dr. Levinson was very busy and sometimes patients had to wait for months. She remembered Bagshot now and was mildly surprised he had called. He had perfect white teeth, with canines that were curiously just a little longer than ordinary, which gave him a slightly and not unpleasantly wild appearance. But, of course, you never could tell about teeth.

"What I called about"—he seemed to have some difficulty in speaking—"is, well, there's a lecture at the Y.M.H.A. tonight. It's a professor from Columbia. 'You and Your Environment.' I thought maybe if you weren't busy. We could have a bite to eat first and. . . ." He dribbled off.

Paulette frowned. Dr. Levinson didn't like personal calls while there were patients in the office. She had been with him for three years and he was satisfied with her work and all that, but he was elderly and had old-fashioned notions about employees' private lives.

She thought quickly. She had been invited to a party that night at the home of an economics instructor at NYU, down in the Village, and she hated going into a room full of people alone and Bagshot was a good-looking serious young man who could talk about books and the latest problems very sensibly and would make a welcome escort. But there was Mr. Gadsden in the chair, and his promise. Of course, it had only been for lunch, but she knew his wife was visiting her family in Cleveland this week. She knew because he had come into the office on Monday and made a joke about it. "Doc," he'd said, "this is one week I'm glad to see you. You may tear my jaw apart, but it's nothing to what my father-in-law does to my brain. Without instruments." He had a wry way of putting things, Mr. Gadsden, when he wanted to. If he was alone, she thought, and remembered about lunch, and had nothing to do for the evening. . . . It would be OK going to the party at the instructor's apartment with the bookstore boy, but it would be dazzling to walk in and say, "I guess I don't have to introduce Omar Gadsden."

"Miss Anderson," Dr. Levinson was calling testily from the office.

"Yes, doctor," Paulette said, then into the phone: "I'm terribly busy now. I'll tell you what—I'll come by after work this afternoon and let you know."

"But—" Bagshot said.

"Have to run," she whispered, making her voice intimate to give him enough hope to last till five o'clock. "Goodbye."

She hung up and went back to the office, where Dr. Levinson was standing with the new shining set of teeth held aloft above the gaping mouth of Omar Gadsden and Mr. Gadsden looking as though he were going to be guillotined within the next two seconds.

❖   ❖   ❖

Christopher hung up the phone. Strike one, he thought. The last whisper over the phone had left him tingling weirdly, but he had to face facts. Strike one. Who knew what would happen to a girl like that before five o'clock of a Saturday afternoon? He tried to be philosophical. What could you expect the very first number you called? Still, he had nothing really to reproach himself for. He had not just jumped in blindly. The invitation to the lecture at the Y.M.H.A. had been calculatingly and cunningly chosen as bait for a girl who was interested in the kind of books *Anderson, Paulette*** was interested in. He had carefully perused the "Entertainment Events" section in the *Times* before dialing Dr. Levinson's office and had studied *Cue* magazine and had rejected the pleasures of the movies and the theater as lures for the dental assistant. And she *had* said that she would come by at five o'clock. She wouldn't have said that if she'd felt it was ridiculous for a girl her size to be seen with a man his size. The more he thought about it, the better he felt. It hadn't been a blazing success, of course, but nobody could say it had been a total failure.

Two college students, a boy and a girl, who made a habit of Saturday-morning visits, came in. They were unkempt and unprincipled and they rarely bought anything, at the most a paperback, and he kept a sharp eye on them, because they had a nasty habit of separating and wandering uninnocently around the shop and they both wore loose coats that could hide any number of books. It was fifteen minutes before they left and he could get back to the telephone.

He decided to forget about alphabetical order. It was an unscientific way of going about the problem, dependent upon a false conception of the arrangement of modern society. Now was the time for a judicious weighing of possibilities. As he thumbed through his address book, he thought hard and long over each starred name, remembering height, weight, coloring, general amiability, signs of flirtatiousness and/or sensuality, indications of loneliness and popularity, tastes and aversions.

Stickney, Beulah**. He lingered over the page. Under *Stickney, Beulah***, in parentheses, was *Fleischer, Rebecca*, also doubled-starred. The two girls lived together, on East 74th Street. *Stickney, Beulah*** was actually and honestly a model and often had her photograph in *Vogue* and *Harper's Bazaar*. She had long dark hair that she wore down loose over her shoulders and a long bony sensational body and a big model's mouth and a model's arrogant look, as though no man alive was good enough for her. But the look was just part of her professional equipment. Whenever she came into the shop, she was friendly as could be with Christopher and squatted unceremoniously on the floor or loped up the ladder when she was looking for books that were in out-of-the way places. She was a great one for travel books. She had worked in Paris and Rome and London and while she bought books about distant places by writers like H. V. Morton and James Morris and Mary McCarthy, when she talked about the cities she had visited, her vocabulary was hardly literary, to say the least. "You've got to get to Paris before the Germans come in again, luv," she would say. "It's a gas." Or, "You'd go ape over Rome, luv." Or, "Marrakesh, luv! Stoned! Absolutely stoned!" She had picked up the habit of calling people luv in London. Christopher knew it was just a habit, but it was friendly and encouraging, all the same.

Fleischer, Rebecca** was just about as tall and pretty as *Stickney, Beulah***, with short dark red hair and a pale freckled complexion to go with it and tapering musician's fingers and willowy hips. She was a receptionist for a company that made cassettes and she wore slacks on Saturdays that didn't hide anything. She was a Jewish girl from Brooklyn and made no bones about it, larding her conversation with words like shmeer and schmuck and nebbish. She didn't buy books by the reviews nor by their subject matter, she bought them after looking at the pictures of the authors on the back covers. If the authors were handsome, she would put down her $6.95. She bought the books of Saul Bellow, John Cheever and John Hersey. It wasn't a scientific system, but it worked and she put an awful lot of good writing on her shelf that way. At least it worked in America. Christopher wasn't so sure it would work with foreign authors. She had endeared herself to Christopher by buying *Portnoy's Complaint* and having him gift-wrap it and send it to her mother in Flatbush.

"The old bag'll sit shiva for six months when she reads it," Rebecca had said, smiling happily.

Christopher wouldn't have dared send anything more advanced than the works of G. A. Henty to *his* mother and he appreciated the freedom of spirit in Miss Fleischer's gesture. He had never gone out with a Jewish girl, not that he was anti-Semitic or anything like that but because somehow the occasion hadn't arisen. Listening to a Jewish girl in skintight slacks who was five inches taller than he talk the way Miss Fleischer talked was intriguing, if not more. June said that Jewish girls were voracious in bed. June came from Pasadena and her father still believed *The Protocols of the Elders of Zion*, so her opinions on the subject could not be called scientific; but even so, whenever Miss Fleischer came into the shop, Christopher looked carefully for pleasing signs of voracity.

He hesitated over the two names. Then he decided. *Stickney, Beulah***. A redheaded giantess who was also Jewish would be too much for the first go. He dialed the Rhinelander number.

❖　　　　❖　　　　❖

Beulah sat under the drier in the living room of the three-room flat, with kitchen, that she shared with Rebecca. Rebecca was painting Beulah's nails a luminous pearly pink. The ironing board on which Rebecca had ironed out Beulah's hair into a straight shining sheet of living satin was still in place. Beulah kept looking nervously over Rebecca's bent head at the clock on the mantelpiece of the false fireplace, although the plane wasn't due in at Kennedy until 3:15 and it was only 10:40 now. The girls did each other's hair and nails every Saturday morning, if other amusements didn't intervene. But this was a special Saturday morning, at least for Beulah, and she'd said she was too nervous to work on Rebecca and Rebecca had said that was OK, there was nobody she had to look good for this weekend, anyway.

Rebecca had broken with her boyfriend the week before. He worked in Wall Street and even with the way things were going down there, he had an income that was designed to please any young girl with marriage on her mind. Her boyfriend's family had a seat on the stock exchange, a *big* seat, and unless Wall Street vanished completely, which was a possibility, of course, he had nothing to worry about. And, from all indications, he was approaching marriage, like a squirrel approaching a peanut, apprehensive but hungry. But the week before, he had tried to take Rebecca to an orgy on East 63rd Street. That is, he *had* taken Rebecca to an orgy without telling her that was what it was going to be. It had seemed like a superior party to Rebecca, with well-dressed guests and champagne and pot, until people began to take off their clothes.

Then Rebecca had said, "George, you have brought me to an orgy."

And George had said, "That's what it looks like, honey."

And Rebecca had said, "Take me home. This is no place for a nice Jewish girl from Brooklyn."

And George had said, "Oh, for Christ's sake, when are you going to stop being a nice Jewish girl from Brooklyn?" He was taking off his Countess Mara tie as she went out the front door. So she had nobody this Saturday to

look good for and she was putting in some extra time on
Beulah's nails, because Beulah had somebody to look good
for, at precisely 3:15 that afternoon, to be exact, if the
goddamn air-traffic controllers didn't keep the plane from
Zurich in a holding pattern between Nantucket and Allen-
town, Pennsylvania, for five hours, as they sometimes did.

The picture of the man who was arriving at Kennedy
that afternoon was in a silver frame on an end table in
the living room and another picture of him, in a leather
frame, was on the dresser in Beulah's bedroom. In both
pictures he was in ski clothes, because he was a ski instructor by the name of Jirg in St. Anton, where Beulah
had spent a month the previous winter. In the picture in
the living room he was in motion, skis beautifully clamped
together, giving it that old Austrian reverse shoulder, a
spray of snow pluming behind him. He was at rest in the
bedroom, brown, smiling, long hair blowing boyishly in
the wind, like Jean-Claude Killy, all strong white teeth
and Tyrolean charm. Even Rebecca had to admit he was
luscious, Beulah's word for Jirg, although Rebecca had
said when Beulah had first reported on him, "John Os-
borne says in some play or other that having an affair with
a ski instructor is vulgar."

"Englishmen," Beulah had said, hurt, " 're jealous of
everybody. They'll say anything that comes into their
heads, because they zilched the Empire." It hadn't been
vulgar at all. On the contrary. It hadn't been like getting
involved with a man in the city, worrying about finding
a taxi in the rain to get there on time and waking up at
seven o'clock in the morning to go to work and eating
lunch alone in Hamburger Heaven and worrying if the

man's stuffy friends would think your clothes were extreme
and listening to him complain about the other men in the
office. In the mountains everybody lived in ski pants and it
was all snow like diamonds and frosty starlight and huge
country feather beds and rosy complexions and being together day and night and incredibly graceful young men
doing dangerous, beautiful things to show off for you and
eating in cute mountain huts with hot wine and people
singing jolly Austrian songs at the next table and all the
other girls trying to get your ski teacher away from you
both on the slopes and off, and not managing it, because,
as he said in his darling Austrian accent, wrinkling that
dear tanned face in an effort to speak English correctly,
"It is neffer come my way before, a girl so much like you."

Beulah hadn't seen him since St. Anton, but his influence had lingered on. She hadn't been pleased with any
man she'd gone out with since she'd come back to America
and she'd been saving her money so that she could spend
three months at least this winter in the Tirol. Then the
letter had come from Jirg, telling her that he'd been offered a job at Stowe starting in December and would she
be glad to see him? Beulah had written back the same day.
December was too far off, she wrote, and why didn't he
come to New York immediately? As her guest. (The poor
boys were paid a pitiful pittance in Austria, despite their
great skills, and you always had to show practically inhuman delicacy about paying when you went anywhere
with them, so as not to embarrass them. In the month in
St. Anton she had become one of the most unobtrusive bill
payers the Alps had ever seen.) She could afford it, she
told herself, because this winter she wasn't going on an

expensive jaunt to Europe but would be skiing at Stowe.

"You're crazy," Rebecca had said when she learned about the invitation. "I wouldn't pay for a man to lead me out of a burning building." Sometimes Rebecca's mother showed through a little in her daughter's attitudes.

"I'm giving myself a birthday gift, luv," Beulah had said. Her birthday was in November. "One beautiful brown, energetic young Austrian who doesn't know what's hit him. It's my money, luv, and I couldn't spend it better."

Jirg had written that he liked the idea and as soon as he was finished with his summer job, he would be happy to accept his old pupil's invitation. He had underlined pupil roguishly. He had some clean outdoor job on a farm in the summer. He had sent another picture, to keep his memory green. It was of himself, winning a ski teachers' race at the end of the season. He was wearing goggles and a helmet and was going so fast that the picture was a little blurred, but Beulah was certain she would have recognized him anyway. She had pasted the picture in a big scrapbook that contained photographs of all the men she had had affairs with.

There was one thing really worrying Beulah as she sat in her robe in the living room, watching Rebecca buff her nails. She hadn't yet decided where to put Jirg. Ideally, the best place would be the apartment. She and Rebecca had separate rooms and the bed in her room was a double one and it wasn't as though she and Rebecca were shy about bringing men home with them. And stashing Jirg away in a hotel would cost money and he wouldn't always be on hand when she wanted him. But Rebecca had had an unsettling effect on some of her other boyfriends, with her red hair and white skin and that brazen (that was the only word for it, Beulah thought), that brazen Brooklyn camaraderie with men. And let's face it, Beulah thought, she's a wonderful girl and I'd trust her with my life, but when it comes to men, there isn't a loyal bone in her body. And a poor gullible ski teacher who'd never been off the mountain in his life and used to avid girls coming and going in rapacious batches all winter long. . . . And sometimes Beulah had to work at night or go out of town for several days at a time on a job. . . .

She had been puzzling over the problem ever since she got the letter from Jirg and she still hadn't made up her mind. Play it by ear, she decided. See what the odds are on the morning line.

"There you are," Rebecca said, pushing her hand away. "The anointed bride."

"Thanks, luv," Beulah said, admiring her nails. "I'll buy you lunch at P.J.'s" There were always a lot of extra men who ate lunch at P.J.'s on Saturday, with nothing to do for the weekend and an eye out for companionship or whatever, and maybe she could make a connection for Rebecca and get her out of the apartment at least for the afternoon and evening. With luck, for the whole night.

"Naah," Rebecca said, standing and yawning. "I don't feel like going out. I'm going to stay home and watch the game of the week on the tube."

Shit, Beulah said to herself.

Then the phone rang.

"Miss Stickney's residence," Beulah said into the phone. She always answered that way, as though she were a maid or the answering service, so that if it was some pest, she could say, "Miss Stickney's not at home. Can I take a message?"

"May I speak to Miss Stickney, please?"

"Who's calling?"

"Mr. Bagshot."

"Who?"

"From the Browsing—"

"Hi, luv," Beulah said. "My book on Sicily come in yet, you know the one?"

"It's on order," Christopher said. He was disappointed with this commercial prelude, even though she called him luv. "What I'm phoning for, beautiful," he said daringly, suddenly deciding to be racy and familiar, put himself right up there on her level, so to speak, "what I'm phoning for is what do you say you and me we hit the town tonight?"

"Hit what?" Beulah asked, puzzled.

"Well, I thought I just happen to be free and maybe you're hanging loose yourself and we could go to some joint for dinner and then split off downtown to the Electric—"

"Oh, shit, luv," Beulah said, "I'm prostrate with grief. This is Drearsville Day for me. I've got an aunt coming into Kennedy from Denver this P.M. and God knows when I can get rid of her." It was standard policy on her part never to admit that she even *knew* another man when asked for a date.

"Oh, that's all right. . . ."

"Wait a minute, luv," she said. "There's a buzz at the door. Hold fast, like a dear." She put her hand over the phone. "Hey, Becky," she said to Rebecca, who was screw-

ing the top on the nail-polish bottle, "how'd you like to
hit the town with a divine—"

"Hit *what?*"

"That beautiful boy from the bookstore is on the phone.
He's invited me to dinner. But—"

"That *dwarf?*" Rebecca said.

"He's not so small, actually," Beulah said. "He's very
well proportioned."

"I don't go in for comedy acts," Rebecca said. "He'd
have to use his ladder even to get into scoring territory."

"There's no need to be vulgar about my friends," Beulah
said frigidly, realizing finally that the whole Sixth Fleet
wouldn't be able to get her roommate out of the house
today. "And I do think it shows a surprisingly ugly side
to your character. Prejudice is the word, luv. It's a kind
of anti-Semitism, if you want to know what I think."

"Tell him to pick on somebody his own size," Rebecca
said, taking the nail polish into the bathroom.

Beulah lifted her hand from the phone. "It was the super
with the mail, luv," she said. "Bills and more bills."

"Yeah," said Christopher dispiritedly, "I know how it
is." He remembered that Beulah Stickney owed him $47
since July, but of course this was not the time to bring it
up. "Well, have a nice time. . . ." He prepared to hang up.

"Hold on, Chris. . . ." That was his name, Christopher.
"Maybe something can be salvaged from Be Kind to Aunts
Day, after all. Maybe I can get her drunk at the airport or
she'll turn out to be suffering from some dreadful female
disease and will have to plunge into bed. . . ." The plane
was due at 3:15, but you never could tell, it might be held
up for engine trouble or darling Jirg, who had never been

out of the hills before, might be confused by the wild traffic of the city of Zurich and miss the connection or go to the wrong gate and wind up in Tehran. Or even, the way things were going with airlines these days, the plane could be highjacked or bombed by Arabs or just fall down into a lake in Labrador. One thing she couldn't bear and that was having dinner alone. "I'll tell you what, you just sit there among all those lovely books like a good boy and I'll get on the horn this afternoon and tell you if Auntie looks like conking out or not. What time do you stay open to?"

"Seven o'clock," Christopher said.

"You poor overworked boy," Beulah said. "Stay near the phone, luv."

"Yeah," Christopher said.

"It *was* dear of you to call," Beulah said and hung up. She always concluded on the telephone with "It was dear of you to call" and without saying goodbye. It was original and it spread good will.

She looked at the clock and then went into the bathroom to experiment with her hair.

❖　　　　　　❖　　　　　　❖

Christopher put the phone down slowly, the palms of his hands damp. The store felt very warm and he went to the front door and opened it. He stared out at Madison Avenue. People were passing by in the sunlight. Perhaps it was his imagination, but it looked to him as though the tall people on the avenue were strolling and the short ones were, well, *burrowing*. He closed the door and went back into the shop, reflecting on his conversation with *Stickney, Beulah***. If luck had been with him, if he'd had a premonition or extrasensory perception or something, he'd have asked to speak to Rebecca Fleischer, instead of Beulah Stickney. The chances were that no aunt of Rebecca Fleischer's was coming in from Denver that afternoon. Now, after having tried to make it with Beulah, he could not call back and ask Rebecca. There were limits. The girl would be mortally offended, being tapped to go into the game as a substitute, as it were, and he wouldn't blame her.

He didn't trust Beulah's ability to get rid of her aunt before seven o'clock. He had aunts of his own and once they got hold of you, they stuck.

Back to the address book. It was nearly twelve o'clock and people would be going out to lunch and then matinees or linen showers or whatever it was girls went to on Saturday afternoons.

❖   ❖   ❖

Caroline Trowbridge was in bed with Scotty Powalter. At one time, Caroline Trowbridge had been Caroline Powalter, but Scotty Powalter had found her in bed with his ex-roommate from Yale, Giuliano Ascione, and had divorced her for adultery. It hadn't been a completely friendly divorce. It had been all over the New York *Daily News* and Caroline had been dropped from the social register the next year, but she and Scotty had what they both agreed was a Big Physical Thing for each other and every once in a while they spent a night or a week together until something happened to remind Scotty of his ex-roommate at Yale.

The truth was that Caroline had a Big Physical Thing with almost every man she met. She was a tall, sturdy, inbred, healthy social-register kind of girl who was crazy about boats and horses and Italians and if she had had to swear to it under oath, she wouldn't have been able to say what was more fun—leaping a ditch on an Irish hunter or crewing a Dragon in a force-six gale or going on a weekend to a sinful little inn in the country with one of her husband's best friends.

Despite her catholic approval of the entire male sex, she oftened regretted not being married to Scotty anymore. He was six feet, four inches tall and built accordingly and the way he behaved in bed, you'd never suspect he came from one of the oldest families along the Main Line in Philadelphia. His family had a place up in Maine with horses and he had a sixty foot ketch at Center Island and he didn't have to bother with anything boring like working. As she sometimes said to her lovers, if he hadn't been so insanely and irrationally possessive, it would have been the marriage of the century.

He had called her the evening before from the Racquet Club, where he had been playing backgammon. When she recognized his voice on the telephone and he said he was calling from the Racquet Club, she knew he had been losing, because he always got horny when he lost at backgammon, especially on weekends. She'd canceled the man she was supposed to go to Southampton with—after all, husbands, even ex-husbands, came first—and Scotty had come over and she'd opened two cans of turtle soup and they'd been in bed ever since 9:30 the night before. It had been such a complete night that sometime around dawn, he'd even mentioned something about getting remarried. It was almost noon now and they were hungry and she got out of bed and put on a pink terry-cloth robe and went into the kitchen to make some bloody marys, for nourishment. She was always strict with herself about no drinks before 11 o'clock, because she had seen too many of her friends go that route. She was dashing in the Worcestershire sauce when the phone rang.

❖   ❖   ❖

What Christopher liked about her, he thought, as his hand hovered over the phone, preparing to dial, was that she was wholesome. In the polluted city, she was a breath of fresh country air. If you didn't know about her and her family's steel mills and her divorce and her expulsion from the social register, you'd think she was a girl just in from the farm, milking cows. She came into the shop often, breezing in with a big childish smile, hanging onto a man's arm, a different one each time, and buying large, expensive, color-plate books about boats or horses. She had an account at the shop, but usually the man with her would pay for the books and then she would throw her strong firm arms around her escort and kiss him enthusiastically in gratitude, no matter who was looking.

She had kissed Christopher once, too. Although not in the shop. He had gone to the opening of a one-man show at an art gallery four doors down on Madison Avenue and she was there, too, squinting over the heads of the other connoisseurs at the geometric forms in clashing colors that represented the painter's reaction to being alive in America. Extraordinarily, she was unaccompanied, and when she spotted Christopher, she bulled her way through the crowd, smiling sexily, and said, "My deliverer," and put her arm through his and stroked his forearm. There was something unnatural about her being alone, like a free-floating abalone. Her predestined form was the couple. Knowing this, Christopher was not particularly flattered by her attention, since it was no more personal than a swan's being attracted to a pond or a wildcat to a pine tree. Still, the touch of her capable ex-social-register fingers on his arm was cordial.

"I suppose," she said, "clever man that you are, that you know what all this is about."

"Well. . . ." Christopher began.

"They remind me of my trigonometry class at Chatham Hall. That distressing pi sign. Don't they make you thirsty, Mr.—uh?"

"Bagshot."

"Of course. Why don't you and I just sidle out of here like true art lovers and go out into the night and snap on one or two martinis?"

They were nearly at the door by now, anyway, so Christopher said, as brightly as he could, "Right on." The owner of the gallery, who was a business friend of his, was near the door, too, looking at him with a betrayed expression for leaving so quickly. Christopher tried to show, by a grimace and a twitch of his shoulders, that he was under the sway of powers stronger than he and that he would come back soon, but he doubted that he communicated.

They went to the Westbury Polo Bar and sat in one of the booths and ordered martinis and Caroline Trowbridge sat very close to him and rubbed her knee against his and told him how lucky he was to have a vocation in life, especially one as rewarding as his, involved in the fascinating world of books. She had no vocation, she said sadly, unless you could consider horses and sailing a vocation, and she had to admit to herself that with the way the world was going—just look at the front page of any newspaper—horses and boats were revoltingly frivolous, and didn't he think they ought to call a waiter and order two more martinis?

By the time they had finished the second martini, she had his head between her two strong hands and was looking down into his eyes. She had a long torso as well as long legs and she loomed over him in the semiobscurity of the Polo Bar. "Your eyes," she was saying, "are dark, lambent pools." Perhaps she hadn't paid much attention in the trigonometry class at Chatham Hall, but she certainly had listened in freshman English.

Emboldened by alcohol and lambency, Christopher said, "Caroline"—they were on a first-name basis by now—"Caroline, have dinner with me?"

"Oh, Christopher," she said, "what a dear thoughtful thing to say," and kissed him. On the lips. She had a big mouth, that went with the rest of her, and she was pleasantly damp.

"Well," he said when she unstuck, "shall we?"

"Oh, my poor, dear, beautiful little mannikin," she said, "nothing would give me greater joy. But I'm occupied until a week from next Thursday." She looked at her watch and jumped up, pulling her coat around her. "Rum dum dum," she cried, "I'm hideously tardy right this very moment and everybody will be cross with me all the wretched night and say nasty things to me and tweak my ear and suspect the worst and never believe I was in an art gallery, you naughty boy." She leaned over and pecked the top of his head. "What bliss," she said and was gone.

He ordered another martini and had dinner alone, remembering her kiss and the curious way she had of expressing herself. One day, when she was a little less busy, he knew he was going to see her again. And not in the shop.

❖   ❖   ❖

Oh, damn, she thought as she reached for the phone hanging on the kitchen wall, I forgot to switch it to the answering service. When she expected Scotty over, she made a practice of instructing the service to pick up all calls on the first ring, because nothing infuriated Scotty more than hearing her talk to another man. She loved him, divorce or no divorce, but she had to admit that he was a neurotically suspicious creature.

"Hello," she said.

"Caroline," the male voice said, "this is Christopher—"

"Sorry, Christopher," she said, "you have the wrong number," and hung up. Then she unhooked the phone, so that if he called again, he'd get a busy signal. She still had the bottle of Worcestershire sauce in her hand and she shook a few more spurts into the tomato juice. She added a double shot of vodka, to calm Scotty down, if by any chance he didn't believe that it was a wrong number.

Scotty was lying with his eyes closed, all the covers thrown off, when she came into the bedroom with the bloody marys. He really filled a bed, Scotty; you got your money's worth of man with her ex-husband. His expression was peaceful, almost as if he had gone back to sleep. The phone on the table next to the bed didn't look as though it had been moved, she noted with relief.

"All up on deck for grog," she said cheerily.

He sat up, monumentally, muscles rippling, and swung his legs over the side of the bed. He reached out his hand and took the glass from her, looked at it consideringly, then hurled it against the opposite wall. A good part of the room turned red.

"Oh, Scotty," she said reproachfully, "don't tell me you're being seized by one of your unreasonable moods again." She backed off a little, being careful to avoid broken glass, and took two swift swallows of bloody mary for her nerves.

He stood up. It was an awful sight when he stood up naked like that in a comparatively small bedroom. It was like seeing the whole front line of the Dallas Cowboys wrapped into one moving in on you. The funny scar on his forehead that he had had since his brother had hit him with a baseball bat when they were boys, and which stood out when he was angry, was turning a frightening bright pink.

"Scotty Powalter," she said, "I absolutely forbid you to touch me."

Thank God he only slapped me with an open hand, she thought as she reeled back into a chair, still miraculously holding onto her drink.

"You're unjust," she said from the depths of the chair. "You're a fundamentally unjust man. Hitting a girl for a little old wrong number."

"Some wrong number," he said. "Who's Christopher?"

"How should I know who Christopher is? This voice said, 'Hello, this is Christopher,' and I said—"

"This voice said, 'Caroline,' " Scotty said.

"Sneak," she said. "Listening in on other people's conversations. Is that what they taught you at Yale?" Scotty wasn't really unintelligent, but his thought processes were cumbersome and sometimes you could fuddle him and make him forget his dreadful intentions by attacking him.

"I suppose he was calling up to remind you you had a date to screw him this afternoon," Scotty said. "Knowing how dizzy you are about little matters like that."

"You're fully aware of what I think about your vocabulary, Scotty," Caroline said with dignity.

"Fuck my vocabulary," Scotty said.

"If you must know, and I don't see where it's any business of yours, anyway, considering the nature of our relationship," she said, "I haven't had a date with anybody since a week ago last Tuesday. And if your poor little brain isn't drowned in the mists of alcohol, you'll recall that a week ago last Tuesday, you didn't get out of this very bed until six P.M. Wednesday." As she spoke, she began to believe herself and tears of self-pity formed in her eyes. It was almost like being married again.

"Who's Christopher?" Scotty said. He began to prowl

dangerously, like a berserk elephant, and sh
the lamps and other glassware in the room.

"I'm perfectly willing to tell you," she s
stop marauding around like some mad beast
You know I've never hid anything *significant* from you.

"Hah," he said, but he stopped prowling.

"He's just a poor little table-model clerk in a bookstore
on Madison Avenue," Caroline said. "He's just a little Shet-
land pony of a man, you'd be ashamed of yourself being
jealous of him if you ever saw him."

"He called you, no matter what size he is," Scotty said
stubbornly.

"Sometimes he calls me when he gets in a book he thinks
I'd like."

"*The Child's Manual of Sex*," Scotty said. "*A Thousand
and Three Indian Positions*. I can guess what kind of bookstore he runs."

"That's hardly the way to talk to a woman who's been
your wife," Caroline said fastidiously. "If you want to see
with your own eyes and convince yourself once and for
all, just you get yourself dressed and I'll take you over to
Madison Avenue and I'll bet you'll take one look and get
down right then and there on your bended knee and beg
my forgiveness for the bestial way you've treated me this
morning."

"I don't want to get dressed," Scotty said. "I want a
bloody mary and I want to go back to bed. In that order.
Make it snappy."

He was like that. Anger aroused other emotions in him.

He was stretching himself on the bed like some huge
beached vessel as she went out of the bedroom toward the

kitchen to make another batch of bloody marys. Her head was ringing a little from that Yale-sized slap along the side of her jaw, but she was pleased with her over-all handling of what could very easily have developed into a crisis. As she shook the bloody marys, she hummed to herself. She might, later on, at the proper moment, remind Scotty that along about dawn he had mentioned the possibility of getting remarried. And she was damn well going to get him to write a check to have the bedroom repapered. And if he turned ugly again this afternoon, as he was likely to do, there was always that dear little man waiting patiently on Madison Avenue.

❖ ❖ ❖

Wrong number, Christopher thought, staring at the dead phone in his hand. Who is she kidding? That was no wrong number. He had an annoyed impulse to dial her again, just to show her that he wasn't being fooled, but decided against it, out of tact. He could imagine all too well why she had said it was a wrong number.

Luckily, a spate of customers entered the store and he was too busy wrapping books and ringing up cash to brood about it.

By the time the store emptied in the lunchtime lull, he had almost convinced himself that it didn't matter at all to him what Caroline Trowbridge did with her Saturday afternoon.

He sat down at the desk by the cash register and took out his address book.

*Toye, Dorothea***. He would never have given her two

stars on his own, although she was pretty enough and if she wasn't exactly five feet, eight inches tall, she was certainly in the neighborhood of five feet, seven and a half. She was not a flashy woman. She was shapely, but in a polite way, and wore simple, sober-colored, almost college-girl clothes, or at least the kind of clothes that girls used to wear in college, and although he guessed she was twenty-eight or twenty-nine, her appearance was demure, her voice low and hesitant, her smile rare. The first two or three times she came into the shop, he had hardly remarked her. But then he had noticed that if there were other men in the shop, even old men or men who at other times seemed to lose themselves in the books, they would slowly begin following her with their eyes and then somehow drift helplessly in her direction. He regarded Dorothea Toye more carefully to see what it was that acted so magnetically on his male customers. He decided that it was probably her complexion. She was always a light tan, with a glow, like a touch of the sun, on her silken skin. She was brilliantly clean. If Caroline Trowbridge looked like a girl just in from a farm, Dorothea Toye looked like a child who had just splashed out of the sea to be dried with a rough towel by her mother. He had been surprised when she had ordered a book of prints by Aubrey Beardsley.

He had been even more surprised when one of his old customers, Mr. O'Malley, who to the best of his knowledge had never spoken a word to the lady, had followed her out of the shop one afternoon at three o'clock and gotten into a cab with her. It was then that he had awarded her her second star. Seeing her get into a cab with Mr. O'Malley heightened his interest in her.

She didn't buy many books, but concentrated for the most part on the small record library against the rear wall, buying albums of every new Broadway musical. At the cut-rate music stores and discount houses farther downtown, she could have gotten the same albums much more cheaply, but as she once told Christopher while he was wrapping the album of *Hair* for her, "I don't go downtown much. I'm really a homebody."

She was an outside chance, Dorothea Toye, but the day was passing swiftly.

He dialed her number. The phone rang and rang and he was just about to give up when it was answered.

"Yes?" The voice was businesslike, but it was Dorothea Toye's.

"This is Christopher Bagshot. . . ."

"Who?" Now the voice was cold and suspicious.

It was a dream of Christopher's that the day would come on which people would not say, "Who?" when he said, "This is Christopher Bagshot."

"From the bookstore, Miss Toye."

"Oh, yes." The voice was warmer but had a hint of puzzlement in it.

"I hope I'm not disturbing you," Christopher said.

"Oh, no, I'm just making myself a bit of breakfast." Christopher looked at his watch. It was nearly one o'clock, and he realized he was hungry. He wondered briefly where Miss Toye could have been the night before to be having breakfast now at one P.M.

"I guess you're surprised, my calling you up like this, I mean," Christopher said, "but I thought—"

"Oh, I get a lot of calls," Miss Toye said. She sounded husky and not demure over the phone.

"I'm sure you do," Christopher said gallantly. "What I am calling about is—I mean, what are you doing tonight?"

Miss Toye laughed peculiarly.

"I could see if I could get some tickets to a show," he said hurriedly, "unless, of course, you've seen them all."

"I'm booked from eight on tonight, honey," Miss Toye said, "but if you want, you could come over right now."

"I can't leave the store," Christopher said, confused by the bluntness of the invitation. "And I don't close till around seven and. . . ."

"Well," Miss Toye said, "I can handle it at seven, if you don't waste any time getting over here. Fifty dollars."

"What was that, Miss Toye?" Christopher said faintly.

"I said my price was fifty dollars." She sounded annoyed at something.

At that moment, the front door of the shop opened and June came in, wearing a raincoat, although there wasn't a cloud in the sky. She waved gaily. Christopher tried to frown in a businesslike way as he cupped the telephone in both hands. He felt himself getting very rosy. "I'm afraid that isn't exactly what I had in mind, madam," he said.

"Look, Mr. Bagshot," Miss Toye said crisply, "you don't give *books* away free, do you?"

June was approaching him swiftly.

"I'll talk it over with my father," Christopher said loudly as June came into earshot, "and perhaps we can come to an arrangement."

Miss Toye's second laugh was even more peculiar than the first one had been. Christopher put the telephone down decisively as June kissed him on the cheek.

"My idea," June said, "is that you close the shop and take me to lunch."

"You know I can't do that." He walked away quickly from the phone and June followed him.

"You have to eat," she said.

"I call the deli and they deliver," he said. He wondered what he could say, without actually hurting her feelings, to discourage her from these raids at all hours.

"You look like someone in the final stages of *mal de mer*," June said. She was studying French at Berlitz in case she ever had the occasion to go to France. "What's the matter?"

"Nothing's the matter. Nothing."

"My God, we're emphatic today," June said. "OK, nothing. You glad I came?"

"As always," he said. His conversation with Miss Toye had done something cramping to his throat and he had difficulty in pronouncing words correctly. Ordinarily, he would have been happy to see June come into the shop, she was a sweet girl, darling, even, at certain times, but her coming in just when Miss Toye was laughing that bruising laugh on the telephone showed an unfortunate, even if unconscious, sense of timing on June's part.

His nose began to run. It was a familiar symptom. Whenever he was under tension, his nose leaked. In school, he always went to exams with three large handkerchiefs in his pockets. He pulled out a handkerchief and blew vigorously.

"Are you catching a cold or something?" June asked.

"Not that I know of." He sneezed. He wondered if any other of Miss Toye's potential clients were affected the same way after a telephone call.

"I know an absolutely fabulous pill that—"

"I am not catching a cold," he said. He blew again.

"You don't have to snap my head off just because I show a normal human interest in your health," June said.

"June," he said, "I'm having a rough day. All alone here in the store and—"

"I'm sorry," June said, instantly contrite. "That's why I came. I thought I might cheer you up. Maybe even help you a little this afternoon. . . ."

"That's awfully sweet of you," he said, aghast at the thought of having June there with Miss Anderson coming in around five o'clock and maybe even Beulah Stickney, too, if she got rid of her aunt. "But it's too complicated with someone who isn't familiar with the stock and all."

"Anyway," June said, "I'm going to have lunch with you. No protests." She certainly was a bossy girl. "I'll go to the delicatessen myself and buy us both a perfectly scrumptious lunch and we'll have a picnic in the office."

There was no getting out of it, so he pulled out his wallet and took a five-dollar bill from it. But June waved it away. "This lunch is on me," she said. "I've had a big week." She worked out of an office that supplied temporary secretarial help and some weeks she made as much as $150. She wouldn't take a permanent job, because she had come all the way East from Pasadena to become a singer. She studied with a man who said he had been responsible for Petula Clark.

Christopher put the five-dollar bill back into his wallet.

"Aren't you insanely happy now I came by?" she asked.

"Insanely," he said.

"Then smile," she said, "and say something nice."

"I love you," he said. That's what she meant when she said say something nice.

"That's better," she said. She kissed him briefly and went out, blonde and small, lovable and intent on marriage, in her raincoat. She always wore a raincoat to protect her throat, just in case.

He thought of Miss Toye and had to blow his nose again.

❖   ❖   ❖

"Isn't this cozy?" June asked as they ate their roast-beef sandwiches and pickles and drank their milk at the table in the little back office. June was against alcohol because of her throat.

"Uh-huh," Christopher said, chewing hard on a piece of gristle.

"Sometimes, when I'm alone," June said, "and I happen to think of this little room, I'm almost tempted to cry."

The reason she was tempted to cry was that the first time they had kissed, it had been in the little back office. If you wanted to look at it that way, it had all started there. The kiss had been wonderful and it had led to other and better things and there was no denying they had had a lot of fun together and she was a pretty and lively girl, nubile and often gay; but still the dark little office was hardly a shrine, for heaven's sake.

He tried to make himself think unkindly about her. When he was exposed to her for any length of time, he felt himself melting in her direction and once or twice he had been perilously close to asking her to marry him. Maybe if before he had met her he'd known a lot of tall girls intimately and had a standard of comparison, they'd be married already.

Sitting there in the cluttered little office watching her lick mayonnaise off her finger with delicious unself-consciousness, he was tempted to forget his whole damn crusade and ask her to have dinner with him that night, even though he'd lied to her successfully and told her he had to have dinner with his mother and father in Westchester that night—they were getting uptight about never seeing him anymore, now that he'd found a girl. But the front doorbell rang just as he was about to speak and he had to go out into the store and stand around for almost a half hour while an elderly couple shuffled around the poetry counter denouncing Allen Ginsberg and finally buying a play in verse by Christopher Fry that must have been on the shelves since the year one.

While the old couple were still fussing around the store, June had come out of the back office, putting on her raincoat, and had whispered, "I have to go now." She had a date with a girlfriend in front of the Museum of Modern Art and then, since he was busy tonight, maybe they'd go to a concert at Town Hall. "Call me tomorrow. And have a nice evening with your family," she said, and kissed him quickly, at a moment when the old couple had their backs to them.

He had a severe twinge of guilt as he watched the brave

little raincoated figure vanish through the doorway. Perfidy did not come easily to him. He even took a step toward the door, to tell her to come back, but at that moment the old lady called, "Young man, I believe we'll take this one," waving the Christopher Fry about like a captured bird.

When he escorted the old couple to the door and opened it for them, he looked across the street and could have sworn that he saw Paulette Anderson walking uptown, holding the arm of a man with wavy gray hair. They seemed to be in earnest conversation.

One more shot, he decided, and then the hell with it.

He went through his address book with the utmost care. He didn't want to have any more Dorothea Toyes sprung on him.

He stopped at the Ms. *Marsh, Susan***. She wasn't preternaturally tall, but she was a good size and you could be sure she wouldn't ever ask a man $50 for the pleasure of her company. She was a dark girl with green eyes who was politically advanced, although in a quiet, unpushy way. The reason Christopher knew she was politically advanced was that the only books she ever showed an interest in were written by people like Fanon and Marcuse and Cleaver and LeRoi Jones and Marshall McLuhan. She had beautiful legs. It was unsettling to sell books of that nature to a girl with legs as beautiful as that.

She had once told Christopher that he had a good mind. It was then that he had put her name in his address book and given her two stars. She had been caught in the shop by a rainstorm and they had got to talking. It turned out she was from a wealthy family in Grosse Pointe that she despised. She had been one of the youngest girls ever to graduate from Radcliffe and had intended to take her master's in philosophy when she had seen the irrelevance of it all. She expressed disapproval of every book Christopher was displaying at the moment in the window and he said, "Actually, the whole world would be better off if they didn't print another book for the next fifty years."

That's when she said he had a good mind. "Books are dividers," she said. "They form a false elite. To immerse ourselves in the masses, we need song, ritual and bloodshed." She had invited him to a meeting that night that she said might interest him, but he had a date with June and he had to decline.

Now, seeing her name in his book, he remembered the rainy afternoon and the quiet beauty of her green eyes and her sensational legs. A girl with legs like that, he thought, doesn't use them just for walking, no matter what her politics are.

He reached for the phone. But just as he was about to pick it up, the front door opened and a huge young man without a hat entered the shop, took three steps into the room and stopped, staring the length of the shop at him with a pensive but at the same time somehow threatening expression on his heavy, handsome face. Six feet, four, Christopher thought automatically. At least.

Christopher moved away from the phone to the new customer, who remained planted and silent in the aisle in a tentlike raglan tweed coat, his face ruddy and athletic, with an old diagonal scar pinkish on his forehead, running down almost into one eye.

"May I help you, sir?" Christopher said.

"No," the man said, continuing to stare fixedly at him.

"I'm browsing. This is The Browsing Corner, isn't it?"

"Yes."

"Well, I'm browsing." But the man never looked at a book, just at Christopher, as though he were measuring Christopher for some unpleasant uniform or deciding whether he could use him for some unpleasant purpose.

Christopher turned away to fuss with a display of books on a table. The man didn't move and the only sound from him was a rather hoarse breathing. He was too well dressed to be a stick-up man and he didn't have the look of somebody who was interested in books. Naturally, Christopher couldn't call Susan Marsh with a customer like that in the shop.

Christopher was pleased when a young couple came into the shop and negotiated their way around the huge man in the middle of the aisle and asked if he had a copy of *The Red Badge of Courage.* Christopher knew he didn't have a copy, but he told the young couple to wait while he looked in back. He stayed in back as long as he dared. By that time, the young couple were gone, but the man was still there, still with that fixed, pensive, animallike stare.

"Have you found anything you like?" Christopher ventured.

"I'm still browsing," the man said. He had the gift of immobility. While Christopher moved nervously from Popular Fiction to Drama to Biography to Greeting Cards, the man stood there, still, mountainlike, only unblinking his eyes flicking in their sockets, to follow Christopher's movements.

This is the worst Saturday afternoon I have lived through in my life, Christopher thought, after it had gone on for what must have been at least half an hour.

Finally, the man said, "Hah!" and shrugged. He smiled slowly. "Thank you," he said, "it's been a nice browse, Christopher." Massively, he departed.

Christopher looked after him, confounded. Christopher! How did the man know his name? He could have sworn he had never seen him before in his life. The city is full of nuts, he said to himself. And it's getting worse.

For some reason, he was trembling and he sat down to calm his nerves. Then he remembered he had had his hand on the phone to call Susan Marsh when the tall stranger had come into the shop. It was a lucky thing he wasn't in the middle of an intimate conversation when the door had opened.

He strode over to the phone, determined not to let himself be shaken. His hand was almost steady as he dialed Susan Marsh's number.

❖ ❖ ❖

Sue watched closely as Harry Argonaut put the machine together on the carpet in her living room. The time might come when she would have to do it herself and there was no room for error. Harry Argonaut wasn't his real name. It was his nom de plume or, more accurately, his *nom de guerre*. He was a small, pudgy, slow-moving man. Although he was only twenty-four, he was already bald. Fred Drabner, who had brought over the detonating device after lunch, was seated in an Eames armchair, watching Harry Argonaut attach the last two wires. The machine was to be used that night in Newark. Newark had been picked for the demonstration because it was one of the most explosive communities in America and the bombing of a bank in the heart of the city would create maximum confusion and with luck provoke some shooting by the police and perhaps a few spectacular arrests of innocent passers-by.

The room was quiet as Harry worked. It was a nice room, luxuriously furnished, because Sue got a whopping allowance from her family in Grosse Pointe. Now she gave almost all her money to the movement, but she had leased the apartment and furnished it before she had seen the light. Since it was on a very good block just off Park Avenue, in a converted town house with high-rent apartments and no doorman, it was a perfect place for making bombs.

Harry Argonaut, whose accent could have come from any part of the country, hadn't told them yet who was going to take the machine to Newark. He gave out information sparingly and at the latest possible moment.

He was caressing the little machine lightly when the telephone rang.

Sue looked inquiringly at Harry, waiting for orders.

"Answer it," he said.

She went over to the leather-topped English mahogany desk in front of the windows and picked up the phone. She was conscious of Harry Argonaut and Fred Drabner watching her intently in the lamplight. All the curtains were drawn and the room looked like evening.

"May I speak to Miss Marsh?" the man said on the phone.

"This is Miss Marsh."

"This is Christopher Bagshot, Miss Marsh."

"Who?"

"From the bookstore."

"Oh, yes." Her tone was noncommittal and she watched Harry Argonaut for signs.

"I was wondering if you'd like to have dinner with me tonight, Miss Marsh."

She thought the man sounded strange, as though the simple sentence was for some reason costing him a great deal of effort to get out.

Harry Argonaut was moving his lips elaborately, silently mouthing the question. "Who is it?"

"Hold on for a moment, please, Mr. Bagshot," Sue said. "A friend of mine is just leaving and I have to say good-bye." She put her hand over the phone. "It's a man called Bagshot," she said to Harry. "He works in the bookstore on Madison Avenue."

"What does he want?" Harry asked.

"He wants to take me to dinner tonight."

"Let me think," Harry said. That was one reliable thing about Harry—he always took time to size up every situation and figure out what advantage might be drawn from it. "Do you know him well?" he asked.

"I've spoken to him four or five times, that's all."

"Do you think he suspects anything?"

"Oh, no. He's a harmless little man." She regretted the little. Harry was no taller than Mr. Bagshot.

"Why is he calling at this hour on Saturday to ask you for dinner?"

Sue shrugged. "Maybe his girl stood him up and he's lonely."

"How did he get your telephone number?"

"It's in the book, for one thing," Sue said. She was used to Harry's intensive questioning by now. "And I have a charge account with him besides."

"Get an unlisted number first thing Monday," Harry said.

Sue nodded. She wondered if Bagshot was still on the phone.

Harry thought for thirty seconds, kneeling on the carpet, his eyes closed in concentration.

"Tell him you can't give him an answer now," he said, "but that you have to pass by his shop in a half hour or so and you'll drop in and tell him then. Go ahead."

Sue nodded. She didn't know what was in Harry's mind, but whatever it was, it was part of a greater plan.

"Mr. Bagshot," she said, "are you still there?"

"Yes." His voice was eager.

"I'm sorry to have kept you waiting so long, but—"

"Oh, that's perfectly all right, Miss Marsh," he said.

"I'm a little up in the air right now," Sue said, "and I'm late for appointment. But I'll be passing by your shop in a half hour or so. I ought to be sorted out by then, and if I can possibly make it, I'd adore having dinner with you." Being in the movement was a lot like being in the theater. The better you were as an actress, the more effective you were as a revolutionary.

"That's fine, Miss Marsh," Bagshot said. The way he said it, you could tell his life was full of postponements, if not worse. "I'll be waiting."

She hung up.

"Well done," Harry Argonaut said.

She flushed with pleasure. Coming from him, that was high praise, indeed.

Without speaking, Harry got up off his knees and went to the hall closet and took out the blue tennis bag that a small boy had delivered to her apartment three days before. She had asked the boy no questions and had put the bag in the closet, hiding it behind a leather-and-canvas valise from Mark Cross that her father had given her as a Christmas present.

Harry brought the tennis bag into the living room and opened it. It was jammed with crumpled sheets of the *Newark Evening News* and the *Newark Star-Ledger*. While Sue and Fred Drabner watched him silently, he took out some of the newspapers and made a nest of those that remained and lovingly fitted the machine into the nest. Then he zipped up the bag and snapped a small padlock through the two overlapping eyelets in the brass zipper tags.

"Now," he said to Sue, "you're going to put on your nicest, most respectable dress and you're going to walk over to Madison Avenue carrying the tennis bag. You'll go into the shop and tell this fellow Bagshot that you haven't been able to get hold of this man you have a tentative date with, but you'll know definitely by six o'clock. You have some shopping to do, meanwhile, you say, and can you leave the bag there until you come back. You've got all that now?"

"Yes," Sue said and repeated word for word what he had told her.

"It's always safer policy," Harry said, "to store material in a place other than the one where the material is assembled. That way, if one cover is broken, all the others remain intact."

Sue wished Harry would let her take notes when he delivered his rare instructive generalities, but she knew it was out of the question.

"After you deposit the bag," Harry Argonaut said, "you come back here. I will not be here and neither will Fred. At a quarter to six, your phone will ring. A voice you will not recognize will say, 'I'll meet you at a certain corner.' If the person adds, 'At the southwest corner of Twenty-third Street and Eighth Avenue, at six-thirty,' you will do the following. You will add ten to twenty-three, that makes Thirty-third Street, subtract one from eight, that makes Seventh Avenue, you will add one hour to the time, that makes seven-thirty, and you will reverse the compass points, that makes northeast corner. Got it?"

"Repeat, please," Sue said.

Harry repeated his instructions patiently. Then he made her repeat them back to him twice, until he was satisfied there would be no mistake. When he was certain that she knew what she was to do, he went on, "At six o'clock, you will go to the bookshop. You will tell the man that you'd be delighted to have dinner with him, but you have to go to a cocktail party, but that you'll meet him at a restaurant at eight-fifteen. Choose the restaurant yourself. Make sure that it is a crowded one, where you are well known. After you have made the contact and delivered the bag, take a taxi downtown to the Village. Get out in front of a restaurant there. When the taxi has gone, hail another taxi and go to the restaurant where you're going to meet the man from the bookstore."

"All clear," Sue said.

"Keep him out as late as possible. If he suggests going to his place, by all means do so. Just be back here at four A.M., for possible further instructions."

Sue nodded, then frowned.

"What is it?" Harry asked. He was terribly alert, even for the smallest signs.

"I have no money for all those taxis," Sue said. "I gave Fred my last ten dollars yesterday. And my allowance doesn't come in before the first."

Harry thought patiently about the absence of money. "Cash a check," he said.

"It's Saturday afternoon," she said, "the bank is closed. Anyway, I'm overdrawn this month."

Harry thought patiently again. "Cash a check in the bookstore. Is he good for a hundred, do you think?"

"I can try."

"Do the best you can," Harry said. "Now go get dressed." He was stuffing the extra newspapers from the tennis bag into the fireplace and once again Sue had to admire him for his foresight. If anything went wrong and the tennis bag were found, with the Newark newspapers in it, there would be nothing in her apartment that even by the wildest chance could connect her with the event. As she was pulling on a soft brown wool dress with a midi-skirt, she could hear the crackling from the fireplace in the living room as the papers went up in flames.

She went back into the living room and put on a tweed coat over the brown dress and picked up the tennis bag. How invariably clever Harry was, she thought. Who would suspect that a well-dressed, aristocratic-looking girl carrying a tennis bag had destruction at her finger tips; saw, in her mind's eye, Park Avenue in ruins, Madison Avenue smoldering in the cleansing fire of revolution? She wanted to ask Harry when she was going to see him again. But she knew better and all she said was goodbye.

❖ · ❖ ❖

One hundred dollars, Christopher thought as he watched the door close behind Miss Marsh. I wonder if I wasn't a little excessive. He took the check out of the cash-register drawer and examined it once more, interested in the handwriting. It was bold but controlled, generous but intellectual. He put the check back into the cash-register drawer and picked up the blue tennis bag and carried it into the back office for safekeeping. He tried to keep his excitement down. The bag was a hostage, a guarantee that she would return. And she had said that she was almost 100 percent sure that she would be free to have dinner with him tonight. And she hadn't been political at all during her brief visit, but sort of twinkly and almost coquettish, especially when he had been enterprising enough to say that it was a shame a girl like her, with legs like that, thought she had to wear a midiskirt, to be in fashion.

It was the most hopeful thing that had happened to him all day, he thought.

❖ ❖ ❖

When Sue opened the door to her apartment with her key, she didn't have the time to be surprised that Harry and Fred were still there. There were four other men in the living room and they immediately turned out to be detectives.

Harry had handcuffs on his beautiful slender wrists, and he spoke to her quickly in a loud clear voice, "Don't say anything until we get a lawyer."

❖   ❖   ❖

At exactly the moment that Sue Marsh was arrested, Beulah Stickney was in the glassed-in visitors' gallery at Kennedy peering down at the floor where the passengers from Zurich were waiting for their baggage before going through Customs. Quite a few miles away to the west, in a one-room apartment on East 87th Street that Omar Gadsden used, he said, when he was kept in town too late to go to his home in Mount Kisco, Paulette Anderson was fighting weakly to keep the silvery-haired commentator from tearing off her cashmere sweater.

"Please," she said plaintively, struggling to sit up on the day bed on which she somehow had been trapped. "Please. . . ." He had gotten one hook of her brassiere undone. It was like wrestling with a man with ten arms. It was obscene for a man with that much gray hair to be so strong. "You mustn't, Mr. Gadsden," Paulette said, half smothered by a shoulder that butted into her mouth. "Really, you mustn't."

"Come on, treasure," Mr. Gadsden said hoarsely, all his ten arms working at once.

It was nice being called Treasure, even nicer than Angel of Hygeia, but she would have preferred it at a distance.

His behavior had come as a complete surprise. He had been fatherly and wise at lunch, suggesting delicious dishes and talking authoritatively about campus disorders and the ABM and Nixon's Southern strategy and integration and the relation of the G.N.P. to ecological decay in America. She didn't remember ever having a more informative lunch. He hadn't even tried to touch her hand in the restaurant. It had been so friendly and he seemed to be enjoying her company so much that she had ventured to say that she was invited down to a party in the Village that evening where he would meet some young people who would be wildly interested to hear his views. And he had said yes, he'd like to go, he knew a nice little place on Ninth Street where they could have dinner first. She had hoped that he would take her to a movie to fill in the time between lunch and dinner, but he said he was exhausted from the morning session with Dr. Levinson, as well he might be, poor man, and why didn't they go to this place of his that he kept for emergencies and play some music on the hi-fi and just relax until it was time to go downtown. Although she was disappointed about the movie, she told herself that she could go to a movie any time and when would she ever get the chance again to have Omar Gadsden for an entire afternoon, with the knowledge that when the evening came, she was going to give her friends something to talk about for months to come.

But in the meantime, Mr. Gadsden was working powerfully on her stockings. There was a fiendish ingenuity to his attack. When she defended one place, the assault shifted, with demonic energy, to another. If this was the way he was when exhausted, he must be perfectly shocking when fresh. If his public were to see him now, she thought, they might take his pronouncements on public morality with a grain of salt.

Suddenly, he stopped. He didn't move away, but he stopped. He looked at her, wrinkling his lovely gray eyebrows inquiringly. His hair was tousled and he looked sad and disturbed. As long as he didn't move, she liked him very much. If you had to do it with an old man, she thought, he wouldn't be a bad one to start with. She lay on the couch, disheveled, skin showing here and there.

"What is it?" he asked. "Are you a Lesbian?"

She began to cry. Nothing as bad as that had ever been said to her before, she said. What she didn't tell him was that she was something even stranger. She was a virgin. She felt that she would die of shame if Mr. Gadsden found out that she was a virgin.

She sobbed bitterly, not knowing whether it was because Mr. Gadsden had asked her if she was a Lesbian or because she was a virgin. He took her in his arms and stroked her hair and kissed her tears away and said, "There, there, treasure," and in eight minutes she was lying naked on top of the day bed and Mr. Gadsden was taking off his shirt. She kept her eyes averted from him and looked at the photographs on the walls, of Mr. Gadsden with President Kennedy and Mr. Gadsden with Mayor Lindsay and Mr. Gadsden with John Kenneth Galbraith. When the moment comes, she thought, I'll close my eyes. I can't bear the thought of doing it in front of all those important people.

Mr. Gadsden seemed to be taking a long time and she looked over at him out of the corner of her eye. He was putting his shirt on.

"I'm sorry," he said. "You'd better get dressed. I can't go through with it."

She closed her eyes to shut out the sight of Mr. Gadsden, President Kennedy, Mayor Lindsay, John Kenneth Galbraith.

But she couldn't shut her ears. "I looked down at you, lying there, so young and perfect," Mr. Gadsden was saying, "and I thought of you in your white uniform performing those humble necessary tasks in Dr. Levinson's office, peering in at my bleeding jaws with all those weird little stumps of teeth, the ugly maw of age, and I thought, Omar Gadsden, you are trading on innocence and pity, you despicable old lecher; it is unbecoming and disgusting."

It was too bad that she was in no condition to appreciate him at that moment, because later on she realized he had never been as eloquent or convincing on any of the programs on which she had seen him.

"Get dressed, Paulette," he said gently, living up to his image. "I'll go into the bathroom until you're ready."

He left the room and she dressed slowly, half hoping he would come out and say he'd changed his mind. She didn't know how she'd ever be able to get this far with a man again.

But he didn't come out until she was fully dressed and had put up her hair, which had fallen loose in the scuffling.

He poured stiff whiskeys and they sat in elegiac silence in the dying light of the late October afternoon. When she reminded him timidly that he'd wanted to go to the party downtown, he said his jaws were hurting him and he was going to stay home and nurse them.

They had another drink and it was dark when she left his apartment, leaving him sunk in a chair, swishing whiskey around his wounded gums.

She remembered that she had told the boy in the bookstore that she'd come in around five. She didn't really make a decision, but she started across toward Madison. She had to go downtown tonight anyway, she told herself.

❖   ❖   ❖

People came crowding into the baggage and Customs area from Immigration in clotted lumps of tourism and there was so much milling around that it would have been hard to pick out your own mother from the visitors' gallery, let alone a man you had only seen for thirty days in your whole life nine months before. Beulah peered through the plate glass anxiously, trying to spot Jirg, with people all around her waving spastically to relatives on the floor below and holding up babies and waving the babies' hands for them.

Finally, she saw him and she took a deep breath. He was wearing a long black-leather coat, down to his ankles, like an SS officer, and a green Tyrolean hat, with a feather. He was warm and he opened his coat and took off his hat to fan his face. Under the coat, he was wearing a bright-green tweed suit. Even from where she was standing, the bumps on the tweed looked like an outbreak of green boils. And when he took his hat off, she saw that he had gotten a haircut for his trip. A good economical haircut that would last a long time, probably until next spring. A wide pale expanse showed under the high, sharp hairline on the back of his neck, and his ears, she noticed for the first time, stuck out alarmingly from the bare pink scalp. Out of a sense of style, he was wearing long pointed Italian blue-suede shoes and fawn-colored suede gloves.

She regretted that she was farsighted.

Before he could see her, she shrank back away from the window to think. She wheeled and ran down a corridor and went into the ladies' room. She looked around her wildly. There was a Tampax vending machine on the wall. "Thank God," she said. She pushed past a square little Puerto Rican lady with three little girls and fumbled for a coin and put it into the machine.

When she came out of the ladies' room, she didn't bother to go back to the visitors' gallery, but went directly to the exit where the passengers came out after clearing Customs. She fixed a wan smile on her lips and waited.

When he finally came out of Customs, he was thriftily carrying his own bags and sweating. He had put on weight since the end of the skiing season and his face was curiously round. He was short, she noticed, almost as short as the bookstore boy. Was it possible that he could have shrunk since last winter? When he saw her, he dropped his bags, making an old lady behind him stumble, and roared, "*Schatzl*," at her and nearly knocked down a child of three running over to embrace her.

The leather coat smelled as though it had been improperly cured, she noted as he kissed her, and he had doused himself with airline lavatory perfume. If I have a friend at

this airport who recognizes me, she thought as she permitted herself to be chucked under the chin, I shall sink
through the floor.

"Here," she said, "we'd better get your bags out of the
way. I'll help you."

"Finally in your country I come," Jirg said as they
gathered up the bags and started toward the taxis. "Where
is the nearest bed?"

"Sssh," Beulah said. "They understand English here."
Her eyes swiveled around uneasily. The people on both
sides of her looked very thoughtful.

"They giff me a big party for farewell, the boys," Jirg
said. For the first time she realized his voice had been
trained for shouting instructions to people caught in distant avalanches. "They know you wait for me. You should
hear some of the jokes they make. You would laughing die."

"I bet," Beulah said.

They got into a taxi, Jirg holding onto the little air
travel bag he was carrying.

"Where to, lady?" the driver asked.

Oy, she thought. "I'll tell you when you cross the bridge
to Manhattan," she said.

The driver gave her a look. "Games," he said. He was
one of those insufferable New York taxi drivers. He started
his car with a neck-snapping jerk.

Jirg put his hand on her knee and looked conqueringly
into her eyes. He had his hat on again.

"And what was the weather like?" she asked lovingly.
"In Austria this summer, I mean."

"Always rain," he said. "Sometimes hail." He stroked

her knee. In Austria it would have sent her through the ceiling with desire. His hands were horny with callus and she could hear him making snags in her stocking.

"Did you enjoy your trip?"

"Filthy," he said. "The plane was all *Amerikaners*. Maybe they are all right in their own country, but they haff no *Kultur* when they voyage. Except for one *Amerikanerin* I know." He leered seductively at her. He had had his teeth fixed since she had seen him last and one molar and one front tooth were pure gold. His hand went up her thigh, snagging thread.

"How was the food on the plane?" she asked, grabbing the other hand fondly, to immobilize it. She regretted not having worn culottes that day. They didn't offer much protection, but they offered some.

"Swiss food," he said. "For cows. And they make you pay for drinks. The Swiss love one thing. Money."

"All airlines charge for drinks in tourist class," she said, sweetly reasonable.

"Drink," he said. "Oh, that reminds me." He smiled benevolently. "I brought my *Amerikanisches Schatzl* a gift."

In the rearview mirror, she saw the taxi driver grimace, as though he had a gas pain. Jirg took his hand off her leg and dug in the air travel bag on the seat beside him and took out a small squarish unlabeled bottle. She recognized the shape of the bottle and felt her duodenum contract.

Jirg proudly held up the bottle. "See," he said, "I remembered."

It was a drink she loathed, a Tyrolean home product made up of odds and ends of herbs and poisonous weeds that grew in dank spots near precipices in the Alps. Jirg imbibed it in huge quantities, like a giant intake valve. She had pretended to be one of the boys in Austria and had expressed her enthusiasm for the foul stuff. He twisted the cork and offered her the bottle. A smell came out of the neck of the bottle like old and ill-cared-for animals.

She took a ladylike sip, managing not to gag.

He took a huge swig. "Ach," he said, nostalgically, "the nights we drank together."

"Hey, lady," the taxi driver half turned his head, scowling. "No drinking allowed in this cab."

"You'll have to put the bottle away, luv," Beulah said. "He says it's against the law."

"It is not believable," Jirg said. "Drinking against the law. He is making fun of me. I believe he is a Jew." Jirg's face turned a sudden Master Race purple. "I haff heard about New York."

"He isn't a Jew, luv, he's an Irishman." She looked at the driver's ticket, stuck in its frame at the back of the front seat. The man's name was Meyer Schwartz. "Put the bottle away, luv. We'll drink it later."

Muttering in German, Jirg put the bottle back in the air travel bag. The driver swerved the taxi in front of a truck, missing it by seven inches.

By the time they reached the cutoff to Shea Stadium, Jirg's hand was all the way under her skirt, sliding under her panties. She was surprised it had taken that long. Luckily, she was in the right hand corner of the back seat and the driver couldn't see what was happening in his mirror.

Jirg panted convincingly in the region of her neck,

while his hand worked expertly between her thighs, his middle finger amorously exploring. She lay back, tense but waiting. Suddenly, the middle finger stopped moving. Then it moved again, two or three sharp scientific probes. Jirg took his hand away abruptly and sat up.

"*Scheisse*," he said, "*vas ist das?*"

"That's fate, luv." Beulah sat up, too.

"Fate? I do not know that word."

"It means what will be will be."

"Speak slowly."

"It means I have the curse, luv."

"Who cursed?" he said. "So, I said *Scheisse*."

"It's a word American girls use when they are temporarily out of commission. Not in working order. Not ready for visitors."

"Four thousand miles I flew," Jirg said piteously.

"Mother nature, luv," Beulah said. "Take heart. It only lasts a few days. For most girls." She was preparing him for the moment when she would tell him it sometimes went on with her for months, especially in the autumn.

"Vat vill I do for a few days?" Jirg whined.

"Sight-see," Beulah said. "I think the boat that goes all around Manhattan Island is still running."

"I did not come to New York to go boat riding," Jirg said. He looked bleakly out the window at the passing architecture. "New York is a pigsty," he said.

He sat in silence, disapproving of New York, until they had crossed the Triborough Bridge.

"We are in Fun City, lady," the taxi driver said. "Where to?"

"That motel on Ninth Avenue," Beulah said. "I forget

the name." She had never been inside it, but it looked clean, efficient and inexpensive from the outside. It had the added charm of being distant from her flat. She was sure there would be ice water for Jirg, probably running out of the taps, which should entertain him for a day or two.

"We are not to your apartment going?" Jirg asked.

"I was going to explain about that, luv," Beulah said nervously. "You see, I have a roommate."

"Does she ski?"

"That isn't the point, luv. She . . . she is neurotically puritanical. Religious."

"So?" Jirg said. "I am also religious. Nobody is more religious than Austria. I will talk religion with your roommate."

"She believes it is immoral for unmarried girls to sleep with men." Beulah was briefly thankful that Rebecca was not there to overhear this comment.

"I did not come to New York to be married," Jirg said warily.

"Of course not, luv. But just to keep peace in the apartment, it would be better if you stayed in a hotel for the first few days. Until she gets used to you."

"In Austria," Jirg said, "I haff slept in the same room with two girls. In the same *bed*."

"I'm sure you have, luv," Beulah said soothingly. "But we have different customs here. You'll catch on in no time."

"I do not like New York," Jirg said gloomily. "I do not like New York at all."

At the motel, which was not as inexpensive as it looked, Beulah got Jirg a single room with shower. He wanted her to go up with him, but she said she was poorly, because of her malady; he could see how pale she was, she wouldn't even have stirred from her bed that day if he hadn't been arriving from Zurich; and if she didn't go home and lie down with a cold compress, she probably would faint right there in the hotel lobby. She gave him $30 in American money, because all he had with him was Austrian schillings and Swiss francs, and told him to eat in the hotel so he wouldn't get lost. If she was strong enough that evening, she said, she would call him.

She watched him follow the bellboy with his bags to the elevator. When the elevator doors slid shut behind him, she sprinted for the main entrance.

She walked blindly cross-town. By Eighth Avenue, she had decided she was going skiing in Sun Valley this winter. By Seventh Avenue, she had decided to take an offer for a modeling job in Brazil that meant leaving by Tuesday. By Sixth Avenue, she decided she wasn't going home before midnight, because she wasn't going to give Rebecca the satisfaction. By Fifth Avenue, she realized that that meant having dinner alone. By Madison Avenue, she remembered Christopher Bagshot. She went into a bar and sat alone over a white lady, trying to decide which was worse.

❖　　　　　❖　　　　　❖

It was past six o'clock, 6:15, to be exact, and Sue Marsh hadn't shown up at the bookstore for her tennis bag. Christopher was beginning to worry. He could not keep open, waiting for her. He was disappointed in her. He hadn't thought of her as a flighty girl who made idle promises. And Miss Anderson hadn't come into the store at five o'clock, either, as she had said she would. He knew he should be angry at the type of girl who treated a man with so little consideration, but what he really felt was desolation.

Then the door opened from the comparative darkness of Madison Avenue and a tall girl with straight blonde hair came into the store. She was wearing a miniskirt that showed a great length of leg, and a hip-length fun fur, more or less electric-blue in color. He had never seen her before and from the uncertain way she moved around the shop, it looked as though she had never been in a bookstore before. He moved briskly toward her. "Is there anything I can do for you, miss?" he said.

She had big gray eyes that seemed to be imploring him. She was beautiful, in a strange, haunted way, like some of those movie actresses in Swedish pictures who have affairs with their brothers or sisters. An incoherent, unreasonable hope stirred in his breast. "Do you have any cookbooks?" she said.

"We have a selection. This way, please."

"Thank you very much," she said, in a near whisper. Her voice trembled. He wondered if she was a young wife who had a fancy dinner to prepare that evening for her husband's boss or somebody and who had met disaster in the kitchen an hour or so before the guests were to arrive. Saturday evening at 6:15 was a queer time to buy a cookbook. He didn't catch sight of a wedding ring, though.

He hovered near. "Just what sort of cooking are you interested in? French, Italian, American . . . ?"

"Oh, any kind."

"There's an amusing one that has come out fairly recently," he said. Because it was getting so late, he resolved to be daring. "*The Myra Breckinridge Cook Book*, by a friend of the author, Gore Vidal. It's quite risqué." He chuckled, to show that she could take his risqué or leave it alone. "Here, let me get it down for you." He reached for the shelf. It wasn't there. He had seen it when he closed the shop the night before and he knew he hadn't sold it since. Somebody had stolen it during the day. "I'm afraid I've sold the last copy," he said lamely. "If you'll give me your name and address, I'll order one and—"

"Oh, there's no need to bother, thank you," she said softly. Just from the tone of her voice, you knew she wasn't the sort of girl who would say she'd come by at five o'clock and never show up, or the kind of girl who deposited a tennis bag and then irresponsibly left it with you while she consorted with New Left agitators who made love in public parks.

The girl took down a huge illustrated book on French cooking and opened it at random to a page on which there was a color photograph of *poularde de Bresse en cocotte*. She stroked the page absently. "Chicken," she said.

"You like chicken?" It was awfully pedestrian, but he had to keep the conversation going. If she had been at the literary-criticism counter, the dialog would have been more inspiring.

"I love it," the girl said. "Chicken. My mother used to kill two every Sunday. Whenever I have chicken, it's like a day I don't have to work."

"What do you work at?" The conversation was getting more intimate in long leaps and heady bounds. Although the picture of the girl's mother wringing the heads of two chickens every Sunday was a little disquieting.

"An actress. A dancer. A little bit of both," the girl said.

A dancer. That explained the legs. "Where are you working now?"

"No place for the moment." She kept stroking the picture of *poularde de Bresse en cocotte.* "I'm up for a part off-off-Broadway. One of those naked plays." She kept looking down at the cookbook and her voice was so low he wasn't sure that he'd heard correctly.

But whether he had heard correctly or not, it was making an effervescent impression on him. To have a beautiful girl, with pretty nearly the longest legs in the world, who had been walking around in the nude all day before dozens of people, just wander in off the street like that. And just before closing time!

"If you like chicken," he said, putting everything on the one throw, "I know a place on Sixty-first Street where they do it better than anyplace in New York. A French place."

"I wouldn't mind a good chicken dinner," the girl said.

"By a lucky accident," he said, "I'm free tonight."

"By a lucky accident," she said, "so am I."

He looked at his watch. "I close up here in about forty minutes. There's a nice bar around the corner on Lexington. Smiley's. Why don't you have a drink there and I'll be right along and then we can go on to dinner at this great place?"

"You're sure you won't forget and leave me there?" she said, sounding dubious.

"You just don't know me, Miss—"

"My name is Anna. Anna Bukowski. I'm going to change it if I get the part."

"My name is Christopher Bagshot."

"It's a good name," the girl said, "for a man who works in a bookshop. What time did you say you'd be there?"

She was eager, to top it all. "No later than seven-fifteen. Are you hungry?"

"I can eat," she said. She gave him the Swedish-actress incest smile and went out of the shop in her miniskirt and electric-blue fun fur.

He raced catatonically around the store, getting things in order before closing up and speeding over to Smiley's Bar. Now he knew that voice in his dream hadn't spoken for nothing.

❖   ❖   ❖

Anna Bukowski walked slowly and deliberately over toward Lexington Avenue. She had to walk slowly to conserve her energy. She hadn't eaten for two whole days now and she was dizzy from lack of food, and every step she took was like dragging through hot tar. She wasn't on a diet or anything like that. She was just flat broke. She was just in from Cleveland and she had had no idea New York was so expensive. She had spent her last money on subway fare downtown for the tryouts that morning and she had walked all the way up from St. Mark's Place after parading around naked all day, which was also fatiguing, even though it didn't seem like much. But people didn't count the nervous strain.

The reason she had gone into the bookstore was to see if she could steal a book and sell it to a corrupt little man in a basement. Somewhere, she had heard that was a thriving industry. But then that young man had stood so close to her she wouldn't have had a chance to steal a rubber band. And she had asked to see cookbooks because she had been thinking about food all day.

Her landlord had thrown her out that morning, too, and kept her bag, and she was standing in all the clothes she possessed in this world, in a miniskirt that was two centuries out of style. If that man in the bookstore was as wild to get laid as he seemed and if she didn't ruin things at dinner, she might be able to swing getting him to ask her to spend the night with him in his place. If he didn't live with his dying mother or something. And that would mean at least breakfast, too, the next morning. As an old dancer had once told her in Cleveland, "I was in Buenos Aires and I was living off coffee and rolls. My stomach was shrinking to the size of a pistachio nut and I had to make a decision, and I made it. I sold one part of me to support another."

When she got to Lexington Avenue, she had forgotten which way the man had told her to turn, uptown or downtown, for Smiley's Bar. Hunger wasn't good for the memory. Well, there were only two ways to go. She chose uptown. She stepped down off the curb without looking which way the lights were on and a taxi made a wild swing, with a loud screeching of tires, to avoid hitting her. She jumped back, but fell down. She was safe, but the day had been so awful and she had come so near to being killed that she just sat there on the cold pavement of the city of New York and began to weep.

A man who had been waiting for the lights to change came across the street and said, "Please, let me help you."

She didn't say anything but, still sobbing, allowed the man to pull her to her feet.

"You really have to watch the lights," the man said gently. "All things combine in an attempt to destroy you in this town."

She sobbed uncontrollably. She was in no mood to hear lectures on safety precautions at the moment.

"What you need is a drink, young lady." She looked at him, conscious of rivulets on her cheeks. He was about forty and wore a nice dark topcoat and a hat.

She nodded. Her tears stopped. If the nice man took her to a bar, maybe it would be Smiley's; it was in the neighborhood. And even if it wasn't, there would probably be potato chips there and olives and salted peanuts and she could put down a little foundation so she wouldn't disgust the man from the bookstore with her gluttony at dinner and ruin her chances for a bed for the night and Sunday breakfast.

"It's very good of you, sir," she said.

The bar he took her to wasn't Smiley's. It was a dark, elegant small place, with candles on the restaurant tables in the rear. There were plenty of potato chips and olives and salted peanuts and she just couldn't help from tearing into them as she drank a bull shot, which was good for dulling the appetite, too, because of the bouillon. Bull shot, Bagshot. It was funny having a bull shot before going to dinner with a Bagshot. She giggled, the liquor getting to her swiftly in her condition. The nice man watched her with a smile on his face as she ravaged three plates of potato chips and two of salted peanuts.

"Have you been on a diet?" he asked.

"Sort of," she said.

"But you're off it now?"

"Thank God."

"Do you know," he said, "I think the best thing I could do would be to march you to a table and order us dinner."

"I'm expected in a half hour or so," she said, although it took a great effort to say no.

"We'll just have one dish," the man said, taking her down off the bar stool. "And then you can flitter off."

She couldn't refuse an offer like that, so she allowed the man to lead her to a table. She asked the bartender where Smiley's was and he said it was just down Lexington Avenue two blocks, so there was plenty of time.

The menu looked so tempting that with a little coaxing from the nice forty-year-old man, now without his hat and topcoat, she ordered the whole thing. Hors d'oeuvres, cream-of-tomato soup, steak with broccoli with hollandaise sauce and French fried potatoes, salad, cheese, and strawberry tart for dessert. It seemed like a lot to cram into a half hour before going out to dinner, but the waiter assured her he would hurry.

❖   ❖   ❖

Christopher was just about to lock the front door and go into the little lavatory next to the back office and shave.

He would be cheating his father of about five minutes' worth of service, but he felt he really had to shave. He had shaved in the morning, but although he was small he was manly and he needed to shave twice a day. But just as he was about to turn the handle of the lock, through the glass of the door he saw Beulah Stickney striding toward him, like a model advertising health food. He stepped back and she entered briskly.

"Hi, luv," she said, morning-fresh, vital and friendly. "Auntie folded like last year's violets. Aren't you the lucky boy tonight? Let's celebrate. The night is young and you are beautiful. Where're you taking your friend Beulah to dinner? I hear there's a new place over on First that's—"

"I'm afraid tonight is out," Christopher said, with a delicious sense of power. "I've made other arrangements. Perhaps if I'm free some night next week. . . ."

"You mean you're feeding another bird, luv?" Beulah asked, a slight edge of what he thought was sharpness in her tone, and what she knew was hysteria.

"If you mean do I have an engagement for dinner with another lady," Christopher said, liking his language round tonight, "you're correct."

"Pah, luv," Beulah said airily, "let's make it *à trois*. It can be a load of laughs. May the best woman win." She didn't ordinarily descend to lures like that, but it was Saturday night and seven o'clock.

"Well. . . ." He hadn't thought about that possibility and it intrigued him. He hesitated, thinking hard. But then the door opened and Paulette Anderson came into the shop.

All I need now, Christopher thought, is for Sue Marsh

finally to show up for her bag and Caroline Trowbridge to come in to apologize for saying it was a wrong number and Dorothea Toye to pass by, offering to cut her price.

"Why, Beulah," Paulette cried, "what on earth are you doing here?"

"This is my friendly neighborhood think tank, luv," Beulah said. "I was just passing by on the way home to change and I saw the beckoning light of literature and I came in to see if he had the new *Harper's Bazaar* or the latest Mailer to read in the tub." Her eyes flashed a clear signal to Christopher, and with a sudden maturity and understanding of women that he had never had before, he knew that she was warning him not to let Paulette Anderson know that she had come in to get him to take her to dinner. And certainly not to let her know that she had been turned down. "What brings you to these parts at this hour yourself, luv?" Beulah asked, her voice rising infinitesimally.

"I was going to invite Mr. Bagshot to a party," Paulette said.

Dental assistants, Christopher realized, did not observe the same rules of feint and parry as models. Paulette looked as though she had had a wearing day and her clothes didn't seem to be on just right, but she had taken her glasses off and there was a winsome fluster to her hair.

"I see you ladies know each other," Christopher said. He hoped they didn't know each other too well.

"We're cap-and-crown sisters, luv," Beulah Stickney said. "I patronize the sainted Dr. Levinson and Paulette holds my hand to keep me from screaming while he wreaks his will on me. I have also taken her shopping in the rag bazaar on Seventh Avenue at wholesale rates so that she can be beautiful enough to invite popular young men like you to parties."

Bitch, Christopher thought. It gave him great pleasure to say this in his mind. "Oh," he said, "so that's how you know each other."

"Well, I must be toddling along," Beulah said. "I'm late as it is." She picked up a copy of the French *Vogue*. "Put it on my bill, luv. The next time I have a toothache, Paulette, you can tell me how the party turned out."

She left, smiling, the air perfumed and polar behind her.

"I'm always a little in awe of her," Paulette said. "Aren't you?"

"Not really," Christopher said.

"Well, I suppose men are different," Paulette said. She breathed loudly. "I hope I'm not too late. But the afternoon was just one thing after another and I just took a chance that you might still be open and. . . . Well, anyway, I'm invited to a party and if you still want to. . . ." She ran down and stopped. The way he was looking at her, with this new light in his eye, she was sure he knew that she had been lying naked on the day bed of Mr. Gadsden's emergency apartment as late as 4:30 that afternoon.

He just remained silent, silent and powerful, looking at her.

"Of course," she said. She was nervous, even if she did tower over him and she had thought of him only as a last resort until this very minute. "Of course, if you don't want to go to a party, I'll understand. . . ."

"I'd love to go, Paulette," he said easily. "It's just that I'm taken for the evening."

"Naturally," Paulette said. "At this hour. Well, maybe another time. Good night."

"*Ciao*," he said. He had never said *Ciao* before to anyone. "Good of you to drop by."

He opened the door for her. She heard it locking behind her.

As she walked heavily down Madison Avenue, she was overcome with the awful certainty that she was going to be a virgin for the rest of her life.

Humming, Christopher shaved. He felt marvelous. He didn't remember feeling this marvelous since the day he got his 4-F classification in the draft. Before going in to shave, he had tripped over the blue tennis bag and put it out of the way under the table. Looking at it, he decided he'd have it delivered on Monday by messenger to Miss Marsh's apartment, with a big bunch of forget-me-nots from that florist on Fifth Avenue. That would be ironic.

He shaved slowly because he didn't want to bleed. Even if he were late, that girl in the miniskirt with the great legs, what was her name, Anna, would wait. Tonight women waited for Bagshot.

❖   ❖   ❖

It would have been all right if the steak hadn't been so good. But it was more than an inch thick and so tender you hardly needed the knife to cut it and it tasted the way steaks look in advertisements. It had just disappeared from her plate while the nice forty-year-old man was barely beginning on his and he had said, "My dear girl, I haven't seen anything like this since I played football in college."

And he had insisted, it was the only word you could use, insisted, that she have another one, and what with the wine and all, and three kinds of cheese that she had never tasted before and the strawberry tart and the Cointreau with the coffee, well, it was 10:30 before she looked at her watch again and there was no use searching up and down Lexington Avenue at that hour like a lost soul for Smiley's Bar. And when she got out of the nice forty-year-old man's apartment at five o'clock the next day, which was Sunday, after a pancake and bacon-and-eggs brunch, served by a butler, there would have been even less use, wouldn't there, to look for Smiley's Bar?

She got the job in the off-off-Broadway naked show and two good reviews, mostly for her figure, if you wanted to be honest, and the nice forty-year-old man was as generous as nice forty-year-old men are supposed to be to tall young naked actresses, and all she had to worry about that autumn was her weight.

Lying idly in bed right before Christmas, reading the "Society" section of the Sunday *Times*, she saw an announcement that Mr. Christopher Bagshot, son of Mr. Bernard Bagshot, the owner of the well-known chain of bookstores, had been married the day before at St. Thomas's, in Mamaroneck, to a girl by the name of June Leonard.

So it had turned out well for everybody. It gave her a nice feeling.